ATLAS

Drugged

(AYN RAND BE DAMNED!)

Stephen L. Goldstein

GRID PRESS
ASHLAND, OREGON

ATLAS DRUGGED

©2012 STEPHEN L. GOLDSTEIN

Published by Grid Press

(An imprint of L&R Publishing, LLC)

Grid Press

PO Box 3531

Ashland, OR 97520

www.hellgatepress.com

Editing: Harley B. Patrick

Cover Design: L. Redding

Front & Back Cover Illustrations: Lawrence M. Butler

Library of Congress Cataloging-in-Publication Data

Goldstein, Stephen L., 1943-
Atlas drugged : Ayn Rand be damned! / Stephen L. Goldstein. --
1st ed.
    p. cm.
ISBN 978-1-55571-709-4
I. Title.
PS3607.O4856A93 2012
813'.6--dc23

2012012079

Printed and bound in the United States of America

First edition 10 9 8 7 6 5 4 3 2

For Alisa

ATLAS

Drugged

(AYN RAND BE DAMNED!)

OLYMPIANS VS. TITANS

In Greek mythology, the Titans ruled the Earth before the Olympians overthrew them. After ten years, Zeus, the head of the Olympians, defeated his father, Cronos, the leader of the Titans. Atlas led the Titans to defeat against Zeus. His brother Prometheus sided with Zeus.

When the Olympians won the war, Zeus punished Atlas, a self-serving protector of the status quo, by making him hold up the world. Prometheus was delegated by Zeus to create man. And since then, he has always been known as the protector and benefactor of humanity.

Prometheus gave mankind many gifts, including fire, which he stole from Zeus—and for which he was severely punished. But he never forsook humankind or gave in to Zeus.

Eventually, Prometheus was freed from his punishment. Atlas never was.

PROLOGUE

Oh Sleep! it is a gentle thing, Beloved from pole to pole!
To Mary Queen the praise be given!
She sent the gentle sleep from heaven, That slid into my soul.
— S. Coleridge, *The Rime of the Ancient Mariner*

JUNE 3, 10 P.M.: WEST 79TH STREET, MANHATTAN. Bored and frustrated, hunched over, elbows rubbing on his desk, head resting in the palms of both hands, Dan Ryan stares at the blank computer screen. *All I need is the first line of my next column and then I can go to sleep,* he thinks. *I've got to get up early so I can watch the masses pay tribute to John Galt tomorrow.* But that's what he's been saying to himself for three hours and it hasn't done him any good. His head is spinning like a wheel with a hyperactive hamster in it. He's tried chanting the mantra he hasn't used in fifteen years (*Could it have expired?*), a half hour of yoga, and a hot bath. In desperation, he considers prayer, incantation, and incense. He's on the verge of giving up—getting into bed and hoping for the best. But he knows himself well enough to know that will never do: at worst, he'll toss and turn for who knows how long; at best, when and if he settles down and inspiration comes, he'll have to get up and write something.

This is not typical of Ryan—and every writer's nightmare: fear of losing "the spark," the sine qua non that makes a real writer a writer or a real anybody an anything. He *always* knows *exactly* what he's going to write before he writes it. A columnist, he *never* suffers from anything as sophomoric as writer's block. But for some reason, tonight, he's got no fire in the belly, no burning desire to write about anything or anyone. The hypochondriac in him wonders if he could be dying; the drama king, if he'll have to become a waiter.

He keeps replaying the scenes from the day for clues about what's troubling him and (hope against hope) for inspiration. But this Friday was no different than every other for the past five years, except for those falling on a full moon when all hell breaks loose. From 6 a.m. to 10 a.m., he refereed the usual political slugfest on his daily radio show, "The Honest Truth," between guests and their real or imagined ghosts, guests and guests, guests and listeners, and listeners and guests and himself. Like every day, he predicted how the comments would align around the day's topic, today's having been "John Galt: Should Atlas Have Shrugged?" The guy he's dubbed "Fuming Frank," who calls in every day at 7:15, can *always* be counted on to rail against the Federal Reserve, even if the discussion is about global warming. Today, he ranted that *only* the Fed shrugs. "Thanks for sharing, Frank. What about John Galt?" Ryan asked.

"Is he still alive?" Frank fired back.

"Have a nice weekend. Goodbye," Ryan said.

Predictably, "Platitudinous Pat" took issue with John Galt—"Wasn't he a vice president?" she asked—and every president going back to Calvin Coolidge, whom she claims as a distant maternal cousin and savior, and to whom she attributes the words of Harry S. Truman: "The buck stops here," "If you can't stand the heat get out of the kitchen," and "If you want a friend in Washington, get a dog." Ryan sent her to *Bartlett's*. But Pat insisted it's a Democratic plot to keep Cal, and her family, from getting the respect they're due.

He advised "Maxed Out" Maxine, who calls in for financial advice because she's again reached the limits on her seven credit cards, to wait until 10 a.m. for "Finding Financial Freedom with Francine," but she said she didn't like Francine but that Ryan once gave her the best advice she's ever gotten—though, when pressed, she says she can't remember what it was.

No, four hours of mental masturbation five days a week never bore or frustrate or unsettle him or leave him without something to write about. As long as he's got a mute button on the control panel and a hefty pay check—*When will they discover I should be paying them?*—he knows he's got the best thing going. What's more, he invariably finds the spark for his weekly column from those that fly from the *vox populi*. So why not now?

He isn't unsettled because he's dreading tomorrow, either, though he probably should be. For one of those "Saturday Specials" that isn't in his contract for him to cover, but which he gets roped into and accepts to keep the peace and his pay check, he's got to get up at 6 a.m. on his day off, meet up with the crew of his radio show, and drag himself to New Atlantis to cover the 67th Anniversary of John Galt's saving the nation. He's done it so many times, it should bore him. But it doesn't.

No, if asked, the clearest he would say about what's keeping him from finding the first line of his column, and the peace he feels he so richly deserves, is that he pictures some troubling, fuzzy, amorphous grayness that gives him a funny feeling in his stomach, like nothing he's ever felt before, a feeling that could foreshadow impending doom or delight, but without a clear cause. *Something's missing*, he thinks.

Finally, he simply goes to bed. *If I can just close my eyes, maybe it will come to me*, he thinks, prays, hopes. *Cut the crap*, he tells his inner demon. *Let me sleep. I need the strength of Atlas. I've got to be up at 6:00 tomorrow morning and somehow get myself through the day.*

ONE

CONGREGATE, CONGRATULATE, MISCALCULATE

SATURDAY, JUNE 4: NEW ATLANTIS, WESTCHESTER, NEW YORK. Some call themselves Galtans. Others prefer Atlantans. Either way, they are all devoted to keeping John Galt alive throughout the year, but especially on the first Saturday of June, every year. It is noon. The sky is cloudless; the sun is intense for late Spring. A line of late-model luxury cars is backed up for two miles on the highway south of the main entrance into New Atlantis. The first car waiting to turn in is a red Ferrari. Behind it is a Mercedes limousine. In burnished gold, over massive iron gates, are the words, "There is no evil except the refusal to think."

The cars that have already managed to enter are crawling, bumper-to-bumper. Taggart Drive winds its way up a gentle, shady slope, through a forest of tall, strong oaks as far as the eye can see. Fresh green leaves of late spring create a stately, comforting canopy. Overgrown lilac bushes are everywhere, long ago timed to be in full blossom on this day by Dagny Taggart. They have never dared disappoint. They have grown to be so many and so full that their aroma overpowers. Parking lots are already full. The only spaces left are on the grass.

Dagny Taggart founded New Atlantis, shortly after she followed John Galt to New York when he declared, "We are going back to the world." Like Atlas, bearing the weight of the world, they had shrugged. They had gone on strike to rebel against (what they considered) the socialist destruction of the economy, sequestered themselves in the valley of Atlantis, and eventually overthrew the government. Dagny said she wanted New Atlantis to be her personal investment in keeping alive the success of (what Galt eventually called) the Rational Restoration of America. "A mecca for the mind and self-interest," she called it, "a place where people of reason can flourish, turn ideas into profit, and never let anyone forget which people are indispensable to the nation." Publicly, Dagny told everyone it was an act of pure self-interest: to see Galt's mission continue and thrive. To *herself*, and only to herself, she confessed it was an act of personal self-interest: to express her devotion to Galt, the only man she ever loved. Upon her death, Dagny left her entire estate to the think tank to manage The Taggart Venture Fund, providing loans to promising profit-making projects.

First located just on the site of property she bought as her suburban summer home, the campus grew to 400 acres. Year after year, like any rapacious CEO gauging market demand and seizing opportunity, Dagny gobbled up surrounding estates to accommodate the growing community of acolytes who came to New Atlantis to be mentored throughout the year—and carry on Galt's work throughout the nation and the world. Every year in June, the same month Galt and his followers had met in the valley of Atlantis decades before, the faithful return.

As cars make their way up Taggart Drive, at strategically placed clearings, passengers see monuments to Galt's strike and the risks others took with him. At the first turn, on the left, is a vintage diesel engine from Taggart Transcontinental, a reminder of the industrial superpower that had to be destroyed so the old order could be crushed and

Galt's new nation could be born. At the next right is the plane that Dagny flew by accident into the secret valley of Atlantis, the trip that began her momentous conversion to the strike—and love and adoration of Galt. At the next left, there's a twenty foot expanse of bridge made out of Rearden Metal, homage to the man who next to Galt was the most creative and imaginative of their generation's industrialists— and to his revolutionary process. And, at the next turn, rests Ragnar Danneskjold's boat, the menacing "pirate" vessel that brought looters to justice, those who live off other people's ideas and inventions, the collective enemy Galt and his comrades finally defeated.

At the crest of the road burns an "eternal" flame, a reminder of Ellis Wyatt's Torch: the ultimate symbol of one heroic man's undying devotion to the power and rights of the individual over everything and everyone. Finally, below, in a burst of dramatic sunlight, a vast, open expanse of manicured lawn stretches in a gentle decline to the walls of d'Anconia Pavilion. The octagon-shaped, flying-saucer-like building dominates the landscape. The huge, gleaming, copper roof is supported by blue-green cantilevers of precious Rearden Metal. A massive gold dollar sign is planted in the middle. The walkway leading to the pavilion is made of railroad ties, another reminder of the Taggart railroad empire—and of Dagny's single-handed restoration of its intercontinental network after she and Galt returned from the valley. A giant replica of Galt's revolutionary motor sits before the main entrance into the Pavilion.

The crowd has been streaming into the 7,000-seat facility since the doors opened at 11 a.m. They parade slowly, wanting to be seen as belonging at New Atlantis. They are dressed as if they were going to church or an afternoon wedding or a luncheon at an exclusive country club. The women wear almost identical, loose-fitting, pastel summer dresses. Yellow seems to be the favored color this year. In spite of the warm weather, some wear close-fitting hats—berets or turbans. The men wear dark, mostly blue, suits with white shirts and monochrome ties, mostly blue or green. The children, mostly teens, are dressed like their parents. There are hoards of young adults in their twenties, who stand out for not standing out. It's a living Norman Rockwell mural.

The lobby is bare except for a towering twenty-four-foot-tall, muscular, gold statue of Atlas on a pedestal in the middle. The midday light from a skylight on the gold creates a blinding glare. Legs spread, his right slightly in front of the left, the Titan stands straight, looking up, as though he wouldn't deign to meet anyone below the heavens eye-to-eye, a self-satisfied smirk on his face. His left hand is pressed against his waist akimbo. His right hand is stretched above his head and out in front of him, lightly bent at the elbow, its palm upturned. His index finger playfully supports a massive, blue-green globe of the Earth, ten feet in diameter, made from Rearden Metal. He gives the impression of a cocky basketball player about to sink a shot he can easily make, but taking his sweet time, spinning the ball just to lord his physical prowess over everyone, the whole world—his opposing teammates, and even his own. This is the ultimate Atlas at the top of his game; a swaggering bully, a poseur, an exhibitionist, a giddy narcissist drunk with power, reveling in himself—and reveling in others reveling in him. On the front of the pedestal are the words, "Drug yourself on self-interest: You can never get enough."

After they pay for their $50 tickets—the motto of New Atlantis is "Nothing is for nothing"—people are given a gold plastic dollar-sign lapel-pin with the number 67 attached to the middle of it and a blue-green plastic bracelet, on which is stamped "To each according to what he produces." For an extra $25, they can buy a bracelet made out of real, blue-green Rearden Metal, an exact replica of Dagny's. Business is brisk, though many of the women are wearing those they have purchased in previous years. It's long been marketed as the best way to "prove" they *really* belong at New Atlantis.

On the middle of the three walls at the back of the stage, a 10'x 20' national flag is mounted—red and white horizontal stripes, a field of blue in the upper left-hand corner with fifty white dollar signs superimposed. Painted in black on the wall to its left are the words, "Congress shall make no law abridging the freedom of production and trade." On the right, "I will never live for the sake of another man, nor ask another man to live for mine." The stage is bare, except for a lectern far forward in the middle, on the front of which hangs a huge gold dollar sign. On the remaining five walls surrounding the audience, stained glass windows carry different messages: "Rational Self-Interest Is Godliness," "Money Is the Greatest Good," "There Is No Evil, Except Refusing to Think," "Mind and Body Are One," and "There Are No Contradictions. Everything Is As It Seems."

Richard Halley's haunting Fifth Concerto is playing, in the arrangement Dagny first heard. At noon, the pavilion is already half-full. For decades, the faithful have returned yearly to renew their vows. But their pilgrimage has been especially meaningful since Galt, Dagny, and their generation have died—and the torch has fallen directly upon their successors. Dagny was the last to die twenty years ago. Every year since then, their heir-apparent, Hilton Manfreed, universally celebrated as "The Prophet of Profit" and senior fellow at New Atlantis, has delivered "Manfreed's Creed," his annual lecture and status report on the state of politics and the free market. Current and former New Atlantans (his preferred label), along with their families and friends from around the world, have come together to drink their yearly dose of what they all call "rational steroids."

At 2 p.m., it is standing-room-only. Three TV screens outside allow the overflow crowd to watch. The music stops. All at once, the crowd falls completely silent. They are all prepared for the ritual they know so well to begin. Over the loudspeakers comes the familiar voice of Manfreed's assistant, Baron Rooky.

"Ladies and gentlemen, please stand, salute the flag, and repeat the Pledge of Patronage with me: I pledge my patronage to the brand of the Corporate States of America and to the profits which it commands. One Emporium, under Mammon, with liberty and lucre for all."

As a "standby" test-pattern counts down from ten to one, simultaneously on three giant TV screens in the pavilion, Rooky announces, "And now, live from the Oval Office of the White House in Washington D.C., the President of the Corporate States of America, the Honorable Hamilton 'Ham' Cooper."

"My fellow profit-seekers, it is my greatest pleasure to speak to you personally every year at New Atlantis, and especially this year on the 67th anniversary of the Galtian Restoration. Like every year, it is important to remember former times, not only with nostalgia, but with a renewed dedication to the seriousness of our mission. Three score and seven years ago, John Galt brought forth on this continent a market-driven nation, conceived in rationality and dedicated to the proposition that people and profit are never created equal."

To everyone's shock, it sounds as though a voice has spoken over the president saying, "bullshit." But it happens so quickly no one can be sure. And the president appears to be unaware of it and doesn't miss a beat.

"Now, we are engaged in a great competitive war, testing whether our market or any markets so conceived and so financed, can remain totally free. We are met on a great staging-ground of that war. And we have come to rededicate ourselves and New Atlantis, so that our markets, under Mammon, shall have increased infusions of capital— and that free markets of free-wheeling corporations, by free-wheeling corporations, and for free-wheeling corporations shall not perish from the earth."

"From all of us at New Atlantis," Rooky continues, "thank you, Mr. President. And now, ladies and gentlemen, it gives me great pleasure to introduce a man who truly needs no introduction, an inspiration to us all: Professor Hilton Manfreed." Bursting into thunderous applause, the audience stands in rapt admiration as Manfreed waddles to the podium. He shows no signs of being the least bit affected by the crowd's enthusiasm, however. Almost contemptuously indifferent to everything around him, the brainy-looking, bald, 4'9", stocky professor deposits a stack of loose papers on the lectern. He towers over the assemblage only once he mounts the booster step put there for him so he can be seen above the microphone.

Like an owl on a tree branch, looking out through his round, horn-rimmed glasses without blinking, mechanically, he surveys the audience quickly from left to right, right to left—then, glares straight ahead. Without small talk or introductory humor, he immediately gets down to business. He taps the microphone, which the audience, still applauding, takes as its cue to be seated. Mimicking a Christian making the sign of the cross, he leads the audience in tracing a dollar sign, in two strokes with his right hand—from his forehead to his upper chest and, from left to right, across his chest—intoning, "In the name of free markets, self-interest, and the holy goal of profit. Amen."

"My fellow New Atlantans, John Galt lives! There is no God but the market. The market is God! Government is Satan!" Manfreed proclaims. The crowd jumps up and erupts in another thunderous round of applause, at the same time repeating in unison, "The market is God, the market is God, hi-ho the dairy-o, the market is God." Finally able to begin after five minutes of vainly trying to quiet the audience, he declares, "John Galt lives through us. We are his prophets. He showed us the way to freedom. We trust in ourselves. We trust in free markets. Markets never fail. Markets are all." Again, the audience goes wild and the applause is deafening. "Decades ago, Galt's Rational Restoration turned our failing, socialistic, anachronistic, government-dominated nation of looters into the Corporate States of America. We boldly changed our name from united to corporate as an act of historical will, the sign of our entirely new beginning, a declaration to the world of our shared sacred values and a rejection of everything that had poisoned our national being. We were cleansed and cleansed ourselves of the stench of stagnant, festering socialism.

"Word of our Restoration could be heard around the world. Nation after nation watched with envy as we dedicated ourselves to ourselves, picked up the pieces of our ignoble past, and converted ourselves into an engine of unbridled prosperity. We liberated every man, woman, and child to follow their self-interest, not the public interest—and to make no excuses for it. We became truly free for the first time in our history. If someone else hurts, we finally understood, that's their problem, not yours or the government's. That's what Band-Aids are for. If I'm okay, but you're not, well it's too bad for you. *Vita sugit*: Life sucks. Suck it up or get sucked up. Such simple, honest, self-evident (but too long ignored) declarations freed us from the mental shackles of ever thinking we owe anybody else anything. We are the source of the greatest transformation of society in human history. We threw off the chains of government. We ended regulations and oversight that have added costs but no benefits to every sector of business. I never tire of relishing in the glory that we have brought upon ourselves.

"At this our yearly time to celebrate together, I am thrilled to report the breaking news that, though it has taken us decades, for the first time in our history, in all of our fifty states and our territories, we have finally done away with the last vestiges of outmoded legislation that imposed undue hardship on manufacturers to prove the safety and effectiveness of drugs. That's right! Consumers in the market are now *totally* free to make their own choices on what is best for them. Scientists and researchers and their employers are now free to develop what may be miracle cures, without having to spend years testing them to the satisfaction of some small-minded government bureaucrat. They will come to market faster than ever before. And once again, the morality of the market will protect the public. Manufacturers' self-interest will guarantee that they will make their products and procedures safe and effective. Otherwise, no one will buy them. In the few instances in which problems may arise, the market will alert the public to hazards and drugs will be discontinued or modified. The market works perfectly—if only people will let it!"

"Yes, yes, John Galt lives!" shouts a man in the audience and the entire assembly applauds and stands, this time stomping its feet. Manfreed looks up and, for the first time, acknowledges the crowd. Once again, he crosses himself with a dollar sign, at which people begin jumping up and down and clapping their hands over their heads. After five minutes of unabated frenzy, Manfreed finally gets the crowd to quiet down and sit.

"In the recent past, we have lifted all environmental regulations and taxes that have stifled the growth of businesses and siphoned off their profits. We have outlawed dreaded unions that have crippled the private sector." Thunderous applause. "They can no longer force wages up and secure benefits or strike and bring business to a standstill." Thunderous applause. "We have eliminated the corporate income tax. There are no more minimum wage laws, occupational safety, leave and overtime laws." Again the audience applauds wildly. "We have liberated business and liberated labor." The audience on its feet begins to chant, "Manfreed, man freed, man freed!"

Suddenly, out of nowhere, over the loudspeakers, a mysterious male voice thunders, "John Galt is dead!" The crowd is thrown into total confusion, near panic. Some people are visibly frightened. People shake their heads, asking each other What? What did you hear? Who's talking? Where's it coming from? Was that the same voice that said "bullshit" when the president was speaking? But no one has an answer.

Obviously disturbed, Manfreed looks around the pavilion, waiting for someone to give him an explanation for the unprecedented interruption. The head of the technical staff rushes out from backstage and whispers in his ear. But from the way he shrugs his shoulders and shakes his head from side to side, as well as the puzzled expression on the professor's face, it appears he has no explanation.

And just when the audience settles down and he prepares to speak, again the voice declares, "John Galt is dead!"

Squinting and looking around the pavilion to see if he can identify where the voice came from, shaken but not wanting to wait too long to suggest that whoever was interrupting had gotten the best of him, Manfreed speaks haltingly, as though waiting for another attack, but continues: "Year after year, we have proven that true democracy rests on Free-for-All economics—unencumbered by regulation and dedicated to the proposition that self-interest is Godliness. You now live in a system that strives to protect your 'natural liberty.' You have been freed from the debilitating, false notion that you are your 'brother's keeper.' And you are free of any guilt for believing and acting upon your self-interest. You know you are only your own keeper. You want nothing from anyone else, nor will you give anything to anyone else. We have liberated each and everyone to go it alone and to fulfill themselves on their own terms.

"We have eliminated government from any role in the destructive act of mediating between the public and business and industry. It's every man for himself. We've proven that, if you can find it on the Internet—and you can find *everything* on the Internet—you don't need government to do it. We have preserved inherited wealth. We have eliminated tariffs. We have ended the false and misplaced idea of consumer protection. Rational human beings can protect themselves. We have totally dismantled the government agencies that intervened between you and the providers of goods and services. You can now have what you want when you want it. Decades ago, we ended what used to be called 'the social safety net'—the welfare-state's Social Security, Medicare, Medicaid, and all the disempowering programs that pandered to people's needs and that enslaved them without their even knowing it. It was a net that trapped them—and from which we liberated them."

Smiling for the first time, regaining his stride after the disturbing, inexplicable interruption, Manfreed continues, "Markets, as we know, protect us in more ways than government can or than we can imagine. Free markets make free agents. Free markets make free men. On the walls around us are written the timeless truths that energized John Galt and that have guided *us* ever since. You now live freer than ever. You all know the benefits that you have enjoyed and continue to enjoy. That's why you're here today—to celebrate your liberation. We have prospered. We have remade our economy. We have remade ourselves. We have drugged ourselves—and continue to drug ourselves—on the libation of total liberation that can only come from pursuing our unbridled self-interest. Each and every one of us is Atlas in our own universe. The world is ours.

"A free market is the closest thing to a miracle mankind can achieve. And yet, ironically, it is the ultimate achievement if, and only if, people get out of its way. Mortals cannot improve upon it, because to intervene and attempt to do so is to fiddle with freedom. Imagine a place where all individuals can express themselves uninhibited and undaunted—a state of nature, in which people are kept from suppressing others. Through the competition of the market, some people may rise and achieve; others may fall and fail. Markets are inherently unequal and always volatile. Their volatility ensures their freedom. And that's true beauty.

"The free market is pure democracy. No one is guaranteed or deprived of a place. In the dynamic of the market, no one can be on top, or even successful, forever. There is always someone with a better idea waiting to raise the bar and force others to meet or exceed them—and make others relinquish their place and fight to regain it, if they choose or can. The market polices itself. The market confers advantage and takes away advantage. The market is king, lord over all: It can mitigate racial differences, bring harmony to the nation, and foster creativity and innovation. Just let the market work, unbridled by regulation, and peace will reign.

"But it has not been easy to achieve the glorious prosperity we celebrate today. I know you have heard this account retold every year.

You know the story. But today, this year especially, *really* put your-selves in the place of Galt, Dagny Taggert, and their fellow captains of industry. Just imagine the moral courage it took for them to do what they did. Just imagine what it was for them to turn their backs on everything they had built. When they acted, they had no idea of the outcome of the risks they were taking. But out of their deepest and most admirable self-interest, Galt, Dagny Taggert, and the other captains of industry—the creative, rational minds who joined forces with them—destroyed what they had created to save it.

Once again, the mysterious voice over the loudspeaker blares out, "John Galt is dead!" The audience is visibly disturbed. Many fidget in their seats. Some stand up and look around to see if they can discover the source of the interruption.

His jaw clenched but pretending not to have heard the distur-bance, Manfreed continues. "They first went on strike, retreated from the world. They brought a corrupt nation to its knees. It had devolved into nothing more than millions of people putting their hands out for whatever charity the government threw their way. Galt and com-pany watched as, one by one, industries collapsed without them and as the strong arm of government foolishly and ineptly intervened, making matters worse—until there was nothing left.

"People across the territory were in open revolt and on the verge of taking up arms. Galt and his allies accomplished their goal. They proved they were the true and only engines of the economy. And fi-nally, he and the others returned, rolled up their sleeves, and rebuilt what they had once destroyed. That's how powerful and creative they were. They rewrote our Constitution. They renamed our nation. They transformed the failed United States of America into a glorious corporate state. They restored fifty deadbeat states into the prosper-ous Corporate States of America we celebrate today and that we will for years to come. They set an example for all of us to follow. They set an example for the world to follow.

"They, we, have accomplished much by committing ourselves to a relentless agenda. Year after year, we have fought reactionary forces. Sometimes, they have even won—fortunately, only temporarily. We *never* give up—and never will."

Again, the voice over the loudspeaker blares out, "John Galt is dead!" Visibly shaken and exasperated, Manfreed says, "At the same time that we have shown that the Free-for-All market benefits everyone without exception, we have fought off criticism—vehement, preposterous attacks—that our system, the perfectly organized market, impoverishes anyone, exploits the poor, and rewards only the rich and powerful. But we never let our defenses down. We never rest. We live in perilous times—more perilous by the minute. We may be challenged, but we are winning. And we will continue to win, as long as we remain committed to our goals and purposes."

Suddenly, Manfreed's microphone goes dead. Then, a loud, uninterrupted, wailing sound emanates from the speakers. He looks up in frustration and disbelief. The audience begins to squirm. A technician immediately runs on stage. He whispers to Manfreed and then, managing to get the microphone working again, tells the crowd it is just a minor problem, people are working on it, and it will be fixed immediately. The wailing stops. Manfreed begins again. Again, his microphone goes dead.

To no avail, Manfreed tries to speak loud enough to be heard in the vast pavilion. He waits, furious. And after two minutes, his microphone appears to be working, so he hesitates but continues: "The Galtian Restoration is constantly under threat from minds that were never completely reeducated and that have passed on their misplaced notions to younger generations. As a result, there are still some looters among us who hold on to vestiges of our shameful past. They make the absurd claim that some people have not prospered because of *us*. They say others have been forced into poverty. Of course, they refuse to accept responsibility for their own failure. The looters' game is to try to foist guilt on you and me—guilt for their failure, their weakness, and their irresponsibility; guilt for our success, strength, and power. They want us to provide for the needs they say they have. And I'm sorry to say that there are still even some people who feel pity and give them what they beg for.

"Let me be perfectly honest with you, my fellow New Atlantans. On this, the 67th anniversary of the Galtian Restoration and the founding of New Atlantis, we can take absolutely nothing for granted. In fact, as never before, we are perilously close to losing the battle others fought so nobly before us and for which we have worked for so long. The whole Restoration hangs by a thread. All of us need to recommit to drinking deeply, to drugging ourselves on all of the principles that have thus far guided our success. We need to take on the world full force and to hold it within our grasp. We all need to become Atlas on steroids in communities across this nation and across the world.

"As you know, in November, we will have national elections. And by what can only be called a fluke of election reform, Cary Hinton is in danger of being elected president." The audience gasps, then stands, chanting, "No, no, Cary, no. No, no, Cary, no." Hoping to quiet the audience, Manfreed shouts, "If she is elected, you can say goodbye to everything we have accomplished over the last sixty-seven years." The audience chants even more loudly "No, no, Cary, no."

"That's no exaggeration," Manfreed continues, struggling to be heard. "The great, integrated, free market that we have created will be destroyed." The audience gasps, then begins to chant, "Cary, Cary, go away, come again another day—not!"

"My friends," Manfreed says, "Cary Hinton is our sworn enemy. She will undo all of the advances we have made and take us back to the Dark Ages of government intervention and socialism. If nothing else, we all need to understand that we are in a constant state of revolution. We can take nothing for granted. We must always be vigilant. Forces are always working against us.

"As many as ten states within our Corporate States are on our active watch-list for takeover by government interventionists, a new generation of looters. Around the world, thirty nations are potentially sliding into socialism. There are always people who will backslide because they have been brainwashed by holdouts who were brought up under a debilitating system of government and economics and never became worthy converts. They are not up to the challenges of accepting responsibility for their actions and letting the Free-for-All market work. They would rather intervene for their personal, short-term interest and blood-suck the energy of others. They are parasites. And we must stop them from taking from the rest of us.

"In part, we are our own worst enemy: Our very success has sown the seeds of the backlash we are seeing. Last year was a banner-year for turning crises into free-market opportunities at home and abroad. To mention just a few: Floods in Mississippi swept away dilapidated houses and businesses—mostly fishing and small farming—on prime, waterfront property, to which owners had questionable title, it turns out. Owners could never afford insurance and could not possibly afford to rebuild. So, a smart developer, true to his glorious self-interest, realized the unique opportunities of the situation and bought up 40,000 acres.

"Free from any government interference, he's been able to get title to the land, dredge it, sell lots, and build state-of-the-art houses and commercial sites. He has almost finished creating a total corporate city. Water, electricity, roads, libraries, schools, parks—everything that was once mistakenly thought to be the responsibility of government is now privately owned. The developer is his own government, meaning there is no government beyond him. It's pure Free for All economics. The beauty of it is, whatever people want they can get—as long as they pay for it, no different than going to a movie or buying groceries. And for the owner, everything, and I mean everything, is pure profit. He is setting the pace for others here and abroad."

The audience applauds. But once they settle down, a tall, young man, with a shock of red hair, probably in his mid-twenties, stands up, looks around, raises his hand to get Manfreed's attention and, without waiting to be called on, asks, "Where are the 25,000 people who used to live on that land in Mississippi going to live? And how are the 7,500 businesses put out of business going to earn a living?"

"Quiet, quiet. Out of order," many in the audience call out.

"Don't you know your place?" the woman next to him yells.

Unmoved, the young man just stands and looks straight ahead at Manfreed.

"No, no, it's all right," the professor replies. Unable to hide his dismay that anyone would presume to ask a question in the middle of his speech, let alone challenge him, but showing no outward sign of anger, Manfreed instantly decides to turn the unprecedented moment into a teaching experience.

"Young man, I won't ask you who you are or where you come from. I just want you to know I feel sorry for you. Have you learned nothing? Are you one of those misguided souls who delude themselves into believing that they are responsible for others? Have you forgotten the first rule of self-interest—that there is nothing *but* self-interest, that we *can* only act out of self-interest, that we *should* only act out of self-interest, and that we don't owe anybody anything? Are you still feeling guilty for your success and the failure of others? Worse yet, are you a looter? Do you want others to be responsible for your failures, and do you want to live off them? Do yourself a favor and free yourself from your regressive, inhibiting, socialist ideas. They destroyed our country once. Don't let them do it again. Honor John Galt." All eyes on him, the young man chooses to say nothing more and sits down.

"Around the world, Free-for-All market successes have occurred, though none as sweeping as what's happened in Mississippi. We can only hope for more like that in the near future. But in Mexico, right on our doorstep, perfect positioning, the sweeping privatization of public services has taken place on a grand scale. And our corporations have been able to cross the border and reap profits no one ever dreamed of. The national gas and oil resources have been sold to a private conglomerate in the Corporate States, and it is already been reaping huge profits. Don't believe press reports of protests and riots because of increased prices. Outside agitators who have been paid to do the dirty work of international companies competing with ours are responsible for all the trouble. Our companies' private security forces have everything under control. Similar privatization deals are occurring on every continent. Our corporations are acting like Atlas—heady with limitless possibility, drugged on the power of self-interest.

"No matter how much criticism we hear, no matter how loud voices may be raised against our fundamental beliefs, let us never forget that all of these breathtaking improvements and opportunities have been possible for one reason alone: Total deregulation of our economy and market, complete non-interference by government, the end of unions. Our government has been converted into a board of directors responsible first and foremost to corporations. The idea was so simple it was lost on generations of leaders here. But now its possibilities inspire almost everyone.

"Some people disparage us by saying we live by the 'law of the jungle.' But I think of that as a positive. They're paying us the highest compliment without knowing it. The flip side of 'the law of the jungle' is 'survival of the fittest.' And that's what we're all about. Now more than ever, each of you needs to carry the message that will sustain and save world economies. Our goal is to convert all nations to the Free-for-All market. As we have proven time and time again, it is a finely wrought machine. It is perfect. It is an expression of 'natural law.' In the perpetual war that we need to keep waging, that we will never be free from waging, government is our sworn enemy. Greed is Good. All good comes from greed. That is all ye need to know."

Expecting the mysterious voice to break in, Manfreed pauses and surveys the audience, hoping to be able to spot the slightest move that would reveal his whereabouts. But there's dead silence and no one so much as stirs.

"We now come to the final portion of today's program," Manfreed says, appearing relieved to be able to begin. "I have the great pleasure of inducting three of our most promising New Atlantis associates into the Circle of Atlas, the corporate body that manages New Atlantis. Will Enrique Reyes, Zora Tremmon, and Albert Swift please come forward? They are living examples of the power of the Free-for-All market in action. They came to New Atlantis three years ago from different parts of the country and the world. Together, they created the most outstanding for-profit proposal we have seen in two decades. They presented it to the board of the Taggart Venture Fund at the end of their first year and received a $500,000 loan. Today, they head a thriving company, and not just a thriving company but a model for all companies and an inspiration for others to bring ideas to market.

"Their product, Atlas Energy, is a high-potency drink sold throughout the world, and their chain of Atlas Fitness Centers is franchised throughout the Corporate States with plans to expand worldwide later this year. They have repaid their loan with interest, as well as a twenty percent share of their profits—and believe me, those are already in the millions with enormous opportunities for growth. And, as I'm sure you realize, they have only been able to achieve their success in such lightening speed and with such spectacular results because, and *only* because, they have been free of government over-regulation. Bureaucrats have not had the power to stand in their way."

With the trio now on the stage, he motions toward them and says, "Enrique Reyes developed the secret formula for the most sophisticated and effective high-energy drink ever produced. It's so powerful that I hesitate to call it just a drink, though that's what they call it for marketing purposes. I would call it a drug, in the best sense of the word.

Believe me. It's everything you can imagine in a liquid that can transform the chemistry of your body and add years to your life. I've been drinking it since it first went on the market, and I've never felt better. Escaping from Cuba, where socialism has suppressed free markets and taken the creative life out of people for more than half a century, Enrique is a scientific genius with a natural aptitude for business. He's proof that you can't extinguish the human spirit. He's flourished in the Corporate States.

"Zora Tremmon was born in the Corporate States to parents who fled totalitarian regimes in Eastern Europe. She created the computer and social network programs that market and manage the sales of Atlas Energy, as well as the franchises of Atlas Fitness Centers.

"Albert Swift, a native of California, created the patented Titan Whole-Body Harmony Machine that is available only at Atlas Fitness Centers. There is truly nothing like it anywhere in the world. Independent scientific studies reveal that regular use lowers body rhythms, harmonizes the brain, and produces unique levels of physical strength.

"The proprietary, thirty-day program developed at Atlas Fitness Centers, combining a regimen of the Atlas Energy Drink and the Titan Machine, guarantees weight loss, energy gain, and total-body toning. It actually cures conditions like diabetes and shows promising early signs of helping reverse the effects of spinal cord injury and Parkinson's."

He shakes each of their hands and gives them a miniature statue of Atlas like the one in the lobby with their name and Circle of Atlas inscribed on the base. "Let's hear a round of applause for our free-market heroes," he adds, looking out at the audience. "You can buy the Atlas Energy Drink as you exit the pavilion. Drug yourself on it. It works like nothing else! Take a Fitness Center brochure to find out how to join the one nearest to you. And consider becoming a franchisee. And now, fellow Atlantans, until next year, good day."

After a lengthy, thundering ovation, the crowd slowly make their exit. Above them, a small airplane buzzes the campus tugging a banner on which are written the words "Beauty is Truth, Truth Beauty." Most people shake their fists at it and shout, "John Galt lives! The market is God!" The red-headed, young man looks up and smiles.

Inside, backstage, an enraged Manfreed, barks at his assistant, Baron Rooky. "How could you let this happen? You've made me look like a fool."

"Me?" Rooky fires back. "I had nothing to do with it."

"Find out who that red-headed bastard is, who said 'bullshit' in the middle of the president's speech, who the hell cut into my speech, and how he did it, or you're out of here. We've got to crush those fuckers completely. And I *mean* completely! This is war. I don't know who's behind this. But no one gets to do this to Hilton Manfreed. There *can* be only one winner. And there *will* be only one winner!"

TWO

Assist, Resist, Desist

SUNDAY, JUNE 5: MIDTOWN MANHATTAN. The gray-blue sky is completely overcast. It's been that way all morning and there are no signs of clearing. It is noon, but there's an ominous feel to it. It's the kind of day you want to come in out of—for the warmth and comfort of whatever you can find. You'll settle for anything. It is late spring, but it feels like winter. It is cold and damp. Nothing is in bloom or shows signs of blossoming anytime soon. Trees and plants are barren of buds waiting to leaf and flower. The landscape seems drained of all color, turned into a study in black-and-white.

From every direction, in what has become a Sunday ritual for years, lines of men, women, and children flock to Central Park. If you were in an airplane, you'd think giant snakes starring in a horror movie were infesting the place. They come not for a concert or just to relax and enjoy the day, as in better times. They are coming to eat. They are the city's fringe population. They are already homeless and destitute—may be barely able to pay their rent or afford to eat, a few bucks away from having to live on the street. The park is their salvation. They and others like them make the trip every day, twice a day, at 7 a.m. and 5 p.m. Sunday is special, an all-day buffet. Feedings start at noon and continue until 4 p.m.—or until the food runs out, which is lately more often than ever. Every day, hundreds more people—too many—come.

Today, the earliest arrivals start lining up at 8 a.m. It's the same story at every entrance. They'll tell you they're going to Cooperville, not Central Park. It's their way of pinning their plight on Ham Cooper, president of the Corporate States of America. Today, there's at least one Cooperville in every major city. It started as a trickle of displaced people ten years ago, to which no one paid much attention. After all, there had always been homeless people—drunks, drug addicts, prostitutes, the poor, *les miserables*. Everyone wished they'd go away, tried to ignore them, and discounted them as human waste. At best, they'd throw them a few bucks. At worst, people felt they had done something to deserve their fate—and couldn't have cared less.

But before anyone realized it, thousands of men, women, and children were on the streets—or barely scraping by—and they squatted wherever there was hospitable vacant land. Their numbers had grown so big so fast, no one knew how to relocate them—or where. They were everyone's relatives, friends and neighbors—working people who had never needed a handout in their lives, even people who had owned small businesses. They came from everywhere—within the five boroughs of the city, the suburbs, and from across the country: Scarsdale, Dallas, Seattle, Chicago.

Something was terribly wrong with the economy. People thought they knew whom to blame. Cursing Cooper became a national pastime. "Cooper doesn't give a shit about us," shouts a woman in her late thirties. "Right on," says everyone within earshot. "That fucker should rot in hell," says a man in his sixties on a walker. "I voted for the bastard," he adds. "I fell for his campaign slogan, 'Free markets free Americans to be rich.' I knew he was a whore for the rich and Big Business. I just never thought he'd sell me out. My company folded. I lost my job, my pension, and my health insurance. I've got nothing. Fuck the American Dream."

At the 59th Street entrance to the park, the north side of Grand Army Plaza, the line stretches down the east side of Fifth Avenue to 50th Street. It's made up mostly of families. "I'm hungry, mommy, and I'm tired of standing," one little girl says above a whisper, looking up at her anguished mother. "We'll be eating soon, sweetheart," she answers reassuringly. "And there will be plenty to eat."

As though protecting themselves from the blinding glare of a solar eclipse, the people look away from the windows of the exclusive stores on Fifth Avenue—too painful a reminder of a world that doesn't exist for them. But they can't avoid taking in the fabled Plaza Hotel. An older woman, probably in her late seventies, points to it and tells a woman in her twenties next to her that she lunched at the Palm Court every Saturday for years. "I just loved the stained glass ceiling," she says. "And what wonderful teas. That was before all my investments were wiped out when the stock market collapsed." *Spare me. And I'm Elizabeth Taylor* the young skeptic thinks to herself. *Why do I always get stuck with the creeps?*

Her driver waiting beside the open door of her limousine, Countess Isabella de Horsch (*nee* Idabelle Sue Raft, formerly of the ruralest of rural Alabama) makes her calculated exit from the main entrance of the Plaza. She doesn't deign to look from side to side but walks slowly, in the measured steps of a bride going down the aisle, making certain everyone can feast their eyes on the product of her three hours' worth of preparation. She and Count Henry bought their penthouse condominium five years ago, shortly after he bought their titles through a Polish website. She, in turn, has done everything her husband's riches and modern medicine can do to banish the backwoods from her looks, if not her psyche or entirely from her speech. The icing on the cake are her four surgeries to make her look like Marilyn Monroe. And she is dressed in a knock-off of the subway-sex dress the bombshell wore in "The Seven Year Itch." She affects Monroe's sultry speech as a way of overcoming a southern twang—well, at least she wishes.

"Wilson, whatevah you do, don't proceed across Central Park South," the countess orders her driver as she brushes the air with her left hand and straightens her dress from under her with her right. "Ah simply can't bay-ah to see all those homeless people on the street. Whah they positively offend the eyes, I must say. Someone has to do something about them. They littah the place just by being he-ah. Human littah, that's what they ah. There ah more and more of them every day. Where *ah* they coming from, Wilson? Can't anybody put a stop to it?"

"Times are *really* tough, ma'am," the driver says.

"Well, they'ah *always* tough. All ah know is that we paid eighteen mil for ah-wah penthouse. It was a steal. The count *always* steals. I mean gets a steal. And ah don't want to have to look at a bunch a bums across the street. It positively offends the eyes."

"I'm sorry, Countess," Wilson replies. "But there's no other route for me to take today. Westbound traffic is completely blocked from 58th Street to 43nd Street and, because of it, westbound traffic on 42nd Street is at a standstill. The Greek prime minister is in town. Two hours ago, I took the count to the Hilton to meet with him. We needed a Secret Service pass to get through security. It's gonna be like this for hours."

"If you must," the countess answers with a sigh. "Let's just hope someone gets rid of these people. They're ruining property values." As they drive along Central Park South, suddenly the countess thinks she recognizes a familiar face among the homeless. *But that's impossible. I must be seeing things.*

The Central Park Cooperville has turned into a city-within-the-city, a full-fledged commune. Everywhere you look are tents, cardboard boxes, lean-tos, sleeping bags—anything that can serve as a shelter or a bed. Several shacks are made out of scrap metal. In "Cooper-speak," they are mansions, the homes of the park's longest and most creative and resourceful residents. Some have even been "sold" when their owners have moved on. There are through-streets and cul-de-sacs, named and numbered. There are playgrounds for kids. Some people have moved close together, making makeshift row houses. Ten huge feeding tents are in the middle of the park, spaced about every four blocks from 60th Street to 110th.

According to a study by the social research firm of Bates & Rich for the deHaven Foundation, an estimated 7,500 squatters actually live in Cooperville at any given time. The average age of residents is forty-five. Forty percent have lived there for three years or more. Thirty percent had been small business owners. Thirty-five percent had worked in manufacturing jobs. Another thirty-five percent were mid-level managers in mid-size corporations. Sixty percent are married or have been married. Thirty percent have a family member with them. The researchers observed, "If the talent in Cooperville resided in one business, it would have one of the most educated and experienced workforces in the nation and would easily be a Fortune 50 Company."

Thirty percent of residents are sixty-five or over. But because Medicare and Social Security were discontinued twenty years ago, they are destitute. Almost everyone in Cooperville has been thrown on the street by circumstances beyond their control—the series of recessions that have gutted the economy in the past ten years. The pattern of dislocation, researchers found, is almost always the same: They couldn't find work after they were fired when their employer shipped jobs overseas. They used up their savings. They lost the equity in their house when the real estate market tanked. Because they owed more than it was worth, they couldn't afford to sell and, eventually, the bank foreclosed on it.

To the researchers' amazement, Cooperville has evolved into a self-sustaining community—what they called "a full-fledged model, a working democracy." Natural leaders emerged almost from the start. Before feedings actually took place in the park, they were the ones who had "the heart" to tell others, especially new arrivals, where and when they could find food, clothing, employment help, and similar resources throughout the city. And before long, as the numbers grew, a core group saw the need for some form of organization to create ways to help people within the park. They elected their own governing body. And when they needed a name to call themselves, they came up with Cooperville. "President Cooper fucked us," the then-newly elected "mayor" said. "It's the least we can do to let him know we know—and we'll never forget."

The "mayor" of Cooperville for the past five years calls himself Mr. B. Like many others, he is fiercely mum about his past. From the way he talks and deals with other people, most say he had to have been a white-collar executive, maybe even the head of something. But he's laughed off every effort to piece together his biography. "You don't wanna know and have got no reason to know," he tells everyone who tries to probe. Whatever he may have been, Mr. B *is* a brilliant fundraiser and organizer. He's found ways people can secretly donate everything from money to cell phones, since private charity is now illegal in the CSA. He created and manages the internal security force to keep outsiders from harassing park residents. Vigilante groups attack homeless for sport. So, Cooperville issues ID's to its residents and has had no choice but to police its perimeter. The CC (Cooperville cops, as they are affectionately known) are armed. Again and again, Mr. B has stood up to anyone who's tried to evict people from the park. Face-to-face, again last week, he told the mayor of New York City, "None of us wants to be here. But as long as we're here, we'll make the best of it. We aren't going anywhere—until and unless it's on our terms. So back off!"

Wilson Brackett, III, the head of Internal Affairs, is as public about his past as Mr. B is private. He'll tell you straight out that he's the black sheep of a Boston Brahmin family who barely graduated Harvard and spent four years after college drinking away his trust fund. Before his money ran out, he met Ryan, his partner of fifteen years, and pulled himself together. Both were investment bankers on Wall Street and doing pretty well. Then, Ryan was diagnosed with MS, eventually couldn't work, and lost his health insurance. Their savings were depleted to cover medical bills, but they managed—until Wilson lost his job when his firm folded. Wilson organizes all services and resources inside Cooperville, including the showers, toilets, electricity, and running water. He staffs the clothes, barber, and laundry tents so those who are looking for permanent jobs, and the thousands who work at day jobs, look presentable and don't smell—especially don't smell. He also manages all the cell phones and wireless communication in the park.

Alma Parks was elected Head of Services unanimously each year for the past three years. She grew up in Cincinnati, the daughter of a prominent rabbi. After graduating from Antioch, she spent five years on three different *kibbutzim* in Israel. When she returned to the states, she got degrees in social work and business. A single mother who raised and educated two daughters and a son, she was always financially strapped but managed to get along. She worked as a guidance counselor in the one public school in New Orleans that hadn't already been turned into a private charter. But as soon as it was, her position was eliminated. She invested all the money she had in an Internet start-up business, which went bankrupt.

Alma is as tough as Golda Meir, as compassionate as Mother Teresa, and as beautiful as Sophia Loren. In Israel, she literally helped make the desert bloom. She worked in a cotton field. She is a fierce egalitarian—the result of her family upbringing, as well as her *kibbutz* experience. Alma coordinates all information about jobs. "That's all anybody wants," she tells everyone. "Just give them a break. They'll work like dogs and never complain."

There is no violence in Cooperville. There is no crime, not even petty stuff. The few who have disturbed the peace or tried to impinge upon the rights of others have been thrown out. No one is asking for anything from anyone, except a chance to work. And they'll do anything—anything to regain their self-respect. Wilson also manages the clean-up crews so there's no refuse and nothing in the park is destroyed. But crews have almost nothing to do. Everyone respects the environment. The park is cleaner than it ever was.

Today, as on every Sunday at 3 p.m., Mr. B gives his weekly "warm-up" (his word) speech to all of Cooperville. In addition to the crowd in front of him, others hear and see him on countless wireless devices throughout the park. "My fellow Americans," he begins in his barreling voice, "it is now illegal to pledge allegiance to the United States of America. So, I ask you to say it silently to yourselves. Some day soon, I hope we'll be able to say those words again—perhaps sooner than any of us might have imagined.

"Your meal today has been donated by several individuals who understand your circumstances and who truly care about you. But you can never know who they are. As you know, in the Corporate States of America, it is illegal to give anything to anyone who needs anything. It's everyone for himself. You can bribe politicians and judges, of course. You just can't help average people. The Corporate Council says to help people is to keep them needy—and that's a crime. So, you could go to jail for it.

"Today, the sky is overcast. It is dreary. But don't think it's bleak. Remember: The sun is always shining behind the clouds. And today is a perfect example of how true that is. Mark your calendar: Sunday, June 5th is a red letter day, the day all of us have hoped for, but none of us could have imagined would have happened in our lifetimes. John Galt is dead." He holds up three newspapers proclaiming the message in huge headlines as the crowd cheers.

"You can read the headline and accounts in every newspaper in America and around the world. It's on every blog and website. It's viral on Twitter. It's on radio and TV. Someone spooked New Atlantis yesterday. They were celebrating their sixty-seven fraudulent, conniving years in power, if you can believe it—the miserable decades we've suffered since Galt and his gang returned to rebuild the economy so they and others could rape it. The 'great' Hilton Manfreed was dishing out his usual free-market garbage when they got spooked. From out of nowhere, a voice interrupted the old coot and proclaimed, 'John Galt is dead!' I wish I had been there to see the bastard's chain pulled. He finally got what he deserved. He got rattled. The whole lousy bunch of them got rattled. They didn't have a clue what to do. It's the first time they've been made to look like fools, the first sign they are starting to lose control.

"You know it and I know it: Sixty-seven long, deceitful years ago, they started plotting to kill the middle class. Of course, that's not what they *said* they were doing, except behind closed doors in the private offices of their 'stink tanks.' Publicly, they called it 'trickle down' economics. But they knew it was a piss-poor excuse for ripping off the country. Their religion is the free market—or what they *called* a free market, really a lot of laws they paid politicians to pass so they could get richer. They promised that what was good for the rich would be good for the poor, that prosperity would 'flow' down to the lowest of the low. They should have called it 'fire hydrant' finances. Like dogs, all they did was pee on the rest of us and turn their backs, without giving a shit.

"For sixty-seven years, they've called everyone on welfare a thief and anyone who wasn't a multi-millionaire lazy. And they never asked why so many people never get ahead. They are so far gone, they think they're as rich as they are because they earned it and deserve it. They think this land is *theirs*, not yours. They won't own up to the fact that they have paid people off. And they've rigged the system worse than a slot machine so you'll never win. Today, the government and our courts are a sham, stacked with their stooges, who protect corporate profits and personal fortunes—to hell, with you, stupid! 'The little people' don't matter. To them, you're throwaway, human toilet paper.

"Sixty-seven long, dreary years ago, they started rolling back everything good about America, all the social progress we'd made. Make no mistake about it: They don't believe all of us are created equal to them. You'll never be able to join *their* country club so you don't matter. And there's nothing you will ever be able to do about it. They won't let you in, even if you could afford to pay the dues. You are not one of them. They won't say it out loud, but, in private, they tell each other how they *really* feel—every Jew is a kike; every Black, a nigger; every Latino, a spic; every Italian, a whop. Everyone who isn't them, just isn't.

"For sixty-seven years, they've sucked the country dry so there's nothing left for you. They treat you like animals—less than animals. They treat their dogs and cats better than you. They throw you their crumbs—and think you should thank them. They killed national health insurance. They've taken away women's reproductive rights. They've ended public schools almost everywhere. Can't afford school tuition for your kids? Too bad! All of you will just have to pick better genes in the next life. They killed your unions and said you'd make more money as free agents. Then, they fired you, moved their plants overseas, and hired foreign workers for a fraction of what they paid you.

"Manfreed and his cronies quote the Declaration of Independence and the Constitution. They praise our dead Founding Fathers. But if you're living and breathing people, with hopes and dreams for a better life for you and your family and need to make a living, they don't give a shit about you. They turned the greatest nation on earth, the United States of America, into the Corporate States of America, a business—no better than a vending machine. They live only to hear their cash registers ring with whatever money you can scrape up. Is your house on fire? Pay the firemen when they get to your house or they'll let your place burn to the ground. Manfreed and his crowd have plundered public assets. They sold America out from under you. They call it privatization and say it is good for the country, but they sell everything at a fire sale to their cronies.

"You *played* by the rules. You *paid* by the rules. You worked. You paid your rent. You paid your mortgage. But you were lied to and cheated. The tragic thing is how many people just like you believed the lies and the bullshit—and did nothing to stop the bastards. You're here because a developer screwed you out of your land in Mississippi. Or you lost everything in a flood. Or you lost your job, couldn't pay your mortgage and the bank foreclosed on your house. Or your kid got cancer and you didn't have health insurance so you went bankrupt. Your stories are different. But the reason you're on the street is the same: The United States of America that used to be *your* country was sold out to the lowest bidder. This was *the* land of opportunity. But it turned into one of monopoly and privilege. Money corrupted people. And people corrupted the system.

"Look up, folks. Look up," Mr. B says excitedly. From out of nowhere, a plane flies over the park, pulling a *John Galt Is Dead* banner. "Repeat after me," he says, "John Galt is dead." The crowd does so, cheers, and erupts into thunderous applause and whistles. "And now, because it is illegal to sing our beloved 'Star-Spangled Banner,' please sing it to yourselves. Don't forget to take your bag of snacks with you as you leave. They've been donated by a very special lady who cares about each and every one of you. I can't tell you her name. But believe me when I tell you she loves you. Until next week, good day and good luck."

As the Cooperville crowd disperses after Mr. B's talk, from her penthouse on Fifth Avenue, Misti Chase shakes her head and sneers as she looks down on Cooperville. Angela Fitzsimmons, president of her co-op, is with her. "Damn homeless," Angela says. "They've turned our beautiful view into a garbage heap."

"I haven't been able to have a dinner party on my terrace in years," Misti adds. Everyone knows Misti is the eyes and ears of the building. She keeps a written log of what's going on in Cooperville. She asked

Angela to come up so she could report what Mr. B had told the crowd. No one more publicly condemns the takeover of the park than Misti.

If anything out-of-the-ordinary happens, "the chaser"—as everyone calls Misti behind her back—immediately notifies the doorman, who calls building security. Since the city's police force has been privatized, the only way a building can protect itself is to sign a contract with a private agency. Full-time, armed guards patrol Misti's co-op twenty-four/seven. They clear the sidewalk if anyone who looks suspicious so much as stops in front of the building. They shoo them on their way or escort them back into the park—anything so they'll move completely out of sight. But as Misti Chase told the doorman when she went out to walk her dog, "No matter where they go, you know they're *always* there, *always* capable of coming back. There's no living from them. They haunt us."

"Times are tough," he replied.

"You don't have to tell me," Misti counters. "My dog gets groomed only twice a month. I only have my dog walker six days a week now. We've all had to cut back."

Misti Chase wasn't always Chase, and she wasn't always Misti. She didn't always live on Fifth Avenue. And she didn't always trash the poor. She was born Myra Cohen in the Bronx. As a college freshman, she had marched for civil rights with The Rev. Dr. Martin Luther King, Jr. She had protested the Vietnam War. She had picketed the White House during Watergate. You could hear her cheering loudly outside the White House when Richard Nixon resigned. Her husband Meyer, who insists everyone call him "Mike," was a prominent proctologist. He made no bones about going into medicine for the money or about choosing his specialty because it was the way he thought he could make the most money. They became richer than they ever imagined they could be.

Misti left to take her French poodle, Fave—named for Fifth Ave—out for her afternoon walk. As usual, she had (what she called) her "Sunday bundle" under her arm, a Burberry shoulder bag ostensibly holding everything she needed to pick up after Fave. If Misti was one thing, she was organized—and always tried to keep up appearances. But as usual, she crossed the street and, after walking two blocks south, she passed a young, red-headed man who stood at the 81st Street entrance into the park. She opened her bag and took out a parcel wrapped in brown paper. Pointing to a trash bin about twenty feet west of them and handing him five dollars, she asked, "Would you be kind enough to throw this in the trash?"

"Of course, ma'am, and thank you very much," he said.

Central Park West has always been the ugliest and most volatile side of Cooperville, the hardest to patrol and keep safe—not from the homeless, but from muggers preying on older men and women. They only want cash. But they can become physically violent if they don't get what they want or if someone foolishly resists. Since the city police force was disbanded, anyone walking on the street is an easy target. No one knows by exactly how much crime has increased, because there is no longer a government agency to maintain records and statistics. Private security forces hired by individual buildings are only responsible for policing the area around them. Between buildings, everyone is fair game. The richest of the rich can afford to pay for personal security and have gotten used to having body guards and bullet-proofing vehicles.

"We live in a jungle," CPW residents now complain. "It's survival of the fittest." Some of the loudest voices anguishing about the deterioration of security were people who had been the biggest proponents of reducing the size of government. "We don't want to pay for a city police force," they insisted. "We don't want our money to go for other people's security. It's nothing but waste, fraud, and abuse.

We can do it better ourselves." Now, a group of CPW residents meets regularly to try to find a solution. Someone suggested creating their own police force, even hiring people from Cooperville, to patrol from 59th Street to 96th Street and from the CPW to Broadway. But no one knew how they could get everyone to pay their fair share for it.

Two weeks ago, in the early evening, a homeless man was set on fire at the corner of 79th Street and Central Park West. Miraculously, he survived without any serious injury. A man came to his rescue, using his jacket to smother the flames. The security guard at the nearest building skulked away into the lobby, pretending he saw nothing. John C., a resident of Cooperville, had been returning from work. Two or three days a week, he was usually lucky enough to find work through a day-labor pool. When three young men demanded he give them his wallet, he told them he had only one dollar. But when they discovered twelve—he had just been paid—for spite, two of them held him down, while a third threw cigarette-lighter fluid on him, then a match. "I can't blame them," he told the man who saved him. "They're young. All they know is the hate they hear. I'm nothing to them. Other people are nothing to them. I don't think *they* think we're human."

Everyone in Cooperville was shaken after learning about the attack on John C., but relieved that he had not been seriously hurt. More patrols were assigned to the west side of the park. But once the initial shock wore off, like everything else, they took it in stride. They really had no choice. They were constantly under attack, real or imagined—the weather, illness, callous potential employers, you name it. Developing a thick skin is the only way they cope. But as hardened as they had become, no one, and least of all LuAnn Buford, was prepared for the shock of Sunday night, especially after Sunday afternoon had ended on such a high.

LuAnn and her husband Billy had only been in Cooperville for six months. They had never been to New York before and never imagined they'd get there the way they did. It had always been their dream someday to get to the "big city," as they called it. Billy had promised, and LuAnn knew he'd make good. She had always said she married him because his word was "as good as gold." "He may not be good lookin' and he sure ain't rich," she told everyone, "but he's honest, and I love him to pieces for that."

Everyone called Billy the park's "Fixer-in-Chief." He was an auto mechanic by trade. But he could fix anything. He had a "tinkerin' kinda mind," he said with a smile. "Gimme anythin' broke and I'll do my damndest to put her back in shape, and most times I can." He was also the world's greatest scavenger. As LuAnn proudly told everyone, "My Billy can make somethin' outta nothin' to beat the band." Before long, Billy had built the best shelter for them in all of Cooperville— and everybody said so. He called it his Taj Mahal, another place he always said he wanted to take LuAnn. After twelve years of marriage, they had no children. But they were devoted to each other. "He's all I got, and all I need," said LuAnn. "Ditto," said Billy.

No one had ever heard shrieks like those that came from Billy's Taj Mahal at about 7 p.m. that Sunday. They sounded like they came from an animal, not a human being. LuAnn had gone for a walk. Billy said he was tired and wanted to rest. LuAnn was only gone an hour when she returned to find his blood-soaked body on the floor. Overcome, she collapsed, and when she came-to about twenty minutes later, she still hadn't grasped what had happened. "Billy," she called, "get up. Get up. Get up." And then came the shrieks and the uncontrollable sobbing. "Oh, my God," she screamed as she ran out for help.

From everywhere people came to find out what was wrong. Before long, the Taj was surrounded by an agitated mob. Who could have done this? Why would anyone do it—to Billy, of all people? Within a few minutes, several members from Internal Security arrived. Immediately, someone went for Mr. B and Wilson Brackett. Several women tried to console LuAnn but she was in a state of shock. They wrapped her in a blanket and held her in their arms as she rocked back and forth, trying to speak but unable to.

People had died in Cooperville, but no one had ever been murdered. So, even when Mr. B and Wilson Brackett arrived, they didn't know what to do. One woman screamed, "We need justice. We need to know who did this." But the two men simply shrugged their shoulders. At another time in another place, someone would already have called the police. But this was corporate New York City in the Corporate States of America. The city's force had been outsourced to a private company, and its only responsibility was protecting corporate assets and executives. If New Yorkers ever wanted justice, it would have to start with their private security detail. Mr. B and Brackett asked the obvious question: "Did anybody see or hear anything out of the ordinary?" But nobody had—or was willing to say they had.

Mr. B couldn't get anyone to donate any land for a pauper's cemetery. They couldn't bury anyone in the park, of course. So, he had arranged for bodies to be sold to New York State Medical School. LuAnn would get half the proceeds. The Cooperville treasury would get the rest. He had just gotten off the phone starting the process, when a TV reporter and her crew stopped him. "What's going on here?" she asked. "Murder," he answered. "The nicest guy you'd ever want to meet—stabbed to death like an animal. I don't know what his poor wife is going to do. He was all she had. I don't know what anyone is going to do. Nothing like this has ever happened before."

Countess Isabella had just gotten into bed to watch the late night news. "This is NewsWatch 11, and I'm Sandra Phillips," the reporter began. "Was it a random act of murder? Or is there a killer loose in Cooperville? And was it someone from outside the park or one of their own? Those are the questions everyone's asking tonight. No one's getting any sleep. Here's my interview with the murdered man's wife, LuAnn Buford.

"LuAnn, tell me in your own words what happened tonight."

"Well, Sandra, I don't know where to begin, but I came back from a walk and saw Billy lyin' on the floor. I musta blacked out, 'cause when I came-to I was lyin' next to him and he was dead. Blood everywhere."

"Come quick, Henry!" the countess calls to her husband who is in the bathroom.

"What's the matter?"

"Ah grew up with this woman, LuAnn, in Mississippi."

"You sure?"

"Ah wouldn't forget someone like her. We were friends, real friends! Listen! Her husband has just been murdered."

"LuAnn, how long have you been living in Cooperville? And how did you wind up there?" Phillips asks.

"We never thought we'd come to this, Sandra, so down on our luck, ya know. We wuz hard workers, Billy and me. He was a mechanic, makin' okay money, sometimes even good money when he took on extra jobs. But I never wanted him to work too extra hard. We always got by, did better than most. We had each other, which is all that counts. I did domestic work and took in sewin' and ironin'. In Mississippi. Did I say we wuz in Mississippi? Well, one day the flood come, like nothin' nobody's ever seen. Wiped uz out. Wiped all of uz out. Imagine, everythin' gone—just like that! We'd lived in our trailer almost free and clear. Paid everythin' on time. Never missed a month. But we couldn't afford no in-surance.

"So, when the rains come and then the flood, we wuz wiped out. The whole area wuz practically, what you call, a war zone. Businesses destroyed. Houses washed away. Nothin' left. Then, one day, a big New York developer comes in and takes over the whole place—acres and acres and acres. Almost no one could afford in-surance. And the few who did didn't have enough. He says people don't own their land 'cause they ain't got proper deeds. So, he buys it up for next to nothin'—all of it. No one protected us. The developer paid off everybody. With no place to go, we just started headin' north, thinkin' we'd find work and a place to live somewhere. But times are tough. That's how we wound up in Cooperville."

"I've had enough of this nonsense," the count says as he shuts off the TV. "Why are you watching those deadbeats?"

"Ah told you. Ah know her, Ah *knew* her," Isabella answers, shocked at his reaction. She tries to turn the TV on again but he won't let her. "Can't we do anything to help her? We've got to do something. Her husband's just been killed. She's got nothing."

"Listen, you piece of white trash," he answers, gripping Isabella's left wrist until she winces. "You're not in Mississippi anymore, and don't you forget it. I've spent a fortune getting the backwoods outta you. So, you just forget 'em."

"Stop, you're hurting me, Henry," she cries, as he twists his fist, burning her skin. He's mad, now, his eyes burning.

"I heard those hard luck stories when I started buying up their land and I don't give a shit. Who do you think she's talking about? Who do you think bought up all those acres and did all those things she said were so terrible? Me, that's who! That's my development, damnit. It's a fuckin' city. It's my fuckin' city. I've made a fuckin' city. And it's just about finished. And I'm about to make more money than I've ever made. Nobody, not them, or you, or anyone else is gonna stand in my way. Not now, when I'm about to cash in."

"We've gotta help her. Ah've gotta help her…"

"Listen you whore, don't you ever tell me what I've gotta do. Don't go near her or any of them, you hear—or else. I found you waiting tables and you'll be lucky to get a job waiting tables if I get sick of you. Just remember who made you a fuckin' countess—and who can unmake you a fuckin' countess."

Sobbing, the countess runs into the bathroom and locks the door. The count goes to the window and looks out on the park. "Cooperville, my ass," he says out loud, laughing to himself but also knitting his brow. "Fuck 'em all. John Galt lives—with a vengeance!"

Mr. B, Wilson Brackett, and Alma Parks meet at 11 p.m. in Mr. B's tent. "We need to come up with a strategy and get the word out," Mr. B says. "Things are never going to be the same for a long time or until someone's caught. Even then, no one is ever going to feel safe again. We've got to assume we've got a murderer loose—and it could be anyone, even one of our own."

THREE

Infiltrate, Intimidate, Extricate

MONDAY, JUNE 6: 10 A.M., NEW ATLANTIS. Baron Rooky, Manfreed's forever genial alter ego, greets everyone at the front door of Holly-field-Smyth House. The Tudor mansion is the first one that Dagny Taggart bought to expand New Atlantis. Its fifteen bedrooms housed the earliest residents. Administrative offices are still located on the first floor. It wasn't the oldest or the biggest of the properties she eventually acquired. But to her, it was the grandest. The circular driveway in front, the massive blue spruce on either side of it, and the broad, flat expanses of golf-tee quality lawn in every direction gave the mansion the same take-charge look she admired in people, mostly men—in particular, its former owner, the late media magnate G. Hollyfield-Smyth, who successfully led the fight against federal laws prohibiting communications monopolies, then cornered the market in no fewer than sixteen metropolitan areas and became the country's chief political king-maker.

In addition to the yearly celebration of the Galtian Restoration for the masses, like the one held two days ago, The Circle of Atlas holds it annual meeting in June in the great hall of the mansion. Dagny conceived of the society as the steward of John Galt's legacy and, next to her investment in the Venture Fund, her most important contribution. She wrote its charter herself, limiting The Circle to fifty members including a five-member executive committee, which she chaired right up to the time she died. Members are limited to two terms of five years, except for her. "We must always have new blood," she said. "Otherwise we'll stagnate." At least five members must be graduates of New Atlantis resident programs. Hoping to spark and maintain the revolution worldwide, she stipulated that there be no less than six members from foreign countries, no more than two from any one. Dagny dictated that members of The Circle are to carry on John Galt's fight against "looters," to manage The Taggart Venture Fund, and to invest in projects of promising entrepreneurs that can provide a revenue stream for New Atlantis.

Perhaps because of the 67th Anniversary, this year forty-six members have made the trip, the largest number in five years. Among the most prominent are the Kork brothers, Daniel and Ridge, from Dallas. They inherited billions from "Big Daddy" Kork, as they called him. But they would be the first to insist that they are self-made, that they always put in an honest day's work—as long as committing securities fraud counts as work and honesty is defined as having friendly judges quash their ongoing indictments. When anyone asks them how much money they have, they always answer that they have no idea, but they just want more of it. Circle member Alfredo Vicenza came from Chicago. Formerly a labor organizer, he became a patron saint of Free-for-All economics when he destroyed the Amalgamated Workers of America, the union he helped found, after he was forced to resign because of alleged improprieties. Sitting next to him in the great hall is Professor Mortimer Lacey, long-time member of the New Atlantis faculty. With a grant from the Kork brothers' foundation, he produced the research that claimed definitively to prove global warming was a myth—findings that coincidentally protected the Korks' oil and gas investment—and that led to the dismantling of the federal Environmental Protection Agency.

When Manfreed walks in, Philip Schwartz, the media mogul, is standing and pointing his right finger accusingly at Walter Baffler, the Internet genius. "They're getting away with murder and you're letting them," he says, while Baffler first shakes his head yes (to indicate he agreed "they" were) then quickly to no (refusing take responsibility). But as soon as Manfreed reaches the podium, everyone takes a seat.

"I'd like to welcome all of you to the annual meeting of the Circle of Atlas and especially those of you who have come from around the world. We all extend an extra-special welcome to Señor Mauricio Valdez from Peru, who is with us for the first time and who has taken the lead in privatizing all of the mineral resources of his country." The Kork brothers clap enthusiastically, having invested $2 billion in the takeover, according to *The Journal of International Commerce*.

"With government regulation out of the way, profits are skyrocketing and production costs have been cut in half. The military has moved swiftly to put down labor unrest. Señor Valdez, you and your country can become a model not only for South America, but for the world.

"And now," Manfreed says solemnly, "let us bow our heads and recite 'The Hoarder's Prayer': 'Our father, who spits on Lenin, trademarked be our name. Our billions come, our bills be paid—in cash, by check, or on credit. Give us this day our daily pay and pile on our profits as we corner markets before markets corner us. And lead us not into insolvency, but deliver us from competition. For ours are the franchise, the profit, and the riches for ever and ever. Amen.'

"I'm sorry to have to report the passing, earlier this year, of Dr. Melany Goodette. For the past fifteen years, she tirelessly led the fight for the complete deregulation of the pharmaceutical industry against the FDA—an entrenched bureaucracy if ever there was one. Dr. Goodette died just three months before her goals were achieved. The FDA is dead. And Dr. Goodette killed it, with the help of New Atlantis and people like you, of course." The group applauds wildly. "As you will soon hear, Dr. Goddette's effort has been a key factor in the spectacular success of Atlas Energy Drink and Atlas Fitness Centers, as well as the millions of dollars we are making as a result."

"Hilton, sorry to interrupt, but we are going to address Saturday's debacle, aren't we?" shouts Philip Schwartz. "The whole world is saying that John Galt is dead. It's embarrassing. My phone has been ringing off-the-hook. It's on the front page of every newspaper, all over TV, and it's the only thing people are talking about on the Internet. I should have said disaster, not debacle. We need a strategy. Do you have a strategy?"

"Debacle? Disaster? Who's side are you on Phil?" Manfreed asks. "Are you going to let some amateurish prank throw you? I can't believe my ears. Let me make one thing perfectly clear: Saturday was not a debacle—for us. But it's going to be for the two-bit nobodies who don't know who they're up against. You have no reason to be embarrassed, Phil. Just look around you. Have you taken the power in this room for granted? Does it look like John Galt is dead? We're stronger than ever—and we're going to get stronger, especially when we crush the enemy."

He grits his teeth, clenches his fist, and pounds on the podium. "We own this country now—and we will forever! We have created a permanent majority who share our beliefs and know how to put them into action." He pounds the podium again. Looking around the room so as to make eye-contact with everyone, he adds, "We're never going to let a worthless bunch of looters take it from us. Never! This afternoon, I'll be on a conference call with the White House to discuss a nationwide strategy to crush the opposition. In a few minutes, I'll tell you what I'm planning to tell the president and the cabinet. Then, you can tell me your ideas. By the time we're through, those half-ass punks will be sorry they ever started up with us. Debacle? Disaster?—for them!

"Now, let's move on to something more pleasant: making barrels of money. The newest members of The Circle are here to update us on the Atlas Fitness Centers phenomenon, for that's what it is, you know—an absolute, one-of-a-kind, super-colossal phenomenon. They are stars of the first order. Talk about making headlines! John Galt dead, my ass! Soon enough, *these* 'John Galts' are going to make headlines worldwide. They have revolutionized health and fitness, mind and body harmony. And they are making money for us—and themselves—hand over fist. In less than one year, they have become *the* major source of funds for all of New Atlantis. Dagny would be so proud! I can see the broad grin on her face, as though she were alive and in front of me. In the best sense of the word, they are drugging the country—soon, the world—as a result of Free-for-All economics. Enrique, I believe you're going to begin."

"Thank you, Hilton. For those of you who weren't here on Saturday, I am Enrique Reyes, and I'm thrilled to be a member of The Circle. With me are Zora Tremmon and Albert Swift. With a grant from the Taggart Venture Fund—which I'm happy to say we've already repaid—we created Atlas Fitness Centers, the most comprehensive health and wellness network anywhere in the world. I developed the secret formula for the most powerful high-energy drink ever produced. Zora, Albert, please pass out samples and our brochure to everyone. Albert created the patented Titan Whole-Body Harmony Machine. As you can see from the photograph, the machine is deceptively simple—an inverted cross. Aside from the fact that it's made of Rearden Metal, so it's indestructible, it is based upon laws of physics that Albert knows but that I'll never understand. And the physical and mental benefits it produces are revolutionary. Zora is our marketing genius. Without her, we'd be nothing.

"Atlas Fitness Centers are more than just places people go to exercise. Oh, people may come to us to get in shape, but they get more than they ever imagined they could find anywhere. Our real goal is— and now I'm speaking confidentially among friends—to advance the mission of New Atlantis. We are strengthening people's bodies and minds to accept the principles of Free-for-All economics. The stronger they get, the more they understand that they are natural leaders who have the right and the ability to seize control of the economies of the world. We train them to become clones of the confident, drugged Atlas in the lobby of d'Anconia Pavilion. Each drop of Atlas Energy Drink they swallow—we call it our 'miracle drug'— makes them more and more potent powerhouses for free markets. They're sold on *everything* New Atlantis stands for.

"Yes?" Enrique says to Count Henry de Horsch, who's chomping at the bit to say something.

"I'm a charter member of the Midtown Manhattan Atlas Center Headquarters," says the count, "and I have to say the service and effectiveness of the program are unmatched anywhere."

"Thank you, Count Henry. We're especially pleased to get your endorsement. And I'm pleased to say we get 100 percent stupendous feedback, as you can see from the testimonials in our brochure. Our economic model is based upon recruiting apprentice trainers. We provide them, free-of-charge, with unlimited amounts of Atlas Energy drink, use of equipment, plus room and board within centers. They provide services to paying customers and collect a percentage of fees for any premium services they provide. Some recent trainees are now successful franchise-owners. They're hooked on it. It's a perfect free-market model. And the proof is, in the nine months since we opened our doors, we now have one hundred centers spread out in all fifty states and are adding locations at the rate of five a week.

"Atlas Energy is catching on like wild fire. We've entered into distribution agreements, so it's being sold in supermarkets, 7-11's, health-food stores, everywhere soft drink and health products are marketed. It's the fastest growing product in all of the Corporate States, and we have plans to launch internationally early next year. We are making seventy percent profit on the Fitness Centers. And our success would never have been possible without New Atlantis and all of the positive effects of the Galtian Restoration. In our unregulated marketplace, the sky's been our limit. The FDA would have made us jump through hoops to prove our claims. And we'd still be waiting for the go-ahead to launch the product. We wouldn't have made a dime yet. But we found nutritionists to back up our claims, and their studies have been a major factor in our success. So, nothing can stop us."

"Thank you for that most uplifting—or should I say cash-register-ringing?—report, Enrique," Manfreed adds, smiling like a Cheshire cat and rubbing his hands over each other like a witch concocting her brew. "Enrique left out—perhaps out of modesty—the specifics of the most important part of the Fitness Center's success. They've already paid back the $500,000 loan from the Taggart Venture Fund, with interest of course, plus $4.5 million in royalties. That's an astounding $5 million payback in less than a year.

"And there's more good news to report. John Galt is not dead, not by any means—and there are no signs that *he* will be anytime soon, so sorry to disappoint our enemies." Pointing to a map of the Corporate States, Manfreed continues: "Texas to North Carolina, you'll notice, is all in the darkest green. That's because we've been able to put governors and legislatures in place who are completely aligned with us. In these states, privatization has taken over the roles of government by more than ninety percent. Power plants, highways and local roads, airports and seaports, schools, hospitals, and other assets and services are now in the hands of for-profit business. And they are making money hand over fist.

"From New Mexico north to Montana and Washington and west to California, in lighter green, there are some trouble spots—mostly in Colorado, California and Oregon, where local areas have tried to reinstall looter government agencies and re-impose regulations on businesses. In lime green, Wisconsin, Minnesota, Illinois, and Michigan are showing signs of discontent. Some unions are trying to reorganize. From Ohio and Pennsylvania north to Maine, we have the greatest challenges. That's why that whole region is in white, without a trace of green. Out of the fifty states, at least three-fifths are firmly or solidly in our plus column. But we cannot take anything for granted, of course.

"Mother Nature has looked out for us this year. We never lose sight of the cardinal principle of Free-for-All economics, 'Every disaster is a buying opportunity,' or put another way, 'Other people's misery is our good fortune.' 'Mother' has helped us beyond our wildest dreams. Wildfires in Arizona, floods in Sacramento, a bridge collapse in Tampa, Florida, and tornadoes throughout the mid-West created new opportunities for turning public assets over to private interests. State and local governments have been starved of revenue for so long, they couldn't rebuild or help individuals affected by disasters to do so. So Count de Horsch in Mississippi, whose private city, Horschville, will soon be completely sold out, and others are making millions and radically altering the landscape of the states forever. Traitorous pranksters can claim John Galt is dead all they want to. Profit-and-loss sheets tell a different story.

"So, now we come to our recent unpleasantness. We take nothing for granted. But we also know we always get stronger when we're challenged. Whoever was foolish enough to break into our sound system on Saturday—and we'll soon know who it is—will pay dearly. We need to ask ourselves, 'What would John Galt do?' And we need to let everyone know that John Galt is more alive now than ever. We need to double-down and act like we're Atlas drugged on steroids and more powerful than ever—because we are. Defeat is not an option. It never is—especially with us. Our enemies should know that by now. But they haven't learned that lesson, which is why we're in power and they're not—and never will be.

"As I mentioned, at one o'clock this afternoon, I will be on a conference call with the White House to discuss nationwide strategies to defeat the enemy. With the election just a few months away, President Cooper has personally told me he wants the opposition crushed. So, I will share with him the surefire two-pronged attack we've developed." Pointing to a fifty-inch TV monitor at the front of the room, Manfreed says, "I believe all of you know the world-renown master of lexipsychographics, Professor Clyde Doppelmann. He's coming to us via a satellite feed. Professor, we're delighted to have you with us. Please explain our media strategy to our most distinguished members of The Circle of Atlas."

"It will be my high honor to, Professor Manfreed." Doppelmann is in his early fifties. His long, ski-slope nose and fluted nostrils lead to a prominent square jaw. His light-brown toupee curls up on his dark-brown sideburns, accentuating what it's supposed to camouflage. He looks straight into the camera. "In my latest book, *If the Pen is Mightier than the Sword, How Come Writers Aren't King?*, I explain that you've gotta have force and power to back up your words or you're just full of hot air. And in my book, *Schlock Doctrine: Feed People Garbage Long Enough and They'll Think It's Caviar*, I explain that Americans are lazy and stupid. We can *always* get the public to believe what we want—as long as we understand the power of lying—and the moral imperative to do it. Lies are the purest example of how the principles of Free-for-All economics can be powerfully applied to every aspect of life. A lie is simply the truth massaged for the benefit of the person promoting it. The trick is to understand the power of lying and *never* to tell the truth. Once you're committed to telling the truth, you're boxed in by facts. As long as you lie, you've got leverage. People will believe lies faster than they'll accept the truth. It's easier to convince people that the sky is green than that it's blue. Tell them up is down and that one and one makes three—and they'll fall for it every time. But tell them that one and one makes two, and they'll try to prove you wrong every time. I believe there are copies of both books for sale in the back of the room.

"The Corporate States need a new tune that the people can hum— a winning new campaign. We need to rebrand ourselves. And based upon my research, our new motto should be 'John Galt created the Internet.'"

"What?" an unidentified voice in the back of the room blurts out.

"Hear me out! It's a perfect application of schlock doctrine. Your opposition is claiming that John Galt is dead. So, don't fall into the trap of saying, 'He's alive.' Studies consistently show that opposites reinforce each other. If you say 'alive,' your listeners will think 'dead.' You've got to come up with a credible lie to make people think John Galt is alive; otherwise, they won't believe you.

"I call the strategy 'Detour Thinking' in *Schlock Doctrine*. The more outrageous what you say is, the more readily it will be believed. Remember what I told you: People will believe lies more readily than truths. Don't ever bother explaining anything to anyone. Repeat, repeat, repeat if you want to be believed. Of course, to the one-tenth of one percent of the population with a brain and willing to use it, you can make the case that John Galt started the Rational Restoration that provided the economic climate for the entrepreneurship that led to the World Wide Web. But don't waste your breath on the masses. The issue will never come up. They are waiting to be duped, yearning to be duped, hungry to be duped. They'll spread the word all over the Internet that John Galt created it. End of story for 'John Galt is dead.'"

"I think it's brilliant," Manfreed says.

"But did John Galt *really* create the Internet?" the Kork brothers ask in unison. They *always* speak in unison in public.

"Absolutely!" Doppelmann assures them.

"A powerful fact, a powerful fact, most impressive, first we've heard of it," they chant.

"Clyde, let's go full steam ahead—fliers, TV, Internet, op-eds," Manfreed says, genuinely excited. "And I'm sure you'll be hearing from the White House after I share the idea. Now, Zora, I believe you're going to explain our 'on-the-ground' strategy."

"Glady, Professor Manfreed," she replies, moving to the front of the room. "In a word, our strategy is to infiltrate Coopervilles around the country and destroy them from within. We're going to recruit physically fit trainees for Atlas Fitness Centers from them, take them into our confidence, and get information that can help us destroy the saboteurs. I mean we all know that the opposition has to be coming from those hell holes, don't we? We'll offer them food, shelter, and the possibility of a promising future. From what we hear, most of them are desperate. So, we can win them over easily."

"Thank you, Zora. I think our two-pronged strategy will crush those bastards once and for all. As Zora says, make no mistake about it: All of our opposition comes right from the hotbeds of socialism in Coopervilles. Now, if you'll excuse me, I have to prepare for my conference call with the White House."

"Professor Manfreed, may I?" Count de Horsch says, without waiting for an answer as he moves to the front of the room. "My fellow Circle Members, once Coopervilles have been neutralized, I plan to move forward with my plans to develop Central Park into a mall and amusement park. It will be a cash-cow, without a doubt. I've been assured by the mayor that my generous bid will be accepted. One of the anchors in the mall will be the biggest Atlas Fitness Center in the world, with an indoor pool, tennis and racket ball courts, and a track. It will have its own hotel for overnight visitors. It's also gonna have a miniature train running around the perimeter. Kids'll love it. The architects should have completed drawings by Friday."

"Thank you, Count," Manfreed interjects, mildly peeved at the interruption. "And now I really must prepare for my meeting. Thank you all for coming. You will be kept up-to-date on all developments."

MONDAY, JUNE 6, 12:45 P.M.: THE WHITE HOUSE SITUATION ROOM. Top advisors to President Ham Cooper are waiting for the start of the 1 p.m. emergency meeting. Hilton Manfreed is present via a satellite feed from New Atlantis. The president has told the Corporate Council, the CSA's real governing body, that he considers the interruptions on Saturday proclaiming John Galt dead a serious, potential threat to his re-election in November. Privately, he's told everyone but Manfreed, of course, that he thinks "the old geezer" is "over the hill" and needs to be replaced as the head of New Atlantis.

Cooper is the fifth former CEO to have become president of the Corporate States of America. He was a high-school freshman when Galt and company returned from the valley. But he has never forgotten the suffering he endured during the strike. His father's oil rigs were taken over by the people Galt labeled looters, so his family lost its fortune—and his inheritance. He tells everyone the government raped them. To him, Galt was God—not *a* god, *the* one-and-only, who had delivered them from evil. When he graduated, he refused to go to college. "I know everything I need to know," he told everyone. "And all I need to know is how to make money anyway I can." His family reclaimed its holdings under the Asset Recovery Act Galt implemented. Cooper capitalized on the deregulation and privatization of energy resources by buying up oil, gas, and nuclear facilities in state after state. His business strategy was "Acquire and Fire." He'd put two profitable companies together, fire half the workforce, raise rates, and make a killing—and there was no one to stop him after all government regulations had been done away with. By the time he was twenty-five, he controlled energy production in ten states and was a multi-billionaire. He had never held public office when he ran for president, but he had all the money he needed to campaign. He won with sixty-three percent of the vote. His winning slogan was, "Less government is too much. No government is just about enough."

Never one for small talk, Cooper takes his seat in the middle of the conference table and holds up one newspaper from a stack of at least twenty-five. "As everyone can see, the whole front page is the headline 'John Galt Is Dead.' How did this happen? Why didn't our friends who own these goddamn rags stop this? With friends like this, we don't need enemies. All the articles go on to say, 'A mystery voice turned the 67th Anniversary Celebration at New Atlantis into a fiasco.'"

Throwing the paper on top of the pile and slamming his hand on the table, he fumes, "This is what the fuck we're up against. It's all anyone is talking about. A mysterious, two-bit voice interrupts the 67th Anniversary Celebration at New Atlantis and we're looking like fuckin' fools."

Leaning forward, his eyes squinting as he looks around the table, Cooper adds, "Something has gone terribly, terribly wrong. Those interruptions on Saturday were no accident. Obviously, hardcore terrorists have made inroads into New Atlantis. And those jokers out there haven't got a clue. They've gone soft on us. Think tank, my ass! We've never had any security problems before. Last year, we put down all those protests in Mississippi over coastal development and nobody said a word. If anybody had a case it was those folks, but nothing, not a peep. Professor Manfreed," Cooper says, for the first time addressing the face on the TV monitor, "what's going on over there in your brain trust? Have you lost control? We can't have this. We can't be made to look like fools. We need a strategy to stamp out these rats. I've got an election I've got to win or you can kiss goodbye to your Free-for-All economics. That bitch, Cary Hinton will put all of us out of business. You listening, Manfreed?"

On the monitor, Manfreed looks like he's been punched in the gut. "President Cooper, let me assure you that everything at New Atlantis is under control. Believe me, I know what a disaster Hinton would be. We've already begun implementing a two-pronged strategy to crush the opposition. Professor Clyde Dopplemann has come up with a powerful media campaign to counter all that 'John Galt is dead' garbage. That's all it is—garbage. Dopplemann's brilliant alternative is 'John Galt created the Internet.' I've told him to saturate the media with the message. We're also going to infiltrate Coopervilles ..."

Cooper, enraged, interrupts him, shouting, "Don't ever call those human garbage heaps Coopervilles! They are displacement camps, illegal, squatter displacement camps. The people there have displaced themselves. They're there because they *want* to be there. Nobody made them go there. Don't *ever* say Cooperville again, you hear?

"Sorry, of course," Manfreed says flustered. "We're going to infiltrate all those displacement…human garbage camp…illegal…squatter heaps around the country, recruit trainees from them for Atlas Fitness Centers, and get information that can help us destroy the saboteurs."

"Thank you, Professor," Cooper says dismissively. "Turn off the feed," he tells the technician, shaking his head in disgust and disappointment. "Is he gone?"

"For sure," the young man says.

"So, John Galt created the Internet. And I'm the Tooth Fairy. Well, gentlemen, it's obviously up to us. The good professor is out-to-lunch. Simmons, what have your intelligence sources turned up?" he asks the head of the FBI.

"Mr. President, this is definitely a coordinated, nationwide sabotage. 'John Galt Is Dead' signs are plastered everywhere in every Cooperv…I mean in every illegal displacement camp. But there's another message they're putting out. In Chicago, Dallas, Seattle, and Boston, planes have been seen pulling a banner with 'Truth is Beauty. Beauty Truth' written on it."

"What the fuck does that mean?"

"That's what our cryptographers are working on right now, sir. We think it's code for a radical gay-socialist-communist-artist cabal. It may even be part of an international conspiracy. In San Antonio, the message they're putting out is '*La belleza es verdad. La verdad, belleza.*' Don't worry. I've got my best experts on it. They'll crack it."

"Mr. President," Homeland Security Director Smathers interjects. "Mr. President, we have been infiltrating the displacement camps for months. Our most up-to-date reports suggest that the squatters are simply unemployed men and women, many with children, who are moving from place to place to find work. All of our intelligence points to their just being desperate people struggling to survive."

"That's impossible," Cooper says emphatically. "I don't believe it for a minute. There's got to be something wrong with your intelligence. Find a way to pin something on as many of them as you can. We've got to have a reason to get rid of that trash once and for all. I can't have them there on Election Day. Of course this is off the record: Do whatever it takes. If you need to, just plant drugs and weapons, then round up suspects and throw them in jail, including the ring-leaders. That way, we can claim they are lawbreakers and national security risks. I don't want to know the details. Keep me out of the loop. It's completely in your hands now. Just get the job done. And get rid of the camp on the Capital Mall—now! That's high priority. It's spoiling my view. I can't go out on the balcony for a little relaxation without having to see those horrible people. Make it an example for the rest of the country. Smathers, contact Manfreed and tell him he's got some great ideas and he should proceed with his plans. But let him know we'll be doing it our way, too. Just don't get specific."

TUESDAY, JUNE 7, 11 A.M.: MIDTOWN MANHATTAN. Countess Isabella leaves the Plaza Hotel. In a plain white blouse, crisply pleated blue skirt, and white heels, she quickly crosses Central Park South. It's windy, so she tries to hold her hair in place with her left hand. She enters Central Park with the care of a lion tamer entering a cage. "LuAnn Buford?" she asks the first person she sees, a woman in her thirties holding a five-year-old girl by the hand. "Can you tell me where ah might find LuAnn Buford, the woman whose husband was killed yesterday, the woman who was on TV last night?"

"No ma'am, sorry I can't," the stranger says, looking suspiciously at her. "But if you keep going on the walk, you'll find someone who can probably help you."

About twenty feet beyond, from a large white tent in which three men are talking, a man wearing a blue-and-white badge emerges. "I'm Richard C.," he says, before Isabella can say a word. "May I help you?"

"Ahm looking for LuAnn Buford, the woman whose husband was killed yesterday, the woman ah saw on TV last night. Ah really need to speak with her."

"Gladly," he replies. "Let me escort you. It's a ways." They walk about thirty feet, when Isabella suddenly holds her chest with her right hand, seeming to have a hard time breathing. "Ma'am, is there a problem?"

"No, Ah'll be all right. It's just the young woman walking ahead of us, with the three children. They're so young. She's so young."

"Ma'am, you know what this place is, don't you?"

"Yes, of course, ah do," Isabella says, fanning herself with her right hand. "Ah can look down on it from my bedroom window. I live in the Plaza Hotel. Ah've just never been down here, this close, seeing people eye-to-eye, like regular people."

"There are thousands of us, ma'am, down on our luck. Most of us were something once. We've all got names, and faces, and stories to tell anyone who cares. Most people don't. They look the other way, don't want to see what's here. Some don't want to know about it. Some think we're just lazy. Some think we've got bugs and disease. Angie and her kids are on her way to the lunch feeding. She wants to get there early to be sure there's enough food for all of them. She's looking after her children like any good mother. Her husband Jeff is out looking for work, any kind of work. I saw him leave this morning. He goes out every day at 6 a.m. Some days he finds work, just for the day. You can tell when he comes back with a smile on his face and can't wait to find Angie and the kids. Most days he doesn't. But he keeps trying. These are good people, ma'am, but they're desperate. They've got no place to go but here. This country isn't for people any more, hasn't been for a long time. It's owned by corporations. They don't give a damn about real people.

"You'll find LuAnn over there," John C. says, pointing straight ahead. "Billy called it the Taj Mahal, because he was so in love with LuAnn. He *really* put his heart into making their place the best in

Cooperville. I warn you, I was with her just an hour ago, she's still in a state of shock. If you'd like, I'll go in and tell her there's someone here to see her. Maybe that'll make it easier for both of you."

"Thank you," the countess replies, shaking her head in disbelief, then waiting outside, assuming LuAnn will come out.

"You're here to see *me*?" LuAnn asks suspiciously. "John C. said 'a fine-looking lady' was here to see me."

"Why, yes, of course, LuAnn."

"I know that voice," LuAnn replies, taking Isabella in from head to toe. "But the face, the face. Oh my God, can it be you? Idabelle? Idabelle Sue Raft?" she says, burying her face in both hands in embarrassment, not knowing whether to laugh or cry. "How did you get here? How did you find me? How did you know? I can't bear for you to see me this way. I, I, Billy, you know about Billy? How could you know about Billy?" she asks, breaking out into tears. "How could they do this to Billy?"

"Calm down, LuAnn," Isabella says, as she hugs her. "Just take it easy. Ahm here for you. Ah know about everything, well everything that was on TV. Ah saw you on the news last night."

"But look at you, Idabelle, just look at you. You look like a rich lady, one fine, rich lady."

"Well actually, ahm not Idabelle anymore. I'm the Countess Isabella de Horsch. My husband the count and I live right over there in the Plaza Hotel," she says, pointing south. "Our apartment looks right out over the park."

"You gotta look out on all of us? Not a pretty sight! A countess, a countess, my word. I always knew our Idabelle would amount to something. But a countess, a countess," she says, again almost collapsing in tears.

"Enough about me. I want to know all about you and what happened last night."

"Well, Billy and I wound up here after we were wiped out in the flood in Mississippi and we lost our land, our trailer, our clothes, our furniture, everything. Then, while the water was still knee-deep, a big developer come in, said we didn't have clear title, or whatever, to our property, so he bought it right out from under us. We didn't have insurance, but Billy could have rebuilt our place. He was an auto mechanic, but he could fix anything. 'Gimme anythin' broke and I'll put her back in shape,' he'd always say. And that wasn't just boasting. He could do almost anything.

"Well, the whole town was wiped out, too. There was nothing left. First the flood, then the developer took everything. Some people had relatives who took them in. We had no one. So, we just headed out, looking for work and a place to sleep. Billy's truck got swamped in the flood, so we didn't even have transportation. We walked and hitched rides through Alabama, Florida, and Georgia. In South Carolina, Billy found work as a handyman at an apartment building for about two months. We had our own apartment, and things were starting to look up. I almost got a job as a waitress. But then, the bank foreclosed on the building, and that was the end of that. We just kept moving north, but we couldn't make a dime. Finally, we wound up in New York City, where Billy always said he wanted to take me, 'cept we had nothing, absolutely nothing and nowhere to go.

"Finally, we wound up here, in the park. They call it Cooperville, you know, after the president, 'cause he and his people don't give a shit about people like us. Pardon my language, but it's the truth. Billy built our place all by himself. He called it the Taj Mahal, because he said he loved me so much. He always said he wanted to take me to the real one, but I knew we'd never have the money. Billy showed it to me in pictures, which was good enough for me. We never had kids. I was all he had. He was all I had," LuAnn says, nearly collapsing. Isabella holds her for about five minutes. Neither one of them says a word.

"Okay, I can go on," LuAnn says. "Last night, I went for a walk. Billy said he was tired and wanted to rest. When I came back, he was on the floor, dead—not just dead, murdered in cold blood. Why did I ever leave him, I keep asking myself? He'd be alive, maybe, if I hadn't gone.

There was nothing anyone could do for him when I found him. Times have changed. There are no police to call. Unless you've got private security, you're not protected. Nobody cares about people like us. Billy's body was sold to a medical school. Look. They gave me $200, half of what they got for him. The rest went to help everyone in Cooperville. That's all a man's worth these days—if he's lucky. They treat animals better."

"LuAnn, ahm gonna help you," Isabella says. She hands her an envelope. "There's $500 in here, and it's just the beginning. Ahm gonna find you a job and help you get an apartment if you want to stay here. If you want to leave New York, ah'll help you get wherever you want to go. Ahm rich now. Ah'll take care of you." They both look up when a young woman peeks through the door.

"Excuse me. I'm Anne Guthrie," she says. "Channel 10 News. I'm looking for LuAnn Buford."

"That's me," LuAnn replies. "And this is my friend, the countess."

"I'm Countess Isabella de Horsch," Isabella says, offering to shake hands.

"Did you say 'de Horsch?'"

"Why yes," Isabella replies, flattered at apparently having been recognized.

"Is your husband Count Henry de Horsch?"

"Why yes, of course," Isabella answers, feeling even more like a celebrity.

"I came here to talk with LuAnn about Billy's murder. But since I found you here, I'd really like to ask you a few questions, if you don't mind. Countess, are you aware of how many people in Cooperville are here, like LuAnn, because, after the flooding in Mississippi, your husband challenged their claims to their land, paid next to nothing for their property, and made them homeless?"

"Ah know nothing about my husband's business dealings. But he's an honorable man. He *always* does right by people."

"Do you think it's *right* to steal other people's land?"

"Why, of course not."

"Why are you here, anyway?"

LuAnn interrupts. "The countess is my friend. We grew up to-gether. She was Idabelle Sue Raft then. She saw me on TV last night and came here to help. Look she gave me $500 to help me get on. And she's promised to take care of me."

"LuAnn, ahm gonna leave you to your guest, but ah'll be back. Nice to have met you, I'm sure—Miss Guthrie, isn't it?" And with that, the countess makes a quick exit.

TUESDAY, JUNE 7, 3 P.M.: TIMES SQUARE, MANHATTAN. On the giant TV screen facing 42nd Street, scheduled programming is interrupted.

"I'm Anne Guthrie, and this is a breaking news exclusive from Channel 10. The wife of a developer brings guilt money to Coop-erville. A phony countess brings cash to her childhood friend, one of thousands her husband defrauded. You're hearing it *only* on Channel 10! During my visit to LuAnn Buford, whose husband was murdered last night in the Central Park Cooperville, I was introduced to none other than the Countess Isabella de Horsch. It turns out the royal's real name is Idabelle Sue Raft, and she was born closer to an outhouse than the manor. The fake aristocrat and her husband bought their ti-tles from an Internet company so they could rip off the poor and still hobnob in society. The unscrupulous count has made millions by stealing other people's property out from under them. Rumor has it that he wants to bulldoze Cooperville so he can buy up Central Park and develop it as a profit-making mall and amusement park. Hear from LuAnn Buford how Count Henry destroyed her life and the lives of everyone else in coastal Mississippi. Stay tuned throughout the day as this story unfolds."

TUESDAY, JUNE 7, 5 P.M.: MIDTOWN MANHATTAN, THE PLAZA HOTEL.
When Countess Isabella returns, Count Henry is sitting on the sofa in the living room, looking straight ahead, not moving a muscle. "Let's go for a walk," he says cheerfully, as though having been awakened from a trance.

"Ah'm a bit tired, hon."

"I insist. Some fresh air will do both of us good. Wilson will follow us in the car, so then we won't have to walk back."

They walk south on Fifth Avenue about two blocks. "Have you seen what's been on TV everywhere for hours?" the count asks coldly, turning to her.

"Whatever do you mean?" she answers.

"All afternoon, they've been running the headline, 'Phony Count and Countess Exposed.' That's you and me. And really, you haven't seen any of it?"

"Oh, no," Isabella says, putting a hand on each cheek. "Why no! Ah haven't seen anything."

"That's not all," the count continues. "That bitch, that bitch reporter Guthrie, who says she talked with you, says that you think it was wrong for me to buy up land in Mississippi."

"That's not what ah said. That's not what ah meant to say, Henry. You gotta believe me."

"I told you not to go near Central Park. I told you to stay away from that piece of trash you said was your friend. Now, you've ruined me, you double-crossing bitch. They'll never get off my ass now." He taps twice on the window of their limo, which has slowly been following them. Wilson stops, the trunk pops open, and the count takes two suitcases out. "I picked you up off the street. You were nothing. I made you a countess. Now, you can go back where you belong. You can be the Countess of Cooperville. Here's a thousand dollars. Get lost. Thank God I never married you."

Without saying a word or shedding so much as a tear, Isabella smiles, squints, shrugs her shoulders, stares at the limo as it speeds away, picks up her suitcases, and hails a taxi.

FOUR

Connect, Protect, Elect

WEDNESDAY, JUNE 8, 10 A.M.: AN UNDISCLOSED LOCATION. What appears to be a cramped communications control room is pitch black, except for reflected light from twelve computer monitors mounted on a wall in three vertical rows of four. A bright blue test-pattern with two black P's appears on all screens. From the back, the silhouette of what appears to be a man is seated at a console, but there is no way to tell the figure's sex, age or anything else about it. The figure leans forward, slides a lever towards him, then punches a red button which turns green. The first monitor in the top row shows the picture of a classical Greek marble sculpture—a middle-aged, bearded man's head and shoulders looking straight ahead.

"The Prometheus Project is called to order," the deep voice declares. "This is Zeus. For verification purposes, please enter your code name and security code now."

In quick succession, the names are typed letter-by-letter on individual screens: O-l-y-m-p-u-s, P-a-n-d-o-r-a, M-e-r-c-u-r-y, A-d-o-n-i-s.

"Adonis, please reenter your security code. Thank you. Access is now verified for everyone. You are all in listening mode. If you have a question or comment, please wait until all updates have been presented and follow the usual instructions when I give you the go-ahead. May I remind you that our identities are completely anonymous, all voices are technically modified so they cannot be recognized or traced, no copies of these transmissions are authorized, and all communication between us is strictly confidential. That said, welcome everyone.

"We have much to celebrate since our meeting last week. As all of you know, months ago, we decided to launch our major initiative, 'John Galt is dead,' to coincide with what so many misguided fools call the annual celebration of the founding of New Atlantis. I will leave it to Olympus to give us a full report on how he turned it into a fiasco. But personally, I can't tell you how thrilled I am that, for the first time, those 'bloodsuckers' are on the defensive in a major way.

"Manfreed and his thugs at New Atlantis still think they can control the media their stooges own and suppress anything they don't want the general public to know. But they're living in the dark ages. Bloggers first put the word out about Saturday's fiasco and the foreign press around the world picked up the story. What's left of our independent domestic press courageously reported the truth, even though they were afraid they'd be attacked or shut down. Actually, they really didn't have a choice. The word is spreading like wildfire. No one can ignore 'John Galt is dead.' As you'll now hear, the backlash has reached all the way to the White House. We won a battle at New Atlantis. We now have to win the war that we already know is shaping up. Manfreed and Cooper are fuming. Olympus, please begin your report."

"Gladly, Zeus. Thank you." A picture of Hilton Manfreed, lips pursed, brow knitted, eyes compressed to slits, appears on screen two. "You are looking at the puny prophet of Free-for-All economics. One smug, pissed off little gnome, completely thrown off his game for the first time—and we did it. I wish you could have been there to see him, choking on the bullshit he's been feeding the nation. You know their ritual: This past Saturday, Manfreed and the thousands of sycophants who flocked to New Atlantis came prepared to celebrate their raping of our domestic economy. They do it every year on the first Saturday in June, the same month Galt and his followers met in the valley every year. They came to be baptized again, to listen to the same old lies and deceptions about how the country is thriving because they insist corporations have reformed the economy. They couldn't wait to get an update on the inroads they've been making to turn the world into their profit center. But they had no idea what they were getting themselves into. They walked right into our trap. Before thousands of their slavish followers, our technology sabotaged them. They had no idea what hit them. We made them look like complete fools. We took control of them on their own turf. Most of the people leaving the pavilion were whispering the same thing to each other: 'What's going on? Something's terribly wrong here! Things seem to be coming apart.' It was a dramatic change from their high spirits when they went in.

"The story turned out to be so big and so embarrassing, no one could ignore it. For once, even the mainstream press, almost completely owned and operated by Free-for-All believers, has been pretty accurate in describing how we torpedoed Manfreed's speech again and again at strategic moments. Every newspaper in the country is running the headline 'John Galt Is Dead' on its front page. They've published the link to the audio and video we posted online. Everyone can hear and see our attack for themselves. Most are even printing a transcript of Manfreed's speech showing where our blast message interrupted the old geezer.

"Of course, what the press had no way of knowing was the total chaos that erupted behind-the-scenes after the program ended. Manfreed was so furious he lashed out at everyone backstage. He would have strangled the head technician if his toady assistant hadn't stopped him. No matter what the poor guy said to defend himself, the old S.O.B. kept screaming, 'You've made me look like a fucking fool. Who are they? How did they do it? How *could* they do it?' He got so red in the face, he looked like he was going to have a heart attack.

"As stupendous as our attack at New Atlantis was, the most important thing to come out of Saturday for us was that it was the first major test of StarWords, our global multi-media interception system—and that it worked perfectly. It proved without a doubt that we can cut into circuits, take out whole communication grids, reword messages, even produce sky-writing—in short, we can now override and cancel any signal anywhere in the world, without a trace. We can invade live meetings wherever they take place. If Manfreed and the White House are upset now, just wait. I don't want to seem to be overstating our case, but we have created the most powerful weapon to publicly humiliate the corporate cabal, to get our message out, and topple the bastards. They have no idea what they are in for. Our invisible eyes and ears can see and hear them everywhere. Our invisible voice can interrupt them. They can't escape from us. And we'll pursue them until we defeat them. We'll follow them like furies. We'll be their conscience and haul them up on charges before the world for everything they've done—and we have the power to broadcast their own words against them, even what they say in secret, or what they think is secret."

"Olympus, I don't have words to describe how I feel right now," Zeus says emphatically. "And I'm sure I speak for every member of the Prometheus Project when I acknowledge the genius of what you have created. Olympus, you promised you'd be able to create a voice for 'the people' more powerful than all corporations combined—and you did. I have to admit, there were times I didn't think it could be done. But I'm in awe of you. I know that what went on at New Atlantis is just the beginning—and the beginning of the end of the tyranny we've endured. You've given us hope, just when things were looking the worst for us. Thank God you're on our side. Pandora, what have you got for us?"

A map of the Corporate States of America appears on the third computer screen. There are two or three green dots and yellow dots on every state. "Congratulations, Olympus. I couldn't believe my eyes when I saw the reports of pandemonium at New Atlantis. It brought tears of joy. So many people have been hurt for so long. So many people are desperate. Finally, I thought, things may be turning our way. As all of you know, my role in Prometheus is to link all Coopervilles to our secure wireless network. In real time, I was able to send all of Olympus's data and information to our existing sites. So, even if outside media didn't pick up the 'John Galt is dead' story, we could get it out.

"Notice the twenty new yellow dots that weren't on the map last week. They are Coopervilles waiting to be cleared for network access. By next week, I hope to be able to report that 190 locations are online and actively participating in our network and in all feeder social media. We will be able to get the word out instantly nationwide to more and more sites to support all of our on-the-ground organizing efforts. Those sites, in turn, will spread the word to their local networks. To start, we estimate we'll be able to reach upwards of ten million people nationwide. Soon, we will have one of the most powerful communications networks in the world built entirely from the ground up. Mercury will have more to add about how we organize and energize people in place, I know."

"Thank you, Pandora. I don't know what we would do without you. If anybody demonstrates the power of one person to reach out to millions, it's you. You're one of the biggest threats to the legacy of John Galt, Dagny Taggart, and the whole gang from the valley. Since you're one of us, I pity anyone you're up against—not!

"Mercury, are you ready to report?" Zeus asks.

"Gladly!"

A picture of a mob of people inside a shopping mall appears on screen four, then dissolves into another and another—making five pictures in all. "The pictures you just saw made front-page headlines and dominated the TV news across the country. One headline captured it best: 'Where did they come from? Where did they go? Nobody knows!' And thanks to Pandora, thousands of people, then hundreds of thousands of people, then millions of people saw them. Those visuals are proof of our on-the-ground strategy and how perfectly it works. When the time comes, everyone will know it isn't only the captains of industry like John Galt who make the economy work and who have the power to strike and shut it down. Average people, whose rights and very existences have been trampled, control the country too.

"Last week, we held another round of targeted 'shop-ins' to bring business to a halt. In Chicago, Philadelphia, Tampa, Des Moines, and Portland, our 'shoppers' swamped five malls. Pandora sent the word out to Coopervilles in those cities that Thursday was going to be 'shopping day,' and the mobs appeared at exactly 11 a.m. At first, businesses thought they were in for a banner day of sales. But as more and more people arrived, for three hours, stores couldn't do any business. We chose malls that were near or across from other malls. The ones we targeted were furious, because all their business went to their competitors. The mobs appeared and disappeared like swarms of locusts. No one said 'John Galt is dead' or anything that might have sounded political. No one could trace anything to us. The events left the victims totally baffled—and scared shitless. When the time comes, they, and the whole world, will know why they and others have been attacked."

"Thank you, Mercury. When the time comes, your ground forces will literally be on the firing lines and will be key to our victory. Adonis, what have you got for us?"

Screen five dissolves into a picture of a young man in his early twenties. His red, curly hair extends down his cheeks. He is bare-chested and naturally muscular. "I have nothing new to report now. I continue to be a trainee at the Atlas Fitness Center Headquarters in Manhattan. I've been there longer than any other trainee. They trust me. Every day, I learn a little bit more about how the centers do business and how crucial they are to the survival of New Atlantis and Free-for-All economics. They are a cash-cow, providing millions of dollars. I've almost seen the secret formula of the Atlas Energy Drink and have picked up bits and pieces of their strategy to 'drug' the country on it. I've almost gotten copies of studies of the effectiveness of the patented Titan Whole-Body Harmony Machine. There's another 'dirty little secret' about Atlas Fitness Centers I've heard alluded to, but I can't say anything until I have proof."

"I want to thank all of you for this week's updates," Zeus says. "I can't tell you how important your efforts are to our ultimate success. You are the *real* leaders of a return to what this country used to be— and hopefully can be again. The Prometheus Project is growing more powerful every day. It will prevail. It *has to* prevail. Its strength is the network of *real* people you have organized. All of us see the faces of despair on every street corner—husbands and fathers desperate to find jobs to support their families, wives and mothers not knowing how they can feed their kids, barefoot kids begging. You see people looking for relief, not because they did anything wrong, but because they did everything right. They played by the rules—worked and provided for their families. All they ever wanted was enough financial security to be able to see their kids live better than they did. But what have they gotten instead? Bullshit! A kick in the ass! They've been treated worse than animals.

"Before we discuss what lies ahead for us—and believe me, there is plenty—I want to remind us all of why we're in the fight we're in. I don't want us to get so wrapped up in strategy and tactics that we lose our souls and wind up no better than our enemies. If I don't, it might look like we're simply butting heads and pitting our way of looking at things against other people's. I believe, and I believe we all agree, that we have the moral high ground in our struggle. Our drug is conscience. We want to put people on moral steroids, not just pump up their muscles and their selfishness. I believe, and I believe we all believe, that somewhere deep inside every greedy, grasping, selfish person is a decent person waiting to get out. We want to help them express their better nature. The only reason to have power is to do good deeds. We are put on this earth to do the best we can so we leave it a better place. Whenever we can lessen the burdens of life, whenever we can help others flourish and realize their dreams, we are acting in the image of God—and man at his best. Every religion that has ever been known to man honors righteous, decent, giving, caring, compassionate people and condemns those who think and act only for themselves. We must fulfill our best destiny. We cannot be for ourselves alone. And we cannot wait for 'the right time' to act, for 'the right time' is *always* now. That said, we'll be relentless in pursuit of truth and justice for all.

"Ever since John Galt and his mafia returned to claim this country as their own, their followers have been drugged on ideas of ruthless freedom. They have turned greed into a national pastime. They treat people like commodities. They dismantled the government, the government that was supposed to represent 'the people,' by exploiting crises. They handed over public assets to private interests because they claimed the government couldn't afford to run and keep them. And once they were in private hands, corporate raiders bled the public of every cent they could. Then, they put their stooges in what was left of government to protect their obscene profits. So, that's where we are today: One nation under corporate greed with injustice for all but the privileged few.

"All we want, all the Promethus Project wants, is justice for people, average people, the people who have always made this country great. Pay strict attention to what I now tell you, because this is the cold, hard truth of what we are up against. This is the 11th hour. All our planning is going to be tested in a matter of days. President Cooper and his henchmen were shaken to their boots after our attack on New Atlantis. He is desperate to win re-election because he knows that, if Cary Hinton beats him, there's enough discontent to break the corporate grip on the country, once and for all. So, Cooper has decided to wipe out every last Cooperville nationwide. You heard me: Wipe them out! Those camps are living proof of how Free-for All economics has failed—and failed miserably. And Cooper's name on them puts the blame for the failure squarely on him—and him alone. We've got him on tape going ballistic when he hears anyone say 'Cooperville.' Well, we'll be letting the whole world hear and see that at just the right time.

"Cooper is clever. Don't kid yourself. He didn't get to be president by being Mr. Nice Guy. He's a shark and a snake—and proud of it. He wants to turn the public against the homeless and destitute, to destroy any compassion others might feel for innocent people down on their luck. He's given the go-ahead for nothing less than an all-out attack on defenseless human beings for crass political purposes. He doesn't care what it takes to carry out the mission or how many people are hurt. He wants to crush them, no matter what the cost. As phase one, he has just approved sending in private, undercover security forces to harass everyone entering or leaving Coopervilles in five states. They will infiltrate them and plant drugs and weapons inside and then use 'suspicion of threats to national security' to conduct raids and arrest people after finding all the contraband they put there in the first place.

"In the process, they will trample people's shelters and throw away what few possessions they have. It's the standard routine of every repressive regime. Anyone arrested will be held indefinitely in stadiums they've already designated and set up as mass jails. They're gonna herd them in there like cattle and let them rot out-of-sight. They're out to make innocent men, women, and children into public enemies so that bastard can stay in power. They figure that, by targeting and destroying a few Coopervilles, they can instill fear in people in other ones so they'll simply leave on their own. As usual, they think they've got it all figured out. They and their cronies don't take responsibility for creating the conditions that led to Coopervilles. Now they think they are so clever, no one will pin the blame for their ruthlessness on them. But they're going to be in for a big surprise.

"We've just heard some promising updates. But I hope all of you realize the seriousness of what we are up against, how we are going to be tested—and how much depends upon each and every one of you. Literally, everything we stand for is at stake. All we want is a people's revolution to take back the country from the Galtian Restoration that has destroyed it. All we want is to see the rights of average men, women, and children restored and the power of corporations and the richest of the rich curtailed. The lives, the hopes, the futures of millions of people are in your hands. The fate of a once-great nation—of the people, by the people, and for the people—is at stake. I trust all of you completely. So I am confident the Prometheus Project is going to destroy Cooper, New Atlantis, and all his corporate cronies before they know what hit them.

"What happened on Saturday at New Atlantis was child's play compared with what we have planned, and yet it took our enemies totally by surprise and completely shattered them. We dealt a psychological blow at the ultimate symbol of Galtian success, the breeding ground for all of the misplaced ideas that have destroyed the country. So, imagine how they will react when Olympus lets out the stops, hits them on multiple fronts, and invades them without their being able to do anything about it.

"Galt's strike will be nothing compared to The People's Strike we'll lead. Let me begin by stressing five critically important points about our strategy. First, everything we do will be legal. We will not surrender our moral authority by stooping to the level of those who have so long oppressed us. You've just heard from Mercury about last week's shop-ins. Last month in Dallas, Indianapolis, and Seattle, a total of 5,000 'shoppers' also swamped shopping malls and shut them down. For five hours, no stores could do any business. There is no law against shopping. So, when mall management called the police, they couldn't arrest anyone. Everyone said they were there to shop.

"Once we are fully engaged, we will bring this country to its rotten knees. We will prove beyond any doubt that when enough people—

simple, average people—put their feet on the ground at the same time in the same place, they don't have to say a word. Their presence alone is the ultimate expression of power. The masses are waiting to be roused. They are desperate for leadership to show them the way. There are still good people in this country, people in business and what's left of government, people who want a return to a country in which 'the people' are sovereign. We know who they are and we won't attack them. But, day after day, relentlessly, we will selectively target every sector of the economy that has screwed 'the people,' until we have driven the message home that the rich and powerful can *only* remain rich and powerful through the will and support of 'the people.' Their fragile hold on the economy and on their personal wealth is no match for the collective power of the masses. By striking corporate interests and threatening their obscene profits, we undercut their stooges, like Cooper, who are in government only to do their bidding. Their whole scam will topple like the proverbial house of cards.

"Second, our unbeatable power comes from 'withholding': We don't use our power actively. We don't stoop to meeting power with power. We become more powerful by not using our power and turning our enemy's power back on itself. Corporations and big-money interests throw their dollars around, paying people off. That's their *only* power. But the people they pay off are insatiable. They can never have enough money to satisfy their greed. Next to our power, they are pikers, small potatoes. Our power comes from 'negative power, negative capability'—the money we *don't* spend, the actions we *don't* take. We have more power than all of the corporations in the nation combined by collectively and systematically stopping commerce whenever we band together and choose to do so.

"Third, we will use passive resistance if violence is ever used against us. Our people will *never* meet physical force with physical force. Nor will they incite others to violence. They will stay silent and go limp. Over and over, as hard as that guiding principle may be to accept, Pandora has made it clear to the network. The minute we meet force with force we lose our moral advantage. We've got Cooper on tape telling his henchmen that he doesn't want to know the details of their plans to destroy Coopervilles or how they are carried out. That's because if anything goes wrong—if anyone's injured or killed—he can pretend he didn't approve of it. He's a coward through-and-through. So, brace yourself for bloodshed. I pray it doesn't happen. But we've got to be prepared. Cooper and his cronies are ruthless. They see their world coming to an end, so they'll stop at nothing. But, if we want to win the day, we can *never* stoop to their level and use force.

"Fourth, we will always be unpredictable. Surprise is the greatest weapon against entrenched power that has grown self-satisfied with its hold on others. They're caught in a straitjacket of their own making. We're guerillas. You've seen what Olympus was able to do at New Atlantis. Well, there's much more to come. And they'll never know where it's coming from—or when. We can appear and disappear in an instant. We'll be gone before they ever know what's hit them.

"Fifth, we will make the opposition look stupid. Laughter can topple dictators more readily than guns. Think of the chaos and embarrassment that would result if fifty pigeons that had been fed castor oil were released during an indoor Cooper campaign rally. Imagine the reaction of an audience at an outdoor concert at New Atlantis if manure was dropped from a plane buzzing it. I'm not saying that those *exact* scenarios will occur—or that they won't. People present at such occasions definitely won't laugh, but everyone hearing about them will double over. And no one wants to be associated with an effort that makes them look like fools or wind up under a pile of dung.

"Let the people and the word go out from every Cooperville that it is a new day in this country. All the Prometheus Project wants is to restore the equal rights of every man, woman, and child in this once-great nation. We'll declare peace when the 'blood-suckers' give us back our fair share of opportunity and prosperity—instead of the crumbs they think they can throw us. They have stacked the Supreme Court with their corporate-leaning toads. They have been whores for banks and investment houses. They have left average people defenseless against predatory insurance companies. They have removed all consumer protections, so individuals are powerless against rip-offs. Talk with real people everywhere and they'll tell you they've had enough—too much. The day is coming sooner than anyone might think when we will rise up—and be able to declare victory.

"Enough from me," Zeus says. "If you have a question or comment, please press Star-1 now. Yes, Mercury?"

"I just want to say that Pandora has put the word out to all Coopervilles and our entire network to be on the lookout for spies and provocateurs. We know for an absolute fact that New Atlantis is out to infiltrate us. Anyone who has any information about plots against us should immediately communicate with her. Don't hesitate, even if you think it's trivial."

"Thank you. Adonis, you have something to add?"

"I just want to assure you that we'll soon be launching a major laughable moment at Atlas Fitness Centers. But I won't spoil the fun."

"Thank all of you for sharing and listening and keeping the faith," Zeus adds. "I know it's not easy, but I know how deeply you are committed. Now I have a special surprise for you." The picture of a woman in her early sixties appears on screen six. On the wall behind her are the words "Beauty is truth, truth beauty."

"Everyone, it gives me great pleasure to welcome Cary Hinton, Ham Cooper's worst nightmare, and the only person in the country who has dared to challenge him for the presidency. I'm not stealing her thunder when I say that she is the *only* person who has the guts to say that she is out to do away with the Corporate States of America and restore an honest, decent, ethical government that truly represents 'the people' first and foremost. Ms. Hinton, as I explained to you, all of the members of the Prometheus Project pledge to participate anonymously and confidentially. And we expect you to honor that and to reveal nothing about your appearance here today."

"Thank you, Zeus. I completely understand and will, of course, honor your pledge. I respect all of you for what you may be willing to do to help me get elected. Let me tell you who I am if you don't know my bio—or remind you if you've forgotten. Otherwise, you might think that I'm just another power-hungry political hack. My story is a story of this country as it used to be—and that I am determined it can, and must, be again in the future, the near future. My grandparents fled pogroms in Eastern Europe, in Belarus to be exact. Eventually, they settled in the Northeast. My father's mother had three brothers. They emigrated first and started a business. She and another brother followed a few years later. Her parents and four sisters came too. My father's father never spoke of his family. Both sides gave up everything they had to come to America. They had to learn English, find work, and build businesses. No one gave them anything, nor did they want or expect anybody to do so. All they wanted was the opportunity to succeed. My grandfather, a tailor in Europe, opened his own shop. Gradually, he branched out from taking in simple alterations and repairs to making custom, high-end clothes. Eventually, he owned four stores. He and my grandmother scrimped and saved so they could provide a better life for their children. My father became a lawyer.

"My mother, whose family had a similar history, became an accountant. Together, they instilled in me, my two sisters and my brother a desire *always* to do our best—and *always* to remember where we came from. Most of all, they *always* told us to be thankful for what we had—and not to be greedy, to remember that there is enough to go around for everyone. They never wanted a handout from anyone—or took one, even when times were tough. And they never simply gave a handout to anyone. They loaned money to people who were willing to work to pay it back, but they never charged anyone interest. They believed it was a source of pride for someone to pay back a loan. And everyone, except one person, did.

"The last thing in the world I ever thought I'd do was run for president of this country. But I found a copy of a journal my mother's father kept from the time he left Eastern Europe until the day he died. One entry changed my life. I'd like to read it to you: 'Today, July 4, 1911, I became an American citizen. Until now, I have lived in America with my family and I've been a good citizen. I am writing this in good English. I've studied hard at night school so my children wouldn't be embarrassed from my accent or because I couldn't read or write. I was the best student in the class. And that's not my pride talking. I got the best grades. I've worked hard at my business. My wife and I have raised a family. We've never cheated anyone. Every day, we've thanked God for getting us to the greatest country on the face of the earth, where we can live in peace.

'But until I raised my right hand and swore allegiance to this great country, I didn't feel I belonged. Today is the proudest day of my life. On my right side was a man from Ireland and on my left side was a woman from Italy. We were all sworn in together. We laughed and cried tears of joy. I pointed to both of them and told them they were Yankees now—and they did the same to me. The room was filled with people from everywhere. But today we all became citizens of the same country. Of course, we are different in most ways. That's why we have so many good restaurants. But we don't let our differences stand between us. Now we are the same in the most important way. This is the land of opportunity. This is *our* land. This is now *our* America. We are now the people, just like the Constitution says. We are Americans.'

"I wept the first time I read my grandfather's words, and could barely compose myself when I finished. And the truth is, I still do. His constant refrain was 'only in America' whenever he or we or anyone enjoyed success and good fortune. When my parents moved into the house they built, when I went off to college, when our neighbors bought their sailboat, he would never tire of saying, 'Only in America could we all live like kings!' I thought about how lucky our family was to have been able to emigrate and thrive here.

"But at the same time that I celebrated my grandfather's exuberance for America, I mourned the loss today of everything for which my grandfather had been so grateful. And I thought about all the Americans who have forgotten the struggles of their families and who have no compassion for others trying to make a productive life for themselves. They act like as long as they got in the tent, everyone else can go to hell. And then I got mad, spitting mad. I thought about how today this country is trashing its founding principles. Believe me: I know American history. I know we've done bad things as a nation. I know the founding fathers had warts—serious ones at that. But whatever their shortcomings, they found the words to inspire others to follow their better nature. And we're a far cry from living up to them today.

"I believe in a meritocracy. That's what the *real* America is. You know, 'all men are created equal.' That's an example of where our founding fathers didn't quite get it right, but got it right enough so later generations could fix it. In their time, they didn't mean *all* people: They excluded slaves and women. But in the end, others took the spirit of their words at face value. The prejudices of their time and circumstances were left behind, and later generations were left with the best words that have ever been uttered on behalf of the human race. I don't care what a person's skin color, ethnicity, sex, lifestyle preference, or anything else may be. All I care about is that people, and I mean *all* people, have an equal chance to prove themselves—and succeed. That's the America I want everyone to live in. That's the America I want to be president of.

"The cynical coup to take over the country in the name of John Galt was hatched in two phases. First, political 'bloodsuckers' used social issues to appeal to fringe groups that would vote them into office. They divided and conquered unsuspecting voters. They targeted one group after another. One year it was immigrants, the next year it was gays and lesbians, another time it was women. They demonized everyone. Once they got political power, those same 'bloodsuckers' turned public assets over to private interests. Roads, bridges, tunnels, levees, dams, airports and seaports—every public works project that could be sold off to private interests was disposed of at fire sale prices. They got 'the people,' the gullible people, to vote against their self-interest.

"And what has the country reaped since the coup has succeeded? Decade after decade, our infrastructure has been neglected. The private sector—much of it now controlled by foreign interests—has put profit above the public interest. Critical structures are now on the verge of collapse—or have already imploded. You take your life in your hands crossing most bridges. Major levees are on the verge of collapse. Boil-water alerts are routinely issued for urban areas. But do the 'bloodsuckers' care? Of course, not! Every bridge that's still state-owned and that collapses is a buying opportunity for them. Every bridge they own that needs repair is a chance for them to increase their profits by raising toll rates and gouging the public to pay for it. The system is totally rigged for them.

"Believers in Free-for-All economics deny science to maintain corporate monopolies. Global warming is a fiction, they insist. So, we should continue to burn fossil fuels, be dependent upon oil companies, and stop efforts to develop alternative fuels. Today, we are no longer a nation of laws but of men. Lady Justice is no longer fair. Her blindfold is off. She winks at those she favors. Her scale is weighted for the benefit of a chosen few. Except for two justices, the Supreme Court is made up of lapdogs for corporate interests.

"To all of you at the Prometheus Project, in short, I want to accomplish one thing: Restore this country to 'the people.' The grand experiment that was launched on this continent almost 300 years ago has been perverted. We've got to take it back. I can't tell you for certain why a relative handful of people was able to stage a coup that enslaved millions of people in the name of freedom and liberty. But they did. Their success wouldn't have surprised our founding fathers. Even they regarded the American Revolution and the Republic to which it led as a fragile, even potentially fleeting, experiment. As every student of American history knows, when Benjamin Franklin left the Constitutional Convention, a woman asked him, 'What kind of government have you given us?' And he replied, 'A Republic if you can keep it.' Well, we haven't kept it. We let it slip through our fingers. We have watched our liberties eroded, justice perverted, and the abiding sense of community—what it always meant to be an American—exchanged for a war between the haves and the have-nots.

"From now until November, I aim to bring my message to everyone in this country—even those who may appear to have fallen for Free-for-All economics. With your help, I believe I can reach enough people to win the presidency. I read my grandfather's journal entry every day to keep my spirits up. I have to honor his memory and the memories of all of our ancestors who endured hardship to come to this great country and who overcame obstacles to provide for their families.

"Please think on my simple message, 'Beauty is truth, truth beauty,' and ask others to do so. It's more powerful than all the messages of Free-for-All economics combined. Thank you."

"Thank you, Ms. Hinton, for taking the time to come to the Prometheus Project. I know I speak for everyone when I say that we support you. And I'm guessing that Pandora can't wait to put your message out to her vast network. This concludes today's meeting. The Prometheus Project is adjourned."

FIVE

Plug, Drug, Bug

WEDNESDAY, JUNE 15, 10 A.M.: MIDTOWN MANHATTAN. The gleaming, white façade of the International Headquarters of Atlas Fitness Centers commands the east side of Fifth Avenue between 64th and 63rd Streets like a parvenu who thinks others don't know he's "just arrived." On a window above the two doors of the main entrance, the Center's name in Garamond font is etched in gold. On the glass of each of six display windows, three on each side of the two doors of the main entrance, there is a gold replica of the Atlas figure at New Atlantis, under which are the words "Drug yourself on self-interest." In each window, bottles of Atlas Energy Drink are arranged in pyramids next to a Titan Whole-Body Harmony Machine. High-definition screens play video of ebullient Atlas clients. Starting at the northernmost window, their testimonials about the miracles produced by Atlas Energy and the Titan Machine are broadcast in the street in sequence. Each one begins with an exuberant, "My Atlas program transformed my life." Then comes a startling specific—like "lowering my cholesterol" or "stabilizing my Parkinson's."

In spite of the stagnant, early-morning, spring-summer heat, about 150 customers have been lining up outside the main entrance for about an hour. The line extends east around the corner of 63rd Street. Preferred clients, Atlas members, have access to the Center 24/7 and use a private entrance. These people are (what the Center calls) "newbies"—less affectionately, "live bait"—and are responding to a full-page ad in yesterday's *Times*. The coupon most are holding entitles them to buy one Atlas Energy Drink and get one free.

The Center's response the day after every major ad runs is perfectly scripted. Nothing is left to chance. As soon as "newbies" enter, they sign in at welcome tables. They fill out a registration card, write the name they like to be called, and receive a name tag that reads "I'm [their name] and I want to be drugged on Atlas." Greeters then escort them to a seat. Today, they've pre-set for 100. So, extra chairs have had to be quickly added. When everyone is seated, either Enrique Reyes, Zora Tremmon, or Albert Swift leads a fifteen-minute presentation on the certified value of the Atlas program.

Today, it's Enrique. On a white board behind him he writes: Drug Yourself on Atlas and Your Only Interest Is Your Self-Interest.

"Welcome all of you. I am thrilled that you are here. And I'm thrilled to be the one speaking with you today. You got that I'm thrilled, right?" he says smiling, with a calculated wink. "These two power-phrases will change your lives, just as they have for tens of thousands of people already. Our goal at Atlas Fitness is to create the next generation of leaders—Super-Atlases who develop their maximum potential so they can seize opportunity and prosper. By coming here today, you've revealed that you are already open to becoming the center of your own universe. By being willing to allow a proven miracle into your life, you can begin the process today. That's right! The miracle is real and available—now. And this is it. This is where it all starts," he says, holding up an 8 oz. bottle of Atlas Energy Drink.

"I can absolutely say it's a miracle because I developed its secret formula. It's my inspiration. I had the privilege of being at New Atlantis, enjoying the freedom to be creative and entrepreneurial when

I hit upon the idea. What do people want, people just like you? I asked myself. A quick, painless, easy, proven way to take control of their lives. And what was the best way to achieve that, I wondered? A power drink, of course. But not just another power drink, one that could be scientifically proven to achieve results. And I was able to develop Atlas Energy because I live in this great country. Free-for-All economics finally did away with all the obstacles that used to make it difficult to bring a product to market because 'the government' was looking over everyone's shoulder—supposedly protecting the public interest. I'd still be waiting for approval, and you would not be able to enjoy the benefits of Atlas Energy, if some government bureaucrat had to approve it. Fortunately, now that we're free of such socialist propaganda, you're able to get a full-strength, unadulterated product that's been scientifically tested and proven by the best researchers we've been able to hire.

"Of course, I drink Atlas Energy every day. I know firsthand that it can alter the chemistry of your entire body. It will add years to your life. And not just years, but quality—the concentrated energy and focus that will permit you to be the best that you can be. But you don't have to believe me. In the back of the room, there are copies of scientific analyses that certify the results users are having—and we also have people right here to speak for themselves."

Three preferred clients always give the in-person testimonials—sales research has determined that two is too few, four or more too many—all of whom attest to the fact that signing up for an ongoing program, including regular use of the Titan Whole-Body Harmony Machine, increases results far beyond simply drinking the drink or doing an occasional workout. Forty-year-old Tom tells the "newbies" that drinking Atlas Energy cured his diabetes. Sixty-ish Emily swears that it lowered her cholesterol. And twenty-five-year-old Tony flexes his pecs, winks, smiles, and says his sex-life has never been better. Tom attests to the immense value of enrolling in free, weekly "Self-Interest

Workshops," which are only available to clients who sign up for a year's fitness program. And Emily adds, "Absolutely, you've got to be committed to your self-interest 110 percent, and the thirty-day program is the best way to do that. Drug yourself on Atlas. Free yourself to pursue your self-interest like so many others. Miraculously, results begin as soon as you sign up."

After every presentation, depending upon the size of the crowd, staff members call out the names of anywhere from ten to fifteen "newbies" and "huddle" with them as a group. They know from experience that there is at least one new center member firm or saleable in every group. As soon as that person signs up, everyone in the group applauds—an affirmation that typically encourages at least two more to enroll. Today, forty-five-year-old Fernando is the first to sign up. He becomes emotional when everyone cheers his decision. "I have a bad heart, but I want to live. From now on, I only want to pursue my self-interest. And I know Atlas Energy Drink will make that possible."

By the end of a half-hour, small-group session, at least five "newbies" in each huddle have typically signed their enrollment contract and paid for their year's program. Anyone who hasn't signed up—"tough cases" in Atlas jargon—is escorted to a private office for a one-on-one consultation ("the massage") with specially trained sales reps. Group leaders depart with enrollees for the Mind-Body Harmony Room, where they make an appointment to receive their free total body fitness assessment in preparation for using the Titan Machine. As they leave the Center, they enroll in their first free "Self-Interest Workshop," and receive two bottles of Atlas Energy Drink, both free because they are now preferred clients.

"Welcome Atlas Fitness Center franchisees," Enrique Reyes says when he goes to the podium before the 100 men and women seated in the Training Room of the Center at 11 a.m. Behind him is a sign that reads Our clients' needs are our dollars. "Give yourselves a round of applause," he adds clapping his hands. "I see John Yates from Philadelphia, Sonya Martin from El Paso, Ingrid Potoff from San Francisco. I could go on, but in the interest of time I'll stop there. Just know that we know you personally, we're joined at the hip, even if we haven't met you in person until now.

"Congratulations! You are now part of a network that is growing daily into the most powerful force for personal transformation. What you have just seen is our weekly sales presentation," he says pointing to the two-way mirror on the wall. "I hope you can help us improve our skills—and take away successful techniques to improve yours and those of your staff. Energy is my business, if you know what I mean. But I am *always* ultra-energized after an enrollment session. It is thrilling to see people turn their lives around right before my eyes. And to think it all starts with a sip of Atlas Energy Drink!"

"Zora and Albert, please join me up here," Enrique continues. Extending his arm around Zora's back and embracing her right shoulder, he says, "I'd like to introduce Zora Tremmon, who, as all of you know, created the computer and social network programs that link all of your centers. She literally holds Atlas Fitness together. Zora was born in the Corporate States, but her parents fled oppressive socialist regimes in Eastern Europe. They knew John Galt and Dagny Taggart personally and were among the first people to join New Atlantis. She's as close to an apostle of Free-for-All economics as you'll find anywhere.

"Albert, what can I say about Albert Swift that isn't already being said around the world? He's been on the cover of every leading business and science magazine. He's the genius who created the Titan Whole-Body Harmony Machine that has totally transformed mind-body alignment. Thanks to Albert, every man, woman, and child in the Corporate States can achieve physical and mental perfection. And soon, after we launch our international initiative, we'll be able to say everyone around the world. On Saturday, June 4, the three of us were inducted into the Circle of Atlas at New Atlantis. It was a thrilling experience. We are proud to say that, by creating Atlas Fitness Centers and the revolutionary programs we—and all of you, of course—offer, we have become the major source of funding for New Atlantis. Through your efforts, we will continue to ensure the ongoing success of the Galtian Restoration and Free-for-All economics. It doesn't get better than that.

"Now, I know that you've all seen headlines reporting what has been called 'a fiasco' at New Atlantis recently. Zora, Albert, and I were there when it happened. So, we can tell you first-hand that it was absolutely nothing. But as usual, the press is having a field-day repeating the slander that 'John Galt is dead' and saying that terrorists attacked New Atlantis. It's just hype and even wishful thinking for some. But just look around! Look at the crowd that's here because of yesterday's ad! Look at how enthusiastic they are! They, we, all of us are living proof that John Galt lives! Let me assure you, it was nothing more than a childish prank. It's been blown all out of proportion. We've been able to narrow down the suspects to two or three disgruntled former employees. We're all in business. We know how one or two rotten apples can spoil things for a whole company. Well, soon enough, they'll get everything they deserve. Professor Manfreed has assured me that he's already launching a public relations effort that will overcome any negativity. Our enemies soon will discover they have tangled with the wrong opponent.

"A little later, all of you will have a chance to tour our facility. We are so proud of it, especially our Elite Services Suites. As headquarters, we hope to set the pace for all of you. Today's meeting, the first of many that, I hope, brings us together throughout the year, is about expansion—and higher profits. We need to generate a 100 percent increase in net profit in the next six months to make New Atlantis stronger than ever. We've got to drug more of the world on Atlas En-

ergy than ever before—for their good and ours. The recent unpleasantness at New Atlantis is nothing more than a blip on our radar
screen, a minor attack. But we take nothing for granted or we'll wake
up one day only to discover that we've lost the war. And make no mistake about it: We *are* at war and we *always* will be. We need to be forever vigilant, on the offensive, taking action.

"So, let's talk sales strategy, pure and simple. At this time, I'd like
to introduce four irresistible members of our powerhouse staff. They
are shining examples of what it takes to produce the best results at
Atlas Fitness. Thor, Rick, Bambi, Cheryl, come up here and let the
folks take a look at you. Display yourselves!" The audience applauds
as they make their way to the front of the room. "Just feast your eyes,
folks, and imagine that you are a prospective Atlas client. Could you
resist falling in love with these four beauties? Yes, you heard me, I
said 'beauties'! Of course, you couldn't! That's the point! But I get
ahead of myself. Now, I'll let them tell you a little about how they sell
themselves—and Atlas. Bambi, please begin."

About 5'7", in her mid-twenties, with short blond hair, in a bikini,
with her shoulders thrust back to accentuate the fullness and avail-
ability of her breasts, like a playful puppy, she bounces her words.
"Hi, I'm Bambi. Just Bambi! Everyone knows me as just Bambi.
Everyone calls me 'The Enforcer.' I'm the one who sees to it that
everyone on our staff, and I mean *everyone,* stays within the physical
standards outlined in your franchise manual—no deviations. To sell
image, we've got to sell flesh. You know from your franchise manual
that male staff must be no shorter than 5'11" and no taller than 6'1".
They must maintain body fat between 14% and 17%. They may weigh
no more than 190. Women must be no shorter than 5'6" and no taller
than 5'8". They are allowed body fat of between 21% and 24% and can
weigh no more than 125. They must have straight, white teeth, well-
groomed nails, and clear skin. Everyone is tested daily to be sure they
fall within the ranges. Any deviations and they are 'off the floor,' as we

say, until they are corrected. Two violations in a two-week period are grounds for an automatic dismissal. No exceptions!"

Six feet tall, in his mid-twenties, tan, with red hair and a swimmer's build, dressed in tight gym shorts and a tank top that accentuates his sculpted upper body, Thor removes the microphone from the podium so he can speak without anything between him and the audience. "Hi everyone," he says smiling warmly, showing perfect rows of gleaming teeth. "My name is Thor Rentgen. They call me 'Thor the Bore' because I train our trainer-recruits and our staff—especially those who serve our elite clients. But I don't take it personally. I'm the one who sees to it that they achieve maximum physical form and that they stay that way. It's my job to see to it that everyone looks irresistible, so Bambi doesn't read them the riot act and no one gets kicked out. Every one of us is an Atlas product. We are showcases for what our clients can be—and should want to be. We need to be living examples of the perfection everyone can achieve. We've *always* got to show our best. I create a personal physical development plan for everyone on our staff. They train at least an hour a day on the Titan Whole-Body Harmony Machine and on special equipment available only to staff."

"Hi, I'm Rick," who walks up and down the middle aisle of the training room, making no bones about showing off his bubble butt. "I guess I should go next because I'm head of sales here at headquarters. We're not selling bottles of energy drink or beautiful bodies. We're *really* selling love. First we get 'em to love us—our bodies, our smiles, our warmth. We are their dream-come-true. We marry 'em. We own 'em. They're ours. They can't believe they could ever be close to anyone like us. We validate them like they've never been validated. Then we get 'em to love themselves—and nobody else. We pump up their pecs and set 'em up for Free-for-All economics. And, man, how the money flows!

"In real estate, they say the three most important things are location, location, and location. But in sales, it's relationship, relationship,

relationship. From the time we meet 'em, we are out to build an unshakable bond between them and us—so eventually we are they and they are us, nothing in between. To get 'em drugged on Atlas we've got to get into their heads. They don't even know what hit 'em, except they never want it to be over. And as long as they can pay, it never will be. And the more they pay, the better life will be for 'em.

"Our special enhancing mirrors, with unique angle adjustments, are designed so clients can see the bodies they *can* have, not just the pathetic excuse for one they have now. You'll never find a harsh, white light bulb in here. Pink-tinted lights make clients' skin look soft and clear and wholesome. People's weight varies throughout the course of the day. Our specially developed scales are 'weight-averaged,' so people's weight will appear five pounds less than it actually is.

"And now let me fill you in about our Elite Client Services. In a word, they are 'gravy.' They have become our most profitable revenue stream. They are a pure example of a savvy business adapting to meet market desires. Our staff began reporting that some of our most exclusive clients, especially corporate executives, wanted private, one-on-one sessions. Especially those who weren't in good physical shape didn't feel comfortable using the Titan machines with other people around. Also, power-clients were often available at odd hours. They need people who work with them to be flexible. They're also used to being pampered. They love to be made to feel special.

"So, our center is open 24/7 to satisfy our elite clients' every need—in person, by phone, email, text message, you name it. Of course, in person is preferred! Our clients have favorites, as you may well imagine. So, staff members, including trainees, are *always* on call for elites. They all live on the second floor. Each has a fully furnished studio apartment. Our elite clients pay extra for a wide variety of personalized services. The sky's the limit.

"Thinking like all good Free-for-All entrepreneurs, we created ten luxurious, private, two-room suites for our elites on the first floor, in which staff may meet with them discreetly. They are in great demand. In fact, we already have architectural plans drawn for additional suites, that are even more luxurious. As you'll see when you tour our facility, there's an exercise room with a dedicated Titan machine in each suite, as well as a bedroom and bath for anyone who wishes to spend the night. We do everything to make them feel at home. Many clients reserve the same day and time each week. Many schedule the same staff member to be with them. Rates vary, depending upon the services provided and the length of stay. But as you can imagine, with elites, price is no object. Staff members receive a generous commission on elite services. Enrique is planning to tell you more about starting your own Elite program, so I'll stop here. Just let me assure you, your bottom line will bulge like you wouldn't believe."

"Hi, I'm Cheryl Watkins," the bouncy ex-beauty queen effuses. "Fly me to prosperity. Just kidding—not! But that's *really* how I feel about my role at Atlas Fitness. Obviously, I'm next. There's no one left. I run our workshops. And I'm not just saying that they are the most important part of Atlas because they're mine. They *really* are our lifeblood. Yes, they are a source of revenue. But importantly, if we build people's bodies and satisfy their needs without reinforcing their belief in Free-for-All economics, we will have failed in our mission. All of you have the list of current workshop offerings, starting with the two foundational ones, 'Drug Yourself on Atlas' and 'Your *Only* Interest Is Your Self-Interest.' So, I want to mention two brand new offerings.

"I am so proud of 'A World without Pity.' We offered it last month for the first time and it has had rave reviews. It is four power-packed sessions, like all of our workshops. But it's unique because of the field component. I'm so excited when I talk about it that I get ahead of myself. First, the goal of the program is to free participants of the emotion of pity. They get to see that it is one of the roots of all evil. They get to recognize how it saps their creativity, most often without their even realizing it. Through a simple but powerful process, participants discover how pity cripples those who pity and those who are pitied. Homework, the field component, is so exciting. Participants have to go out into the world around them and make a list of every situation in which they find themselves showing any signs of compassion, caring, feeling—anything on the continuum of pity. Then, they learn how to work through it. One of my favorite exercises is called 'Laugh 'til it hurts.' It's so simple. Participants take turns describing a pitiful situation of their choosing—and then the whole group laughs at it. It works like a charm! At the end of four weeks, they understand that they don't have to think twice about anyone else. They are truly free for the first time in their lives. They understand that pity is for suckers and charity is for dupes. And they've developed senses of humor.

"We're two weeks into the first offering of our 'Profit without Pity' workshop, and we're already getting rave reviews. It's a natural follow-up to 'A World without Pity.' Participants say their lives are completely transformed. Once they understand the power of living without pity—that they don't owe anybody else anything, and nobody owes them anything—they are liberated to take everything they want when they want it wherever they find it, without answering to anyone. They've learned to see greed and selfishness as positives—and to be proud to be called grasping and self-centered. At the end of four sessions, they'll actually speak a different language. It's *that* powerful. As the song goes, they'll 'accentuate the positive, eliminate the negative, latch on to the affirmative, and not mess with Mr. In-between.' They'll have a whole set of empowering mantras, like 'My ends justify my means' and 'Winner takes it all.'

"During your visit today, I hope you'll review the training manuals for both of the workshops and purchase them in quantity for your staff. I'm available to train them in delivering the programs on-site at your centers, of course."

"Everyone, let's give Thor, Rick, Bambi, and Cheryl a thunderous hand," Enrique says, leading the applause. "Now you see why headquarters is so successful! Our Elite Client Services program has evolved and is still evolving. But already it is our top priority—and a major source of increased revenue. We leave it up to each staff member to cultivate and maintain clients. As Rick said, it's all about relationship, relationship, relationship. If you want your cash register to ring, never lose sight of that fact or let your staff forget it. During the course of today, please sign up for your private session with me to discuss implementing your Elite program. I'll give you all the details, suggested commission rates, and other incentives.

"I'm also pleased to announce that we will soon be launching Atlas Super Energy Drink, the next generation of our miracle-in-a-bottle. As its name suggests, it is extra-potent and extra-effective. It is also twice as expensive as regular Atlas Energy. But enough from headquarters for the moment. Let's hear updates from the field. Don't wait to be called on. Feel free to stand up—and tell us who you are."

A man whose head is shaved and who appears to be about 6'3" jumps up like a jack-in-the-box. "I'll be the first. Hello, everyone," he says, extending his arms in an embrace that takes in the whole room. "I'm Alex Henderson from the Sacramento Center. I am thrilled to be here and to be part of Atlas Fitness. It's the best damn franchise— ever. Anyone who says you can't make it in the Corporate States is a socialist fool. We've doubled our membership in the last three months. We're running out of space and are looking at moving into a new facility—probably renting with an option to buy. We've got two, that's right two, secret weapons. First, we're got the hottest women and men in all of Northern California on our staff. Make that *all* of California! Let me tell you: Flesh sells. I am very interested in your Elite program, so please schedule me for your first one-on-one. And second, we don't wait for people to come to us. Our hotties go everywhere there is to go. I've got an RV filled to the brim with Atlas Energy Drink and we sell bottles hand-over-fist right from there. We go into neighborhoods. We go to malls. We're outside of movie theatres hustling crowds. We get their names, phone numbers, and email addresses. And before long we've got 'em coming in to try out the Titans and buy more drink." The whole audience stands and applauds. "Go, Al. Go, Al. Yes, yes, yes," they chant.

A woman with a sour puss gets up even before Henderson sits. "Well, I don't want to put a damper on all of Al's success. But we've got a major problem. I'm Cheryl Atkins and this is my business partner Mike Paul. We're from the Chicago Center. Unfortunately, we're across from Grant Park, which these days has been turned into a Cooperville. You know what that means—a steady stream of dispossessed, stinking riff-raff. For those of you who don't know Chicago, it used to be a showplace. The Art Institute, the Museum of Natural History, and the Aquarium are all there. But now everywhere you look, there are people living in tents, cardboard boxes, and even in the open in sleeping bags. The Memorial Fountain, the beautiful landmark, was turned into a bathtub until the city shut off the water and drained it. Now, they're pissing in it for spite. Hundreds of them go out during the night and put 'John Galt Is Dead!' stickers everywhere, including all over the front of our building. It's like an infection. It's the biggest drag on business you can imagine. And we're hurting."

"We've even got unreformed do-gooders passing out food and giving those bums money," Mike Paul adds without standing up. "They're only making matters worse. Those lazy sons-of-bitches need a good swift kick in the ass so they'll go out and get a job. I've heard all their talk about there not being any work, but they're full of it."

"Cheryl, Mike, and anyone else whose business is suffering because of a Cooperville," Enrique says, "don't worry. You'll hear from Professor Manfreed in a few minutes about how Washington is going to take care of all those deadbeats once and for all. I promise you!"

A tall, tanned man in his forties calls out, "Enrique, I've got a different problem, and I'm really concerned about it. I'm Richard Foster from the Indianapolis Center. We've been getting reports of bad reactions to the Energy Drink—like diarrhea, vomiting, and stomach upset."

"I'm shocked," Enrique replies. "And of course that can't be. People must have the flu or something. You've all seen the scientific evidence of the effectiveness and safety of Atlas Energy. There's absolutely no basis in fact for any negative reactions to the miracle formula."

"Enrique, sorry to hit you with some more bad news. I'm Elinor Ridge from the St. Louis Center. We've had complaints of severe lower back pain after clients use Titan machines."

"Enrique, I can answer this, if you don't mind," says Albert Smith. "Clients are obviously not using machines properly. It is impossible for Titans to cause physical damage of any kind. The physics of their engineering is so precise and reliable, that using it can't hurt anyone, even if they tried. It would automatically compensate for it. That's how innovative Titans are. I know it sounds eerie, but they almost think."

"I'll vouch for that," Thor Rentgen adds. "The only time I've ever had clients complain about lower back pain is when they've done exercises outside of their Titan regimen. They're told not to deviate from their Atlas program, but of course too often they do. Some people don't want to listen. So, you've gotta make absolutely certain that your clients know they have to follow their regimen precisely."

"We value all of your observations—yes, even something that might be critical or negative," Enrique says dismissively. "But as you know, we stand 100 percent behind Atlas Fitness. Well, unless we have any more non-problem problems—and I repeat that we welcome them—let's move on to expansion. As I mentioned, we need to get to 200 centers fully operational by December 31 of this year. That's a tall order in a little more than six months. But the more people who drug themselves on Atlas, the more profitable we'll all be. And I don't have to remind you that the bottom line is our bottom line, our *only* bottom line. And the best way to expand is for each of you to clone yourselves. Open another branch. Spread the word.

Reap the profit. Let's take a twenty-minute break. And during that time, please schedule your one-on-one meeting with one of our staff members to discuss your center's expansion strategy, including putting in place an 'Elite Client Program.' Believe me, that will pay off more than you can ever imagine. It's now 11. Be back at 11:20 sharp."

After the break, when everyone is seated, Zora Tremmon makes a grand entrance into the training room, smiling at all the franchisees and walking backwards down the middle aisle with both hands outstretched, palms open. "Waaay to go," she says. "I see that everyone signed up for a one-on-one expansion strategy session." Pointing to the sixty-five inch TV screen on the wall, she says, "In a few minutes you're going to have the honor and privilege of hearing from the god of Free-for-All economics, my idol and mentor Professor Hilton Manfreed. But first, I can't tell you how delighted I am to meet all of you in person. I feel as though I know all of you from our emails and videoconferences. I know it's heresy to say it these days, but there's nothing like face-to-face time between people working together.

"Every time I hear Professor Manfreed speak, I get high on our mission and purpose. Of course, I drink Atlas Energy faithfully every day. But the professor is his own kind of drug—and the more you absorb his wisdom, the more successful you'll be. You all know him as the father of Free-for-All economics, the inspiration for the ongoing Galtian Restoration. Without him, I don't know where we'd be today. Oh yes I do. We'd be wallowing in socialistic bombast and none of you would be here. His sweeping vision of the world is directly responsible for the success of Atlas Fitness. So, I'm thrilled to be a part of Atlas Fitness, because it 'gives back' to New Atlantis.

"Professor Manfreed," Zora continues, "we are thrilled to have you with us."

"Thank you, Zora," he replies, grinning broadly. "And as usual, thank you for your glowing introduction. Knowing that someone like you is carrying the torch of John Galt's vision, following in my footsteps, means everything to me. You are our future—and so is every franchisee of an Atlas Fitness Center. So, let me say right off the bat that no one should have any doubts that the spirit of John Galt is alive and well. Don't believe any of the nonsense you've heard about our being on the verge of being destroyed. Quite the contrary! Of course, our enemies—we've *always* had them and we *always* will—want you to believe we're about to go under. They'll keep lying about us—and the rogue press will continue to twist and exaggerate their claims. But it won't do them any good because our message is positive and most citizens of the Corporate States know it. It's the only message that people want to hear because it liberates them from servitude and frees them to pursue their dreams without guilt.

"Our enemies are guilt-inducing predators who try to subjugate the rest of society. They are orchestrating the downfall of western civilization. They say they want to protect the environment. But they scream that the sky is falling down without reliable scientific proof—unless you think that just because someone has won a Nobel Prize they're credible. Then, they concoct rules to end crises they fabricate and that simply take money out of all of our pockets. The bounty of the Earth is to be conquered by the strong, not redistributed to the weak as their reward for simply breathing in and breathing out. There are no disasters—natural or man-made. They are buying opportunities. Human beings rule nature. We're not just one of many equal species in the scheme of things. And the strongest among us are destined to thrive and rule the weakest.

"Our enemies preach social responsibility so they can take what you've got and give it to the weak and lazy. Do you see the pattern here? Of course you do! You'd be on the giving end of the equation if John Galt were really dead—but you're not and you won't be as long as I've got anything to say about it.

"Remember this above all, a cardinal principle of Free-for-All economics: There's no such thing as an economic downturn. I know that you've been hearing for years that totally free markets exploit people, throw them out of work, and simply make the rich richer. But again and again, research has proven the validity of 'The I-Factor,' the natural law of inequality. Nature abhors similarity and equality. Only the unique survive. You have a moral obligation to think 'I'—that you are all there is—and to protect your 'I' from the deadly 'we' mentality.

"Let me tell you a story about a family that, as the saying goes, 'had it all,' but then had it taken from them, literally stolen, in the name of equality, doing right by others. In sixty years, they grew a small farm into a major agribusiness—HarvestCo in Southern California. Their laborers were migrants who chose their way of living, chose to marry, chose to have children, and chose to work where they were working. Everything was working just fine. Things were the way that had *always* been. The business thrived. Everybody knew their place.

"But then, outside agitators came in like snakes and tried to form a union. They poisoned the workers. They claimed the business was exploiting them, that it was underpaying them, should have been providing healthcare, should have seen to it that children were going to school not harvesting in the fields. They had a bagful of 'shoulds' for everybody and everything. They claimed that all the growers in the area were acting illegally because they said they conspired to set wages. So, they said workers had a right to join together to fight their exploiters and oppressors. You know, they just spouted all the socialist, communist rhetoric we've heard for years. There's nothing new in economic class warfare. You'll keep hearing it until they finally give up or we crush them once and for all, which may happen sooner than you realize.

"They demanded, and demanded, and demanded. They demanded what they called a 'living wage' for everyone, some figure they made up. It was way more than the minimum wage, which they weren't getting anyway. They demanded housing with electricity and inside plumbing and free rent. They demanded that a nurse be present in the fields at all times and that a doctor be on call. And they demanded that children under sixteen be able to go to school. Well, none of those demands were met—or were ever going to be met. So, they flexed their muscles, and for the first time ever, just before the harvest, workers packed up and walked out. They targeted only HarvestCo to make an example of it for all the other growers. Eventually, everyone else caved in and met their demands.

"But we didn't. I say 'we' because my family owned HarvestCo. My father said he would never give in to demands. We were forced into bankruptcy. And the only way we could settle our debts was to sell our land, literally dirt cheap, to a developer who built cheap tract housing. My family lost everything after decades of working and building equity. I was robbed of my inheritance. I was born to wealth that was stolen from me. I was in my teens when it happened, but I never forgot it. How could I?

"You've got a God-given right to hold on to everything you've got. You don't owe anybody anything. You've got a right to run your business the way you want to—and that's that. If someone doesn't like it, they can quit or not come to work for you in the first place. If customers don't like it, they can spend their money somewhere else. The market trumps some government intruder in your affairs telling you what to do and how to do it. Follow your arrogance. There is too much 'we' in the world, not enough 'I.' Life is a competition. You live and die in your own skin. In the end, no one's on your team but you.

"I know all of you have heard about the recent unpleasantness at New Atlantis. So I want to reassure you that we are in the process of implementing a dynamite, two-part strategy to put an end to our opposition. All of you are key to the success of part one: Getting rid of the blight of Coopervilles. They are a black eye on Ham Cooper's presidency. He even goes ballistic when he hears the word. We can't have any of them around before the next election. They have to be eradicated, along with all the human trash living there. It makes me physically ill to see what they've done to Central Park, just a few blocks from you.

"We need all of you to help bug Coopervilles near you. Send someone in, or go in yourself if you can stand it, hire as many people as you can for a few hours on different days, even if it's just to sweep your floors. The important thing is to pump them for information. We need to find out who the leaders are and what they're planning. Transmit any intelligence you get to Atlas Fitness Headquarters as soon as you can so it can be forwarded to the proper authorities.

"Part two of our strategy is, well, I think, brilliant. And I can say that because I didn't think of it. It is the work of Professor Doppelmann, the world's leading expert on psycho, psycho-lexicality—or something like that. We are about to blanket the country with a public relations campaign that will overpower our enemies. The phrase 'John Galt is dead' is going to be on land, sea, and in the air. No one will be able to escape it. We're going to…"

Everyone in the training room becomes visibly agitated. "Professor Manfreed, I'm sorry to interrupt," Enrique says openly troubled. "But you said that 'John Galt is dead' is going to be on land, sea, and in the air?"

"That's impossible," Manfreed replies. "Of course, I said, 'John Galt is dead.'"

"I'm sorry, Professor, but you said it again."

"Let's move on. You all know what I actually meant," Manfreed says, dismissively.

Suddenly, the video connection is lost and the screen goes black. A strange voice repeats, "John Galt is dead." The audience is noticeably confused. Multiple hands raise. "Let's wait to ask questions until after lunch," a puzzled Enrique says. "Be back at 1:30."

SIX

Invade, Raid, Crusade

WEDNESDAY, JUNE 22, 4:30 A.M.: WASHINGTON, D.C. In the summer, even before dawn, everywhere in the nation's capital feels like a steam bath. There is no refreshing, evening cool—ever. The heat of the previous day never evaporates entirely. After the sun goes down, it morphs into an invisible, cloying, omnipresent, wet, gray sultriness that enshrouds people, places, and things. Nothing escapes. Memorials and buildings weather the discomfort in their stride. Lincoln, Jefferson, and the White House are indifferent. But living, breathing people fare badly. A languor overtakes everything they do, even how they move their eyes. Rain, fierce or gentle, makes matters worse. After it, the air feels heavier and stickier than before. Breezes intensify the heat. You can take temporary refuge in air conditioning. But you know you're only fooling yourself. The heat always gets you when you go from place to place. It is relentless and unbeatable.

Today, as every day shortly before dawn, the daytime heat is waiting to ambush Cooperville and its residents on the National Mall. Rows of stately elms provide some relief to those lucky enough to camp under them, but they pay the price of waking to gobs of early morning dampness. Commonly referred to as "the capital of destitute

America" and a black eye for Free-for-All economics, the Washington
Cooperville is now a fortified city-within-a-city. Tourists don't come
here anymore to luxuriate in history and genuflect before marble
monuments. From a healthy distance, they gawk and squawk. More
than one can be heard wondering what diseases the population carries. At row after row of makeshift housing, they shake their heads,
disapprovingly from side to side, in disbelief that anyone—let alone
families with children—can be living so tentatively, in such squalor,
in spitting distance of the president and Congress. And they are personally affronted that such sights—especially crowds bathing in the
reflecting pool—have ruined their trips to the capital. "Why doesn't
somebody do something about getting rid of such an eyesore?" most
can be heard asking. "Why don't they get off their lazy asses and find
jobs?" From time to time, trucks with sound systems drive around
the Mall harassing them with messages like "Get to work, you bums"
or "You're pieces of shit."

Inside Cooperville, people are used to it. They develop hard skin.
They have to. It's the only way they can survive. The camp's official
greeter, Malcolm—residents go only by their first name—tells every
new arrival, "Don't get plugged in by the catcalls. Focus on surviving
and doing whatever it takes to move on. And don't talk about the past.
We've all got one. Don't pile your tale of woe on top of other people's.
You can tell your story outside to anyone who will listen, for whatever
it's worth. Inside, talk about the present. Talk about the future."

For their protection from assailants and vandals, over the years, residents have sealed off the perimeter of the Mall with a series of six-foot
high, makeshift barricades made out of railroad ties, garbage cans, fenc-
ing, barbed wire, almost anything to thwart an intruder. Two unarmed
guards trained in the martial arts are stationed on the north at pedes-
trian entrances from Constitution and Pennsylvania Avenues and on
the south at Independence and Maryland Avenues. There is no access
from the east and west. No vehicles are allowed in Cooperville.

Today, except for a few early risers, the only people moving about before sunrise are members of the volunteer force who guard and patrol the encampment day and night. Like doting parents looking in on their sleeping children, they move up and down rows of tents, cardboard boxes, sleeping bags, and lean-tos people call home. Occasionally they straighten the flap at the entrance of a tent to restore privacy to those inside or cover a sleeper who may have rolled beyond his lean-to or her sleeping bag. But they also watch and listen for anything out-of-the-ordinary that might spell trouble—a deranged or suicidal resident or an attacker from the outside.

"How's it going?" asks George, who's a half-hour away from the end of his eight-hour shift, when he sees Roger pacing back and forth in front of his tent.

"Things just don't feel right, George," the young man in his early thirties replies.

"Have you been eating?" George says. "It looks like you're losing weight. Do you feel ok?"

"I'm restless, haven't been able to sleep in the heat, can't find a comfortable spot," Roger replies, rubbing his bloodshot eyes and combing his disheveled hair with his right hand. "Plus, Adam, my eight-year-old has been sick. We don't know what's wrong with him. But he's got a bad cough."

He's got the yearning look, George thinks to himself. *I've seen it over and over, just before people crack.* "Take it easy, man. Just take it easy for as long as you can. Things have got to get better. They've got to."

Every day by 6 a.m., Cooperville teems with life. No one knows the exact number of its refugees—people come and go, mostly come and stay in the last five years—but it is probably about three thousand. They are all ages. There have been marriages, deaths, births, and divorces. Some children have known no other home. Daily, billowing smokestacks confirm that breakfast is being served from 6 to 9 a.m. in fifteen different communal food tents arranged like a spine straight down the Mall. Individual grills also sizzle. Everywhere, "unity circles" form spontaneously—the hopeful just hold hands before the start of another day drawing strength from each other that their lives will change for the better; others repeat the Lord's Prayer or share epi-grammatic wisdom from the Buddha, Kahlil Gibran, or fortune cookies, anywhere they can get it. People finish their morning ritual quickly. Daily, by 6:45 a.m., trucks and vans line up at entrances to pick up day laborers. A few minutes delay can mean the difference between having enough money to eat meat at dinner—or settling for what they're serving in the soup line.

At precisely 5:30 a.m., under the cover of darkness, four mounted officers from the District of Columbia police force appear at the south entrance of Cooperville. "I'm Commander Platt. We have a warrant to search this place," he declares dryly, brandishing a piece of paper he takes from his breast pocket.

"There's nothing to search for here," Jason, one of the guards replies. "There's just a lot of people trying to live as best they can."

"Fuck you, you piece of shit. We don't care about what you, or any of your kind, have to say. We've got our orders—and they come from the top. We'll find the drugs and guns if we have to search every miserable shack in this hell-hole. This place is gonna be history when we get through. We know who's here and what's here, mister, and we're gonna find it. So, get out of our way."

Jason immediately sounds a shrill, wailing alarm that sweeps over Cooperville. And word spreads like wildfire that they are under attack.

"You shouldn't have done that. Now, you're just gonna make real trouble for everyone. Let's go in boys," Platt says, signaling their advance with the forward motion of his right hand and spurring his horse to proceed. Following closely is a battalion of about 300 security forces on foot, who appear as if from out of nowhere from the shadows. Meanwhile, Cooperville volunteers move quickly through the encampment, trying to reassure and calm people, many of whom were asleep and are still groggy.

"The D.C. security forces are coming through. Remember, no matter what they do, do not resist. Do not provoke. Stay calm. Don't give them any reason to use violence," the volunteers repeat.

Like an invading army, the capital police split into two single lines moving south, one on the east side of the camp, the other on the west. Residents stand at attention, watching in disbelief as officers kick and poke at whatever is in their way, including anyone who might still be asleep.

"Please, don't destroy my house," one frail woman in her sixties pleads. "I haven't done anything wrong. I don't have anything to hide."

"House?" a young officer sneers. "You call this cardboard box a house?"

"But it's all I've got," she says crying.

"Not anymore," he says as he bludgeons it to bits. "There now. I guess you're gonna have to apply for a home improvement loan."

Slowly, as the force makes its way throughout the camp, they shine blinding flashlights directly into people's eyes. "What kind of drugs are you hiding?" "Where are your weapons? We know you've got 'em. Hand 'em over now and maybe we'll go easy on you." But as they speak, they don't wait for answers but kick and smash everything in their way. They subject people, especially attractive young women, to body searches, making obscene gestures and comments to each other. "Hey, I think you'd like being searched, wouldn't you?" one young officer says to a teenage blond.

"Touch her and you're dead," her father says, emerging from their tent.

As they move, they tell everyone they've already accosted to remain standing in line in single file. But no one has to be told not to move. Adult men and women are mute, in a state of shock. Several have collapsed. Whimpering children hug their parents, dolls, and Teddy bears. Infants can be heard crying, instinctively sensing dread. They have been repeatedly warned about the possibility of attacks. But no one was prepared for anything on this scale. Like a tornado wreaking havoc, in one hour, by 6:30 a.m., Cooperville is wasted. Not a shelter left standing. Whatever people called their personal possession smashed and scattered. Food tents leveled. Outhouses toppled. All that remains are two long lines of bewildered men, women, and children, as far as the eye can see—and no sign of drugs or weapons.

"By the authority vested in me by the District of Columbia security force, I now order the complete evacuation of these premises," Commander Platt shouts, and his words are repeated to his men down the Mall: "Evacuate now. Evacuate now. Move 'em out now." Like cattle drivers, the guards push and poke people to move north.

"Where are you taking us?" "Why?" "We haven't done anything!" "What are you doing to us?"

"Why, didn't your travel agent tell you?" Commander Platt says to the first group to exit. "All you pieces of trash are goin' to a new home. Me and the boys made reservations for you in RFK Stadium. You'll be real happy there. We made it look real nice for ya."

When they reach the north exit, guards push the two lines of people into a single column eight or ten abreast. Outside, their route is cordoned off and lined with additional security. Slowly, for three miles, they shuffle along Independence, Pennsylvania, and North Carolina Avenues, until they enter East Capitol Street and are within sight of RFK Stadium. Watching from the middle of the street as the crowd approaches, Platt sneers to his assistant, "It's goin' without a hitch. These people are just a bunch of fuckin' sheep. Look at 'em. They haven't got any fight in 'em."

But suddenly, as the crowd is directly in front of Platt, from out of nowhere, a bugle blares. Scared, Platt's horse suddenly rears up on its hind legs. The commander, who has been loosely holding the reins, is almost thrown out of his saddle. When the horse's front legs come down, his right hoof strikes Adam, Roger's son, who is at the front of the pack, on his forehead. His skull cracks open like a walnut.

His brains ooze out. He is killed instantly. As blood spouts from what is left of his mouth, his legs and upper body twitch for several minutes before falling limp. Cell phone cameras crop up from everywhere taking still and videos of the scene. D.C. security guards cannot confiscate all of them, though they try.

"Adam, Adam," his mother cries uncontrollably before fainting, while Roger falls to his knees, cradling his son's broken body in his arms like Mary holding Christ in Michelangelo's "Pietà." About twenty people driven from Cooperville surround the grieving parents. Twice as many people, yelling "child killer," surround Platt's horse and begin lashing out at the commander with their fists and whatever rocks, glass, and pieces of wood they can grab in the street. As nearby officers attempt to come to Platt's aid, more and more attackers turn on them. Finally, two men pull Platt from his saddle and drop him on the ground. The crowd begins kicking and stomping on him. He menaces his pistol at them and fires a warning shot in the air. At that, his horse rises up again and almost crushes him. The crowd opens a space, a bystander swats the horse's rump and it runs off. The assault on Platt continues. A line of D.C. police surrounds his attackers and begins clubbing them. But the crowd moves around them.

"Let them go," Roger pleads. "Otherwise we're no better than they are."

"You'll pay for this," Platt shouts, shaking his fist at the crowd as two of his men help him hobble away.

"We already have," Roger replies.

Posted on Twitter, Facebook, and other social media, the picture of Roger holding Adam goes viral. The headline with it reads "Justice for Adam. Damn Ham." Angela Bellmonte, the first TV reporter to arrive on the scene, approaches Roger, who continues to cradle the corpse of his son in his arms and refuses to let go as others try to ease it away from him. She says nothing, but quietly motions her cameraman to "roll it."

"My son, my Adam, is dead," Roger says, as though in a trance, walking the last few blocks towards the stadium, cradling Adam, his wife at his side. Then, he looks plaintively at Bellmonte and says, "I'm not a father anymore. I don't have a son. I don't have a son. I had a son. But just like that, I don't have a son. He had a cough he couldn't get rid of. His mother was dead tired from staying up with him. The little guy had open heart surgery when he was born and he had a chronic heart condition. We went bankrupt after our health insurance company dropped us. I just got a job washing dishes. But they came this morning and drove us out of Cooperville like cattle. I was getting ready to go to work. It only pays minimum wage. But at least I could buy enough food to feed the three of us. There's no telling how long it will last. I worked almost my whole life. My family never asked anyone for anything. When I was nine, I delivered newspapers. We lost our home and business. We were completely wiped out. With the economy the way it is, I haven't been able to find steady work for three years."

Then, Roger suddenly collapses. Adam's lifeless body falls across his chest. His wife screams for help. Four men come running, pick up the corpse, and begin fanning Roger until he comes to. They take their shirts off and square off, two by two, and put the body in their makeshift sling. In the confusion after Adam is killed, about half of the mob from Cooperville breaks through the police line and scatters into side streets. With no place else to go, the remaining crowd heads to RFK, now forming a funeral procession behind Roger and his wife. Stunned police still on duty doff their hats as the body passes. By now, East Capitol Street is swarming with media. Bellmonte, who has moved to the entrance of the stadium, is reporting live outside as the mourners approach.

WEDNESDAY, JUNE 22, 1 P.M.: UNDISCLOSED LOCATION. In the control room of the Prometheus Project, Zeus is on the board, watching the

TV monitors, one hour after giving the order to begin all phases of "The People's Strike for Adam."

Monitor 1 shows mobs surrounding the White House, chanting, "John Galt killed Adam!" and "Down with Cooper!" No fewer than fifty different videos of a grief-stricken Roger holding the lifeless Adam have been posted on YouTube. Viewers are warned that the content is bloody and graphic. But already, ten of them have each had more than one million hits. Every TV station in the country has interrupted programming to broadcast live coverage from RFK Stadium. The afternoon editions of domestic newspapers carry the headline "Kid Killed at Cooperville." Media around the world have picked up the story.

On Monitor 2, Mercury provides changing images of crowds of "shoppers" gradually and casually strolling into malls in Phoenix, Seattle, Oklahoma City, Dallas, Chicago, Philadelphia, Atlanta, Boston, Charleston, and Indianapolis. Eventually, they add up to a crowd of at least 5,000 in each location, all of them heading for Gayle's Department Stores. The owners of the upscale national chain are known to be major supporters of President Cooper and the agenda of Free-for-All economics. As head of the National Association of Free-Market Retailers, Mortimer Gayle, grandson of the department store's founder, worked with Hilton Manfreed to eliminate minimum wage and worker's compensation laws, as well as unemployment compensation.

By 1:15 p.m., there is no room for any more customers to enter the ten Gayle's on the Prometheus Project hit list. Shoppers overwhelm salespeople with a battery of questions. They insist upon trying on blouse after blouse, pants after pants, barely able to get to fitting rooms because of the crowds. They ask advice about dry cleaning versus hand-washing of delicate fabrics, want clarification of exchange policies, and ask for discounts. Ultimately, they buy nothing. Legitimate shoppers who can't get waited on begin loudly complaining. By

2:30 p.m., it is clear that Gayle's is not going to transact any business anytime soon.

An agitated Mortimer Gayle is interviewed by Channel 10 News from the chain's Atlanta headquarters. "I want all of our loyal customers to know that Gayle's is open for business, will *always* be open for business, and will not be shut down by gangs who believe in mob rule," he says emphatically. "These are the Corporate States of America, not some half-baked developing country at the mercy of terrorists. We know how to deal with guerrillas who want to bring down our way of life—and we will do so. In the interest of national security and public safety, we are closing the ten stores that have been targeted for attack. But we will reopen soon. You can count on that."

On Monitor 3, Adonis shows a tall young blond woman entering the Manhattan headquarters of Atlas Fitness Centers, guiding two Saint Bernards yoked on a common leash. Slim, she is dressed in a black leotard and announces she wants to buy a twelve-pack of Atlas Energy Drink. As she waits for the salesperson to fill her order, the dogs start to squirm and tug on their leashes. "What's the matter?" she asks, trying to calm them. "You want to explore a little bit, I know," she says, freeing them. As they run through the facility, it becomes clear that they have massive, uncontrollable cases of diarrhea. Before long, they have christened the better part of the center with their explosions and have released an overpowering smell. Grousing clients pack up and flee the premises en masse. "Bad dogs, bad dogs," the woman says, as she apologizes to the disgruntled staff. The center closes for business until further notice.

Meanwhile, the center's phones ring off-the-hook, reporting similar attacks of dog shitting at Atlas Centers—fifteen and climbing—to those who have to begin to clean up. Zeus chuckles as he watches. "There's nothing like a good sirloin steak with Ex-Lax sauce to do the trick."

On Monitor 4, Pandora coordinates the updates from across the country, documenting "people's brigades" that have closed down forty-five branches of the Bank of the Corporate States. Starting at 1:30 p.m. on the East Coast, unusually large numbers of potential depositors have been swarming facilities, saying they want to open accounts. At the same time, online withdrawals of funds, estimated to have been $40 million in just five minutes, caused the bank's website to crash, freezing all transactions nationwide.

On Monitor 5, at 3 p.m., Zeus watches as pandemonium breaks out on the floor of the National Stock Exchange and all trading is halted after 475 million shares are sold off in ten minutes and shares of targeted companies drop by seventy percent.

On Monitor 6, starting at 4:30 p.m., "passengers" fill subway stations throughout the five boroughs of New York City but don't board trains. Crowds of irate and anxious commuters spill into the surrounding streets, bringing traffic to a standstill.

On Monitor 7, Olympus reports that crowds have packed the terminals of CSA, World, and National airlines in Los Angeles, Chicago, Dallas/Fort Worth, Chicago, Atlanta, Charlotte, and New York. No one can check in for flights. Planes have been delayed indefinitely. Flocks of pigeons that have been fed castor oil are let loose and are shitting everywhere, so people are fleeing the terminals.

On Monitor 8, Zeus is watching domestic and international TV feeds, reporting that the viral message on social media is that "The People's Strike for Adam" has brought commerce in the country to a virtual standstill. Unconfirmed reports are also circulating that President Cooper is about to address the nation to declare a national emergency.

WEDNESDAY, JUNE 22, 9 P.M.: THE WHITE HOUSE. The Cooper Administration has issued a written statement condemning "The People's Strike for Adam" as an act of treason. "Anything that strikes at the economic lifeblood of the Corporate States of America amounts to an act of war, whether it originates on our soil or from foreign sources," President Cooper says. "I have instructed the FBI, the CIA, and the National Capital Security Force to launch a consolidated investigation into the acts that paralyzed the nation today. My fellow Investors, let me assure you that I will not rest until we have brought all of the perpetrators of these un-American attacks to justice. They will pay— and pay dearly!"

WASHINGTON, D.C.: THE NATIONAL MALL. Throughout the night and into the next morning, bulldozers can be heard smashing and clearing debris from the Mall Cooperville. An eerie, orange light from there can be seen throughout the capital. Anything that can be burned is thrown onto scores of bonfires. An army of dump trucks hauls off anything that can't be incinerated. Scavengers among the crews salvage a girl's doll, a baseball glove, clothing, even pots and pans. Before deciding to keep something, they ask among themselves about how much they think it might sell for. The next day, by 6 a.m., ashes are all that is left of Cooperville.

As the nation recovers from "The People's Strike," the media question the ability of the Ham Cooper Administration to continue to lead the Corporate States. Some pundits, even those who have typically towed the party line, suggest that the nation may be poised to move in a different direction. "Is John Galt, in fact, *really* dead? Are we on the verge of a revolution?" John Trigmore, op-ed columnist for *The National News*, asked in a Thursday, June 23 column. "Has Cooper lost his grip?" more than one commentator wonders.

In the meantime, the Prometheus Project has declared Friday, June 24 a national day of mourning for Adam. In the name of "The

People's Strike," it has asked all working people to stay home and all businesses to close. A memorial has been scheduled at RFK Stadium for 1 p.m. Pandora has coordinated arrangements through her network of local supporters in Washington, D.C. and surrounding areas. The National Television Service has agreed to provide live coverage of the event and a feed to all domestic and international media. Reports of the killing, which is being called an assassination, and of the details of the Friday memorial have gone viral on social media. Comments and visuals are in the tens of millions. Some sites have crashed for hours. Internet platforms are also reporting that the White House has declared the day of mourning a treasonous, rogue action punishable by law, and has advised the public not to attend.

FRIDAY, JUNE **24**: WASHINGTON, D.C., RFK STADIUM. Beginning at 9 a.m. on Friday, crowds flock to the stadium. About 1,500 former Cooperville residents have been living there since their camp was destroyed two days before. On the floor level, a mini-Cooperville has already appeared. There are about 100 makeshift shelters improvised from sheets and cardboard boxes. A large white sheet with the words "Cooperville 2" flies from the stadium's flagpole.

By 1 p.m. the 46,000 seats of the stadium are filled and the overflow crowd has spilled into the streets outside, where they watch the service on three billboard-size screens. Busses have brought attendees from across the country. Most, if not all, are wearing black armbands. Many are carrying signs that read "Justice for Adam," "Down with Cooper," and "John Galt Killed Adam." It is a typical hot, sticky Washington, D.C. afternoon, but no one seems to care.

As four men slowly carry Adam's closed coffin into the stadium, the audience stands. They are followed by fifty or so children singing the chorus of Michael Jackson's "We Are the World":

We are the world/We are the children/We are the ones who make a brighter day/So let's start giving/There's a choice we're making/We're saving our own lives/It's true we'll make a better day/Just you and me.

The simple pine box is placed in the middle of the stadium, on a raised catafalque made of orange crates. A single piece of black cloth is draped lengthwise across it. Behind it are four chairs. Two are occupied by Adam's parents, Roger and Anne. An unidentified man and woman sit beside them.

"Please be seated," Adam's father says, coming to the microphone facing the coffin. "Good afternoon everyone here in or outside the stadium, as well as the millions of you who are watching around the country and the world. My name is Roger. I am Adam's father. Anne is Adam's mother," he says pointing to his wife. "Does anything look lonelier than the coffin of a young boy, forever lost to us? Can you imagine any loneliness greater than what Anne and I feel? She brought him into this world on the happiest day of our lives. And now, on the loneliest day we will ever know, his cold body lies in a pine box. He belongs to the world now, but he is lost to us forever—alone, a little boy lost, alone without his parents, to wander through eternity.

"Parents are not supposed to bury their children. It is against the law of nature for a father to see his son's frail body crushed in front of him under the massive weight of a horse. I was supposed to protect him, but I couldn't. I wonder if he knows that I would have, but couldn't. It all happened so fast. If I had known, I would have thrown myself before the horse. But it all happened so fast. It is against the law of nature for a mother whose warm body gave her son life to know that life has been drained from him for the cold of death and to know that he will be lowered into a cold grave.

"Today, the whole world knows Adam's name and how he was brutally killed. But let me tell you about who Adam was when he was

alive. Oh, how we celebrated when Anne and I learned she was preg-
nant. She had an easy pregnancy and birth. But shortly after Adam
was born, the doctor discovered that he had a congenital defect that
affected his heart rhythm. He never needed surgery or medication.
But we had to watch him carefully. He couldn't play sports or get
overexcited without possibly endangering his life. Long-term, we didn't
know what his prospects were. Otherwise, Adam was an average kid,
though he was much smarter than average. He was gifted. He was always the smartest in his class and he couldn't wait to get to school.
He said he wanted to be a doctor, because he wanted to make sick
kids better. He said he *really* thought he knew how to do that. He even
told his doctors that.

"Adam was killed on Wednesday. But we died as a family two years
ago. For ten years, I had been a software developer for an international
technology company. But on a Friday at 5 p.m., I received an email
informing me that my services were no longer needed, because it had
decided to outsource all of its technical operations overseas. Since,
thanks to Cooper and his corporate cronies, there is no unemployment insurance, within six months we had used up our cash and available savings. I couldn't pay our rent or health insurance. We could
barely afford to eat. We had no one to turn to or any place to go.

"I did the only thing I knew. Adam, Anne, and I packed up everything that would fit in our van—Thank God it was paid for—and we
headed north from Tennessee. I found odd jobs along the way, so we
were able to eat. But we slept in the van. We started out in the middle
of summer. I had hoped that we'd get settled somewhere in time for
Adam to start school. But we couldn't stay anywhere long enough.
Anne did the best she could to teach him. I told you he was gifted,
and something inside him started to die when he couldn't go to
school.

"Finally, we wound up in Washington, D.C. and Cooperville. For
the first time, we were with thousands of people who understood what

we were going through, because they were going through it, too. I've been able to work at day jobs, washing dishes or doing light construction. You can forget software development. No one's hiring. We signed Adam up for school in the fall. Though we had a long way to go, we were starting to pick ourselves up. At least we weren't moving from place to place and living in our van. Oh, by the way, I sold the van shortly after we went to Cooperville, and that gave us some breathing room for a few months.

"Then, Wednesday happened. I still can't believe it. From out of nowhere, men with flashlights and sticks attacked helpless men, women, and children, most of whom were sleeping. They gave us no time to collect our things and made us march into the street. By now, the whole world has seen what happened, not just to Adam, but to thousands of human beings. In Adam's name, I beg you to never let this happen again."

As Roger returns to his seat, people in the audience jump to their seats and shout, "Ad-am, Ad-am, Ad-am. Nev-er a-gain. Ad-am, Ad-am, Ad-am. Nev-er a-gain!"

"My name is Frank," the next speaker says. "Ever since John Galt returned and the Corporate States of America was established, it has been illegal to pledge allegiance aloud to the United States of America. So, I ask you to observe a moment's silence and to repeat it to yourselves.

"We are here because President Cooper and the Corporate States of America assassinated Adam, an innocent child, in the name of greed, profit, and personal ambition. They have drugged the country on Atlas until they've gone mad with power. We are here because we want the world to know that if you kill one of us, you kill all of us. We are here because President Cooper and the Corporate States of America have failed us. They destroyed Cooperville and have sent us here because they don't want the world see how we suffer from the disaster they created.

"Just two days ago, none of us dreamed we'd be here. But look around, this is now what some of us must call home, thanks to President Ham Cooper and his thugs. That's right, let the whole world see this open-air jail, where we have been forced to move. I was living in Cooperville in Washington, D.C., as I had been for the past four years. I was trying to survive. I knew Adam and his parents from the first day they arrived on the Mall. I watched how they cared for each other as a family—and especially how George and Anne doted on their son. I saw how determined George was to find work and how he went without eating more than once so Anne and Adam could eat—especially Adam. Yes, that's how bad things get for some of us in the Corporate States of America. We actually can't afford food or a decent place to live or clothes or medicine or all the things that many of you watching take for wanted.

"Everything changed for all of us in Cooperville during the predawn raid Wednesday. Based upon lies, trumped-up charges, that we now know came directly from Ham Cooper, District security forces attacked and began destroying our shelters, scattering our belongings, and rounding us up like common criminals. They treat their dogs better than they treated us. They claimed that we were a national security risk because we were hiding drugs and weapons. But they knew those were lies. They put us on a forced march to this stadium, through the streets of the capital, to get us out of the way. That's because we are living proof of the brutality and failure of policies of the Corporate States of America. But the world is now seeing the truth.

"Adam, well, innocent Adam wasn't even lucky enough to get to this hellhole. He was trampled to death. It is fitting and proper that we should be here, in RFK Stadium, to remember the short life of Adam, who was killed before he had a chance to grow up and make something of himself. In 1969, this stadium was renamed for U.S. Senator Robert F. Kennedy, who was assassinated the year before as he campaigned for the presidency of the United States of America.

To those of you who are too young to remember, the U.S.A. was totally different from the Corporate States of America. Its policies and government were 'of the people, by the people, and for the people'—not, as they are today, for the benefit of corporations and the rich, to hell with everyone else. RFK would be ashamed of what we are today—and he would have fought against it if he had lived until today. And so, as a fitting tribute to Adam's life and memory, I ask you to commit yourself to challenge the warped values of the Corporate States and to return to those that made this nation great." As he takes his seat, the audience stands and applauds and shouts, "John Galt Killed A-dam. John Galt Killed A-dam. John Galt Killed A-dam."

"Thank you, everyone," the woman says, as she replaces Frank at the microphone. "My name is Irene. I too lived in Cooperville on the Mall before I was forced out two days ago and made to walk through the streets barefoot to get here. That's right! The Cooper thug who pulled the stakes of my tent out of the ground so it collapsed on me wouldn't even let me put my shoes on when he told me to march. 'But I'm barefoot,' I told him. 'Too fuckin' bad, bitch,' he answered.

"Today is an unofficial national day of mourning for Adam. And the White House has declared it an act of terrorism. But I'm thrilled to report that, at this hour, there is a nationwide work stoppage. Nothing is happening anywhere. The Corporate States of America is completely shut down. Maybe now, Cooper and his thugs will understand who *really* makes this country possible.

"I want to ask five of the children who used to live in Cooperville and who are now are pretty much in jail here to come forward." They line up in front of the coffin and each one holds a single white rose. Irene takes the microphone out of the stand and places it in front of the children as they speak together, then one at a time.

"We speak for all the children of Cooperville, who only want a chance to live, and play, and grow up to be good people."

"I speak for the children from the North."

"I speak for the children from the South."
"I speak for the children from the East."
"I speak for the children from the West."

Then, together, all five say, "We speak for the children from everywhere. We speak for Adam. All of us are Adam." One by one, they put their roses on the coffin and walk away.

Over the loudspeaker, a voice announces that this concludes today's ceremony. The pall bearers begin moving Adam's coffin out of the stadium, followed by Roger, Anne, Frank, Irene, and a line of fifty children. In the sky, out of nowhere, the following words appear: "Adam lives. John Galt Is Dead." The audience breaks out in deafening applause and chants the message until the procession is out of sight.

SEVEN

Excoriate, Bloviate, Celebrate

SATURDAY, JUNE 25, 10 A.M.: THE WHITE HOUSE, EAST ROOM. President Cooper agreed to meet with his Corporate Council, fifty heads of the nation's major corporations and his de facto bosses, who demanded he meet with them. The usually quiet, staid group is noisy. People have congregated in threes and fours. Some are shaking their fists. Others are shaking their heads, lips pursed, brows knitted. They ignore the president when he comes in, until he taps the microphone at the podium and asks them to take their seats.

"These are difficult times for all of us, I know," he begins.

"You said it!" someone yells from the back of the room.

"Thank you all for coming on such short notice," Cooper continues, trying to ignore the interruption. "I invited you here to assure you face-to-face that we have everything under control."

"Mr. President, Mr. President, I'm Jonathan Smythe of Consolidated Industries," a tall, totally bald man in his early fifties says as he pops up from his seat in the front row. "Mr. President, first of all, with all due respect, *we* asked for this meeting—not you. Second, it appears to us as though you and your administration have lost control. You're looking like impotent fools, with all due respect. And you're making us look like a bunch of idiots for supporting you. Something's gotta give. You've gotta keep a lid on things for us. You need to protect our markets. Can't you control a bunch of malcontents? Frankly, I'm beginning—almost all of us are beginning—to think that John Galt, and everything he stood for, *is* dead, just like all those fuckin' anti-government banners are saying. And we're coming to the conclusion that you've killed him. At least that's what everyone's thinking, even if they're not saying it."

"Mr. Smythe, I don't take your comments personally," Cooper answers dryly.

"Well, you should!" Smythe snaps back. "Who else do you think they were meant for?"

"Obviously, you're upset and you have every right to be," Cooper continues. "But you're just plain uninformed and misinformed. So, let's set the record straight. Anyone who thinks like you is simply falling for the terrorist propaganda that the media love to pick up and throw in our faces. You know who runs this country now—and who has for sixty-seven years. You know that all the power is on our side everywhere—at the national level and in the states, right down to cities. Nothing, absolutely nothing, has changed. It took us a while, but we've got the courts sewn up with people who think like us. There hasn't been a ruling against corporate interests in decades—and there isn't going to be. We've got what's left of the Congress and state legislatures in our pocket. And you know my White House is *always* on your side. There may be grumblings from time to time from loudmouths and troublemakers stirred up by outside agitators. But we've been able to crush them in the past and we'll do it again. Only this time, we'll put them out of business for good!"

"But Mr. Cooper, I'm Harold Klein of International Networks," another member of the audience says, as he jumps up, shaking his head back and forth quickly. "Surely, you understand that the killing of the young boy Adam is a game-changer. He is now a symbol for everyone who is against you—against us. The whole world was watching yesterday, literally the whole world. People who didn't know anything about John Galt or Coopervilles or Free-for-All economics are suddenly calling us greedy and grasping fascists. They're saying we're all cold-blooded killers. We're losing the PR war. Even if it *was* an accident that the kid was trampled, and of course it *was*, no one in his right mind would have intended to do something like that, it has turned almost everyone against us—and by everyone, I mean the world, *literally* the world. All you hear on the news is that the CSA is run by a bunch of child-killers. I've been getting calls from my associates all over the world asking what the hell is going on here. And you know what that means—they're worried about their investments. Some are even threatening to back out of deals. I can't have it! I just can't have it! I won't have it!"

"Gentlemen, gentlemen—and lady, of course—I fully understand your frustration. So, let me outline our counteroffensive, which is why I asked you to come here today," Cooper says—again forgetting that they called for the meeting. "We are not sitting by and getting steamrolled by a bunch of lazy, homeless, deadbeat tramps. By the time we get through with them, there won't be anymore camps, no one will slander me anymore by calling those dumps Coopervilles, and the country will get back to normal. My administration will be stronger than ever after this recent unpleasantness.

"First, at 1 p.m. today, right here in the East Room, I am going to speak to the nation and hold a press conference about the facts in the Adam case. The FBI has completed its initial investigation, and let me assure you we have proof that the whole thing is a put-up job. My administration is not responsible for that kid's death, and everybody's gonna know it by the time I'm through. We own the press. So, this will be a cakewalk. I'll speak, they'll ask questions, I'll answer, and the whole matter will be put to rest.

"Second, we're gonna pull out the stops for this year's July 4th Presidential Gala. By the time we're through with the fireworks,

Adam and his fuckin' family will be nobodies again and we'll get back to the business of business. That's what I'm here for. We make the world safe for business and keep a lid on 'the people.' You know that! That's what I've *always* been here for. And that's what I'll continue to be for when I'm re-elected.

"Ham?"

"Yes, Mortimer," the president says to the head of Gayle's Department Stores. "Ham, I lost millions when those mobs shut down ten of my stores. Real shoppers saw TV reports and were so scared, they stayed away. My employees were afraid there might be violence. We were afraid of lawsuits if anyone got hurt. We had no choice but to shut everything down. And we stayed closed Friday, not because we wanted to, but because those guerrillas—that's what they are you know, terrorist guerrillas—called for a nationwide shutdown during the bullshit they put on at RFK Stadium over the death of that kid. It made me fuckin' sick. I went on TV and they made me look like a greedy bastard. Even my wife said I looked bad. Who's in charge of this country now—our companies or mobs of people?"

"Mortimer, that's why I'm speaking to the country and holding a press conference this afternoon. I'm gonna pass out the FBI report. And by the time I'm finished they'll get the facts in the Adam case and we'll look like victims of a subversive conspiracy, not greedy bastards. Everyone will know who's *really* in charge. There won't be any doubt."

Abner Richards, an investment banker, says, "Bullshit! To anyone who falls for the bullshit about greed, I say bullshit. I'm proud of being greedy. I don't care what people call me. All I care about is the bottom line. You goin' soft on us, Cooper? Is that the problem? You lost your spine? Are you the *real* problem? We don't have a single, goddamn thing to apologize for. We've got billions at stake. You better use this as a chance to ram Free-for-All economics down the throats of the fuckin' people, whether they like it or not. If we've still got socialist looters who think they're gonna bleed us, to hell with them.

Round 'em up and put 'em in jail. Come on strong, Cooper. This is war, and we'd better win it. The problem with the cleaning out of the Mall Cooperville was that the cops didn't come on strong enough in the first place."

Aristotle Khouris, an ethnic Greek living in Rome, rises and slowly, in an impeccable British accent, adds, looking intently at Cooper, "I agree with everything that's been said about coming on strong. It's our only option. This Adam affair couldn't have happened at a worse time, but we don't have to take it lying down. We've got trillions of dollars on the table. Let me repeat, trillions, not billions. I have spent the last three years putting together the three-country European strategy that will make every one of you richer than you could ever have imagined and I'm not about to see it destroyed.

"All of you already know the plan: After the November election, the Worldwide Investment Trust is ready to force countries A, B, and C—you all know who they are—into default by calling loans they have no chance of repaying, never had any chance of repaying. The government will lose the confidence of the people. The generals are in our pocket, will overthrow the civilians, and declare martial law. Then, under their extraordinary powers, they'll open bidding to privatize all public services and resources, because the state treasury won't have money to keep the country going. But we know who will win them.

"We've already taken out unofficial contracts on state-owned power companies, seaports, airports, national lotteries, state-owned media, national banks, railway systems, and airports. Everything will be sold at fire-sale prices. If there are any protests from state workers who'll lose their jobs or who have to take a pay cut, the military will take care of them too. Assets are supposed to be auctioned, but that's just for show. After that, there's nothing between us and trillions of dollars. All the money the government used to collect will turn into our profits. It will implement the corporate state model, just like the

CSA, and we can keep replicating it around the world, faster and more easily after A, B, and C are successfully taken over. I repeat," he says, looking directly at Cooper, "nothing and no one can be allowed to stand in our way. We've worked too long and too hard for this and too much is at stake."

"Aristotle, I refuse to take your comments personally. One thing you learn being the head of the CSA is that you've got to have a thick skin. You know, everyone here knows, my administration and I are not going soft on anything. We came into office to continue Free-for-All economic policies. I'm not going to waste time listing all the accomplishments we've had since I became national CEO. But I'll remind you, in case any of you have forgotten, who was responsible for pushing to rename the country the Corporate States of America in the first place. So, I'll leave it at that. Unless any of you have further comments or questions, we have to clear this room while it's set up for my address to the nation and news conference. I hope all of you will attend."

SATURDAY, JUNE 25, 1 P.M.: THE WHITE HOUSE, EAST ROOM. Twenty-five members of the press and all but five of the members of the Corporate Council who just met with Ham Cooper are in the room when the president steps up to the podium and speaks to the nation.

"My fellow Americans, investors in the Corporate States of America, I am speaking to you from the historic East Room of the White House," Cooper begins. "In good times and in bad times, in this very room, much of our glorious history has been written and reported. It is the duty of every president to speak honestly to everyone who has a stake in his company. And today is no exception. I am proud to say that the Corporate States of America remains the shining example of a company of collective interests. The bottom line is—and ultimately we all know that the bottom line is all that counts—the more dedicated we are to our corporate good, the stronger and more profitable we all will be. You know the guiding principles of the Galtian Restoration. You know how they have changed this country and the world for the better. You, we, are all living proof of the greater good that flows naturally from a free-market nation.

"Unfortunately, I have to look all of you in the eye and tell you the sad, honest truth: There are enemies among us—not just people who disagree with us, we always welcome open, honest, constructive debate—but forces whose sole purpose is to overthrow the CSA and all the good we stand for. Here's the proof, right here in my hands. I am holding up the complete and objective FBI report—'The People's Riot on the National Mall'—on the events that recently took place in and around the National Mall. Every stakeholder must feel confident that those who lead their enterprise are open, honest, and transparent in their dealings. So, let me be blunt and absolutely clear: My administration is in no way responsible for any violence that occurred on the Mall. As the FBI report makes clear, the events of this past Wednesday were intentionally provoked by illegal squatters and outside agitators. Everything that occurred was part of a well-orchestrated plan to discredit those of us who represent you honestly, ethically, and sincerely.

"Early Friday morning, acting upon only the most reliable and pressing intelligence collected over a period of months, capital security forces entered the illegal encampment on the Mall. They were searching for drugs and illegal weapons that they had every reason to believe were there."

Cooper holds up the FBI report. The camera focuses on it, while he turns the pages.

"Just look at conclusive evidence of the violent plot that was being hatched on the Mall. Yes, just blocks from the White House. Here you see photographs of the hundreds of items that were found. I know you'll be as shocked as I was when I first saw them. You're looking at full-fledged terrorist weapons: AK-47 assault rifles, semi-automatic pistols, revolvers, rifles, machine guns, knives hidden in belt buckles, hairbrushes, and combs. There are even playing cards with metal tips that can cut someone's throat. There's pepper spray. There's nothing innocent about the meat cleavers and box-cutters that we found. They weren't being stocked to make dinner or unpack household goods. Make no mistake about it: The Mall was an arsenal waiting to be unleashed until security stopped the plot. It was a violent revolution waiting to happen.

"Take a look at the photographs of the drugs that agents found—marijuana, cocaine, heroin, and mountains of prescription painkillers. Drug deals were helping to finance the Mall camp. Detailed kidnapping plots against corporate officials were also found. So, no matter what anyone tells you, people who took over the National Mall—your mall, a treasure that belongs to everyone—were not innocent victims of our economic policies, as they've led the press to report. They were criminals, pure and simple. If anything, we tolerated them for too long, because we're decent and humane and we give people the benefit of the doubt. In our defense, we waited until we had absolutely irrefutable evidence against the violent perpetrators before we acted, because we must always be accountable and honest. Because we believe that foreign agitators infiltrated the Mall encampment, I have asked the CIA to investigate and report to me immediately on all aspects of the international plot. As you can see, on the grounds of national security—protecting each and every one of you, as well as the nation's capital—we had every reason to search the Mall and move people living there to RFK Stadium, where they could be held and processed before they were prosecuted. They posed a real and immediate danger. That place could have erupted in violence at any time.

"My fellow investors, the next conclusive proof from the FBI report will no doubt astonish you as much as it did me, particularly after the fictitious story that the media have made up about what happened to the young boy Adam. Anti-government, subversive elements have seized upon the incident to attack me and my administration, but they are lying to the nation and the world about what *really* occurred in order to advance their self-serving political agenda. We have still photos and video, showing conclusively that the horse was in no way responsible for his death. If anything, it was the reverse. Adam collapsed—and the screams of the people around him scared the horse. It reared back on its hind legs and then fell forward, only when provoked. Adam was already dead when the horse's hoof came down on him. Adam was a sickly child from birth. For his whole life, he was weak. He had a congenital heart defect. His parents should have provided for him and protected him, instead of neglecting him.

"That brings me to another important, but sad, point: We are looking into bringing charges of parental child abuse against Adam's parents. I have asked the FBI to turn over all the incriminating evidence they have regarding…whatever their names are…to the District security forces to determine if further criminal prosecution is warranted. And, if it is, and I believe it is, let me assure the nation, they will be prosecuted to the full extent of the law. My administration is 100 percent, categorically, against child abuse. It simply will not be tolerated.

"The FBI report also deals with a dangerous group of criminals that calls itself the Prometheus Project. Using the legal surveillance and clearing of the illegal encampment on the Mall and the death of Adam as a pretext for rebellion, those guerrillas orchestrated an attack on private businesses, threw the stock market into chaos, and brought transportation, the lifeblood of business, to a standstill. They claim that they are 'the people.' And they have set out to show the decent, law-abiding, productive investors in the prosperity of the Corporate State of America that they and 'the people' they represent are really in charge and that the nation must be governed in the interest of something they call 'the common good.'

"Well, I have news for them. They are in for a big surprise. Our opposition may delude themselves into thinking they are Prometheus—protectors of others, people with social consciences. But every true citizen of the CSA is an Atlas, and not just *an* Atlas but an Atlas drugged on boundless self-interest. We are the freest people in the world. We know no limits. And we will trample anyone who tries to hamper us.

"It is illegal to do anything to bring business in this country to a standstill. In fact, it's unconstitutional. We just celebrated sixty-seven glorious years of the Galtian Restoration that made protecting business the primary concern of government. It is the primary concern of my administration, of course. If businesses are not making profits, nothing else matters. I swore an oath to protect this country's corporations, and nothing—not a person, not a mob, not even the death of an eight-year-old boy—will stop me from fulfilling my responsibility, especially after we have discovered the lies and deceptions behind his death.

"Finally, my fellow investors, the FBI report on the riot blames the District security forces for over-reacting to the violence that erupted in and around the Mall. It states, and I am reading directly from the report, 'District security personnel should have shown greater self-control in responding to the provocations of the rioters.' As a result, I have ordered the head of security for the District to implement a comprehensive training program in crowd and riot control for all security personnel. And now, I'll be happy to take questions from the press. Let me see, the first on my list is Maya Fitzpatrick of *News of the Nation*."

"Thank you, Mr. President. Who were the people living on the Mall Cooperville?"

"If you don't mind," Cooper says visibly infuriated, "the proper term is illegal encampment. I refuse to be slandered by having my name attached to something for which I am in no way responsible. To rephrase your question, Who were the people illegally encamped on the Mall? They are deadbeats, people who refuse to work, people who want 'the government,' someone else, anyone else, to take care of them.

"Bernard Brill of Truth-dot-com ..."

"Thank you, Mr. President. Are you sorry that Adam died?"

"Of course, I'm sorry. But as you heard me say before, my administration is in no way responsible for what occurred, directly or indirectly. We're not guilty of anything. I am most sorry that he was there in the first place. He and everyone else had no business illegally camping out on the Mall. If his parents hadn't put Adam's life at risk, he'd still be alive.

"Angelina Pescadore of The International News Syndicate ..."

"Thank you, Mr. President. Do Coopervilles—I mean illegal encampments on the Boston Commons and in Santa Fe, New Mexico pose similar national security dangers? And if so, what are you doing to protect the nation?"

"Ms. Pescadore, all illegal encampments are under surveillance. At the moment, none has posed a threat to national security comparable to what was detected on the Mall. People illegally squatting would be advised to leave all encampments immediately rather than allow themselves to be used as pawns by outside agitators. We can't guarantee their continued safety. We have taken an oath to protect the nation—and protect it we will.

"Baird Williams of National Television Syndicate ..."

"Thank you, Mr. President. Some studies have shown that most, if not all, of the residents on the Mall had actually been previously employed, had owned homes, but had been dispossessed as a result of economic policies enacted by your administration and previous administrations. Are those studies accurate?"

"Baird, you know better than that. Of course, they are not accurate. They are absolute lies. They are nothing more than socialistic propaganda. Anyone who wants to work in this great country can do so. Anyone who wants to start a business has free rein. We've gotten rid of almost all regulations on business. This is the greatest nation on earth for making money. If you can't make it here, you can't make it anywhere. But this is not a country for loafers and looters and people who want everyone else to 'do it' for them. That's who's *really* trying to discredit our policies with the false studies you've quoted!

"Susanna Rutledge of United Markets News ..."

"Thank you, Mr. President. The members of my trade association are extremely concerned after the Prometheus Project's 'People's Strike for Adam.' They've lost billions of dollars. And they don't know when or how the attacks are going to be stopped. They've asked me to ask you how your opposition managed to shut down the country and how you're going to handle it."

"Susanna, first of all, they are not 'my' opposition, as you say. They pose a much bigger threat to the stability of the nation. They are opposed to *all* of us, to everything we all stand for. They are attacking the fundamental principles upon which the CSA was founded. How the Prometheus Project works and how we are going to stop them is top secret information, which, of course, I am not at liberty to disclose. But let me assure you that ..."

Suddenly, transmission from the White House is interrupted. Cooper's microphone goes dead. He taps it, scratches his head, and looks around for assistance. Aides immediately rush up to his side, but no one is able to restore power. Then, a picture of Adam being trampled by the horse that killed him replaces the live feed.

A voice from the back of the room shouts, "Mr. President, Mr. President, I'm Roger Fitzpatrick."

"I'm sorry, but I can't hear you," Cooper answers, cupping his hands over his ears.

"Mr. President," Fitzpatrick repeats, raising his voice so the whole room can hear him. "Mr. President, visuals positively show Adam standing and being struck by the horse. One of the pictures is on your monitor now. The pictures are all over the Internet. There's absolutely no denying it. How can you possibly say he collapsed and scared the horse?"

"I'm sorry, but I can't hear you," Cooper answers abruptly while leaving the podium. Backstage, he asks his press secretary, Rhea Pullman, "Who's that Fitzpatrick guy, and how did he get in? You were supposed to screen the media for ringers. Another mistake like that and you'll be out on your sweet, fat ass—and you know I mean it. Now, call the FBI and the CIA and tell them to find out who pulled the plug on the transmission and how the picture of that fuckin' kid got on the screen."

MONDAY, JULY 4, 7 P.M.: WASHINGTON, D.C. The stage is set for the national birthday celebration open to the general public. Twenty billboard-size TV screens have been set up so that the events may be seen on the Mall. Since the Cooperville on the Mall was leveled, crews have been working around-the-clock to remove debris and plant sod. Cooper has personally inspected the progress almost daily. "I want every memory of that fucking trash heap of human waste gone in time for the 4th," he told his staff. "I want the public to be able to enjoy a concert and fireworks again. And I want the whole world to see that we're still in charge."

Privately, Cooper told his inner circle that, in this election year, he sees the evening as make-it-or-break-it for his administration. "Spare no expense," he commands his chief-of-staff. Irate because of the growing backlash from the killing of "that little bastard," as he refers to Adam, he has already fired the head of his re-election campaign and his White House press secretary. He told both of them together, "We still don't know why the feed at my press conference went dead, how the picture of 'that little bastard' got on the screen, or who that hostile last guy was. You gave me a list of people to call on. Everything was supposed to be orchestrated. Our people own the media.

So, if you can't keep me from getting shit on, there's something wrong with you. Bottom line is: You don't produce, you're outta here. Business is business. You've got twenty minutes to pack up and get out. "

Since 5:30 p.m., guests have been arriving for the exclusive July 4th Presidential Gala at the Washingtonian Hotel. Paying $1,000 a person, the 400 confirmed guests are a Who's Who of Free-for-All economics, national politics, and international business. Count Henry de Horsch, the evening's principal honoree, arrives early so he can attend a brief run-through of the program. He exits his limousine, followed by a stunning brunette in her mid-twenties. Her hair is pulled straight back in a severe boyish cut. A single, emerald-cut diamond, of at least eight carats, graces her neck. The count helps her gather up the material of her evening gown so it doesn't touch the ground and takes her by the hand. They slowly make their way down the red carpet. The staff member who precedes them makes sure that no photographers are able to take a picture, at the insistence of the count.

Next, Hilton Manfreed, accompanied by Baron Rooky his assistant, Enrique Reyes, Zora Tremmon, and Albert Swift exit the Atlas Fitness corporate Hummer. The words "Drug Yourself On Atlas" are written on all three sides and on the hood. Aristotle Khouris's limousine arrives, preceded and followed by security details in separate SUVs. With him are Horst Breckvold, the head of the Worldwide Investment Trust; Maximilian Lipper, chief strategist for TransWorld Energy; and Prince Siegfried IV of Moldavia.

In the lobby, during cocktails, Jonathan Smythe of Consolidated Industries, who had been openly critical of President Cooper during the Corporate Council briefing at the While House two weeks ago, tells Harold Klein of International Networks, another one of the president's critics, that Cooper has lost touch with reality. "I couldn't agree with you more," Klein replies. "In business, it's strictly 'what have you done for me lately?' And Cooper's been nothing but a liability. I know what he hopes to accomplish tonight, but I doubt he can bring it off."

Khouris introduces Breckvold, Lipper, and Siegfried to Smythe and Klein, then leads his guests to their table. "Who are those guys?" Smythe asks Klein. "They're the ones engineering the takeover of countries A, B, and C. Breckvold is the one who will call the loans. Lipper and Siegfried—he's a real prince but he's been living in exile for twenty-five years—have got the money and connections to buy up the assets. They'll lose billions if Cooper loses the election."

Inside the Grand Ballroom, forty tables of ten sit in a horseshoe around a raised platform. The name and corporate logo of each table sponsor are embossed on the 12" high gold dollar that serves as each table's centerpiece. Around it are ten bottles of Atlas Energy Drink, one for each guest. Suspended from the ceiling over the platform is a 30'x10' backdrop that reads "July 4th Made Possible by Gayle's Department Stores."

At 8 p.m., the Grand Benefactor of the event, Mortimer Gayle, goes to the podium and addresses the crowd. "Ladies and gentlemen, fellow investors, those of you here with me in the Washingtonian Hotel, on the National Mall, and, of course, watching on TV nationwide, I am especially delighted to celebrate the founding of the Corporate States of America with you this year.

"What you are about to see is the premiere of an original pageant, 'Atlas Drugged: The Birth of New Atlantis.' Developed at Atlas Fitness Centers, it is a collaboration of some of the finest creative minds in the Corporate States of America. The script, music, and choreography were developed by Bambi Broderick, Thor Rentgen, Rick Michaels, and Cheryl Watkins of the New York Headquarters of Atlas Fitness. The musical accompaniment is provided by the nationally celebrated ensemble, the Gross National Product."

To thunderous applause, Broderick, Rentgen, Michaels, and Watkins appear dressed as early British colonists. Together they chant, "We are the founders of a new nation, conceived in liberty, and dedicated to the proposition that all of us are free to be unequal."

They then shed their costumes and reveal the suits they are wearing underneath.

Grabbing top hats and walking sticks as props, they each put on a different mask—Andrew Carnegie, Andrew Mellon, J.P. Morgan, and John D. Rockefeller—and chant: "They call us robber barons. But they don't really know us. We're all just average guys you'd like to know. Of course, we play by the rules: We made them up. But now that we have prospered, we are being looted."

They clutch their throats with both hands, strangling themselves and appear to wither and collapse. While they are on the ground, the men strip down to thongs; the women, to bikinis. As they slowly rise, in unison they say, "We see hope in a man named Galt." They then hold up bottles of Atlas Energy Drink in their right hands, grow visibly stronger, flex their muscles, and twirl globes of the world on their fingers. "We are Atlas drugged. We are the new John Galts. Drink with us. Get drugged with us."

They then open the bottles of Atlas Energy and all sing, "We've got the whole wor-ld in our hands. We've got the whole wide wor-ld in our hands. We've got the whole wor-ld in our hands! We're drugged on Atlas En-er-gy!"

There's thunderous applause and people jump to their feet. Then, in unison, Broderick, Rentgen, Michael, and Watkins say, "And now, ladies and gentlemen, the president of the Corporate States of America, Ham Cooper."

Cooper rushes onto the stage, shaking the hands of the performers as they leave. Basking in the adulation of the crowd, he makes no effort to stop the applause or signal people to sit. Instead, he beams and stretches both arms up and out in an extended V and makes smaller V's with the index and middle fingers of both hands. After about five minutes, people begin sitting down, so Cooper asks them to continue doing so: "Thank you, thank you, my fellow investors in the Corporate States of America. Please be seated.

"I cannot tell you how thrilled I am to see all of you here tonight, once again celebrating Independence Day. Ever since John Galt defeated the leeches and looters and reclaimed this great land of ours in the name of creative and productive men and women, independence has had a special significance. First, it is freedom *from* everything that stands in our way, principally the government and all the obstacles that it tries to put in our way. Second, it is freedom *to be*—on our own, accountable to no one, owing nobody anything. Once people grasp the true meaning of independence, they experience the liberation that comes from enlightenment, and they pity those who have yet to come to their senses.

"John Galt set an example for everyone to follow. He opened the door to riches for all those who have the guts to follow him. It is no exaggeration to say that John Galt created the Internet. Don't let anyone tell you he didn't. Wherever there is money to be made, John Galt lives. He lives through Atlas Fitness Centers, which are revolutionizing mind-body harmony and are strengthening the next generation for their roles as leaders in the Corporate States and around the globe.

"And, of course, John Galt lives through Count Henry de Horsch, the man we are honoring tonight. He is without a doubt one of the most successful corporate titans of the CSA. He sets the pace for others to follow. He is proof of the principles of Free-for-All economics. Count Henry, please join me here on the stage."

As the count makes his way to the podium, an unidentified voice comes over the sound system and announces, "My fellow Americans, especially those of you watching around the country, the People's Court is now in session." Cooper and Count Henry look out on the audience helplessly. Cooper taps on the microphone. The count looks for wires to unplug. The hotel's sound technician rushes onto the stage.

"Stay calm," the voice continues. "But don't try to leave the room. No one is in danger." Nonetheless, the ballroom is thrown into complete chaos. As people run for the exits, they discover that the doors have been locked, so they go back to their seats or remain standing by the exits. "No one will be hurt," the voice continues reassuringly. "All of you, just return to your seats. You will be able to leave very shortly. As I'm sure you've already discovered," the voice continues, "all cellphone coverage has been blocked within the ballroom. Sit down, now—and listen very carefully. The future of all of you, and of everyone in this country, depends on what you are about to hear.

"In the name of 'the people', we accuse President Cooper and his administration of the death of Adam—and we demand justice. The recent attack on the Cooperville on the National Mall was planned and carried out on the express orders of Ham Cooper, a man who is not worthy to lead this country. He is criminally responsible for the death and violence that took place.

"We accuse Count de Horsch of fraud in the development of Horschville. His massive land grab was totally illegal. We have copies of forged documents executed by de Horsch that prove he has no title to his city. They have been turned over to the proper Mississippi and federal authorities.

"We accuse Hilton Manfreed of plagiarizing. All the ideas in his first book, *What's Mine Is Mine and What's Yours Is Mine*, come from the thesis of one of his students who died in a car accident before he was able to get his degree. He is an academic fraud. The People's Court now rests its case. Now, let all of 'the people' demand justice. You are all free to go. The doors are unlocked. But do not forget, or try to deny, what has taken place here and the undeniable truths that have been exposed."

As though fleeing from a terrorist attack, the president and the count are surrounded by security and escorted out of the ballroom. No one can find Hilton Manfreed. The count and his date disappear into his limousine, but not until he tells Ham Cooper that "he'll pay" for this. "You've lost control, man, and I'm paying the price. You better see what you can do to make things right. I've got billions at stake."

Turning to his date, the count adds, "Well, the night's over, Cinderella. It's time to fork over the goods," he says as he reaches to unclasp the diamond necklace. "You can change into your clothes right here."

"Why you cheap piece of trash," she says once she's in her own clothes.

"Wilson, stop the car. Here's the thousand bucks I promised you," he says practically throwing a wad of bills at her. "This should be more than enough to cover tonight. Take a cab home."

"Keep it, you piece of shit," she says, throwing it back at him. "Your money is dirty. I got principles. But you're a fraud. And you're gonna lose everything."

Back on the Mall, the fireworks display is just about to end. But the finale doesn't go as planned. The last burst of red, white, and blue was supposed to show the face of Ham Cooper. Instead, it proclaims "John Galt Is Dead" across the night sky, no less than three times.

Standing alone on Capitol Hill, the young red head smirks as he watches the confusion break out among the audience on the Mall and chuckles aloud as he watches video of "The People's Court" and the fireworks on his wireless device going viral on social media.

EIGHT

Devastate, Berate, Orchestrate

FRIDAY, AUGUST 5: THE FLORIDA PENINSULA. Tuesday, August 2, the sky was a brilliant, clear blue until 4 p.m. when an unbroken cover of steel-gray clouds suddenly created a canopy over Key West, Florida, obliterating what had promised to be a typical, made-for-tourists sunset. With the clouds came the unique mugginess locals knew was the harbinger of an impending storm, confirming the rumors that had been swirling for the past two days. Fishermen returning from the day's catch had been telling stories of a monster—presumably a hurricane—already moving through the Caribbean.

There was no way to know the intensity or extent of the storm for sure, however. After three failed attempts within the past five years by agents of the Corporate States of America to overthrow the Cuban government and clear the way for businesses to privatize the country's assets, all communication between Washington and Havana came to an abrupt end, including tropical storm tracking that was routinely shared on humanitarian grounds, even when the countries were bitterest enemies. In addition, ten years ago, the National Hurricane Center in Miami was privatized, its assets sold to CallUS.com, a company that specialized in creating Internet-based businesses, specifically call centers.

In short order, the most experienced meteorologists were fired to save money and increase profits. The site posted almost no original weather analysis, but typically repackaged data and information from other sites. Free weather reports disappeared. Only people who could afford to pay could get updates and were prohibited from sharing them or making them public. In the biggest blow to what had once been a model agency, "Hurricane Hunters," the Air Force Weather Reconnaissance Squadron, which flew directly into the eye of storms and provided lifesaving information, was discontinued because it wasn't considered profitable enough. Finally, just last year, CallUS.com declared bankruptcy. While its assets are tied up in court, nothing can be done to replace it, leaving hurricane-prone regions of the CSA defenseless.

So, Wednesday morning, August 3, when residents and visitors in Key West woke up to a pitch black sky, they had no idea what they were in for. Fearless conchs, as residents affectionately call themselves, typically take storms in their stride. They stand pat and snicker at people who run scared. Nothing gets them to evacuate. "Just another storm in paradise," long-time Duval Street resident John Macalister reassured his friends visiting from Syracuse, New York. "We'll get some heavy rain, probably a good deal of flooding. But it won't amount to much." Local TV stations ran banners across their screens, advising people to stay put, but few paid any attention.

By 8:30 a.m., fifteen-foot waves were crashing across the island's wharf. Within half an hour, all streets were under at least six feet of water. Key West looked like a game of pick-up sticks. Buildings that had withstood years of storms were swept away, reduced to rubble. Victims sat perched in trees or hanging on to branches. Everywhere, people—the lucky ones—clung to anything that could float. But heavy rain pelted them, and, with heads bobbing, they struggled to stay alive in water churned by merciless winds. Many had already lost consciousness and drowned. Dead, bloated bodies and the carcasses of hapless pets already outnumbered the living. All power to the island gone. All communication severed.

As the storm made its way north, local, on-the-ground reports pieced together an unimaginable story: the Florida peninsula was either being hit by two storms at once—one on the east coast, the other on the west—or by one storm that split in two. No one could say for sure. But either way, the net effect was the same. On the east coast, the eighteen-mile stretch of bridges connecting the Florida Keys and the mainland was completely destroyed, so there was no way to escape—and no way to bring victims relief, except by helicopter. Using boats was not possible because most docks had been swept away. The trendy art deco district of South Beach on Miami Beach and high-rise buildings along Biscayne Bay were leveled. A tornado destroyed the MacArthur and Julia Tuttle Causeways.

The story was the same as the storm relentlessly made its way up the east and west coasts of the peninsula; city after city leveled. In Fort Lauderdale and surrounding cities, all the bridges over the Intracoastal Waterway had been blown away. Residents of the flooded barrier island have no water or power or any way to reach land or be reached. Palm Beach, the playground of the rich, is no more—its palatial oceanfront mansions now piles of rubble; its residents, homeless. Causeways from the mainland were blown away, so there is no way to help thousands stranded on the island.

Fort Pierce, Cape Canaveral, Titusville, Daytona Beach, St. Augustine, Jacksonville—city after city has been flattened. On the west coast, Naples, Fort Myers, Sarasota, St. Petersburg, Tampa, and Clearwater have been leveled. Two-thirds of the Florida peninsula are cut off from the mainland. I-95 from the Keys to Jacksonville is impassable. I-75 from Fort Lauderdale to Tampa and the I-4 corridor from Tampa to Daytona were swept away and are no more. The Sunshine Skyway Bridge over Tampa Bay has collapsed.

After two of the most destructive days in U.S. history, about twelve million people in Florida are estimated to be homeless and/or living without water or power. About twenty years ago, claiming that existing building codes, written specifically to ensure that structures could withstand hurricane-force winds, cut into their profits, developers successfully lobbied the state legislature to eliminate them.

Frequent gas leak explosions and fires raging out of control are creating panic. Scores of victims who have ignored warnings to stay out of the water because of downed, live power lines have been electrocuted. Vehicles are strewn everywhere, often piled on top of each other. It's being called "the rich man's hurricane" because almost all of the damage has been done to the most expensive private property. Reconnaissance planes and helicopters surveying the damage are recording video of unimaginable devastation and human desperation. Refrigerators and stoves are strewn everywhere. Clothing is scattered, caught in trees, blowing like flags in the wind.

Children's dolls and toys are piled in heaps on land. Some are floating in stagnant pools, clutched tightly in the arms of dead boys and girls. "Help!" has been painted on the rooftops that survived intact and on sheets—and spelled out in scattered debris to draw the attention of aircraft. At the sight of planes possibly bringing help, victims wave furiously, drop to their knees and clasp their hands as though praying, but collapse in despair when they disappear.

The truth is: No help is coming from the government. No help *can* come. There are no public relief agencies at any level—local, state, or federal—to provide assistance because of a disaster, any disaster. A cardinal principle of Free-for-All economics is hands-off government and personal responsibility—no big brother, every man for himself. The market replaced the government. If you could afford to pay for protection, you were supposed to arrange to get it on your own. If you couldn't afford it, you were out of luck. The Corporate States of America abolished all national search, rescue, and aid agencies. And state and federal governments followed suit and disbanded theirs. What survived was a patchwork of for-profit businesses that provide fire, fire rescue, flood, general disaster aid, and related services, to which individuals annually subscribe for a fee. The problem is that most of those corporations have been devastated from the storm and, even if they hadn't been, they didn't have anywhere near the resources they'd need to function after a widespread disaster.

This morning, Friday, August 5, a few helicopters and small boats of private companies from outside of Florida are beginning to land and offer assistance to anyone who can pay. They have limited supplies of canned goods and water. But most people who have money don't have access to it. So, when about fifty victims in the rubble of what used to be Worth Avenue in Palm Beach were told that "money talks, nobody walks," they became so incensed, ten of them wrestled the pilot and two crew members of one helicopter to the ground and held them down, while others ran off with the provisions they carried. Similar scenes are occurring everywhere.

SATURDAY, AUGUST **6, 10** A.M. By video link from Tallahassee, Governor Cris Cott of Florida and, from the Press Room of the White House, President Ham Cooper hold a joint press conference in the aftermath of the recent hurricane.

Malcolm Scott of Floridanews.com: "Governor Cott, four days after the most devastating hurricane in U.S. history has destroyed at least two-thirds of Florida and left an estimated twelve million people homeless, destitute, and cut off from the rest of the country, no help has been forthcoming from the state. Victims are desperate. There are reports of riots and looting in affected areas. What is your plan of action to help them?"

Governor Cott: "Mr. Scott, your question suggests that help in some form *should* be coming from the state, that whenever and wherever there's a problem, government is going to come to the rescue. So, I'm delighted to be able to set the record straight: Government has no role to play. Anyone who thinks it does is guilty of a pre-Galtian, socialist, inhibiting, looter mind-set. The overwhelming majority of the country has evolved way beyond it. You and others who think like you are a tiny minority of reactionaries. Storm preparation is a personal matter for families and individuals, which they can address by being responsible and buying appropriate goods and services from for-profit businesses. The same applies to the aftermath of any disaster. It's the law of the marketplace. The state has no role in it."

President Cooper: "Well said, Governor Cott. Let me add my unconditional support. The federal government also has no role to play. After so many years, I'm shocked that anyone in the CSA still believes in socialism. Why should residents of California or New York or anywhere else have to pay to help people in Florida? If you live in a place where there might be bad storms, it's up to you to protect yourself. That's a basic principle of Free-for-All economics. It's what has made the CSA great and what will keep it great. This is no time to question or abandon the core principles that have made us the envy of the world. It's taken too long for us to get where we are to abandon our beliefs because of one disaster."

Angela Rothbart of *The People's Voice*: "Governor Cott, there are countless reports of people without their medications. Medical personnel on the ground fear the outbreak of infectious diseases. Serious injuries are not being treated. People are dying. Surely, this is a public health crisis of a magnitude that only government can deal with."

Governor Cott: "Ms. Rothbart, who should be responsible for making sure they have enough of their prescriptions on hand at all times? Can you honestly expect the government to send out reminder notices or, better yet, deliver medications to people's homes?"

Angela Rothbart: "Governor, thousands of homes were destroyed. High winds and tornadoes scattered everything over miles. Victims may have had all the medications they needed, but they were blown away."

Governor Cott: "Ms. Rothbart, Ms. Rothbart, private health providers are flying hundreds of medical relief helicopters into affected areas. They will bill insurance companies for services if people have proof of coverage. Anyone without coverage or proof of coverage may pay in cash or with a credit card. So, your statement that this crisis is so big only government can deal with it is totally and completely misguided."

Melinda Farkas of *The Washington Reporter*: "Mr. President, surely you are aware that polls show massive disapproval of the way Washington and Tallahassee are responding to the crisis. How do you explain the serious disconnect between your position and public opinion?"

President Cooper: "I think I can answer for Governor Cott and myself. When people are hurting, for whatever reason, even the most enlightened may look to blame others. That's human nature at its worst—and weakest—giving in to emotion instead of accepting full responsibility for people's personal failure. They refuse to look in the mirror to find the source of their problems. They cannot bring themselves to accept that the uncomfortable position they're in is proof of their own weakness, foolishness, and basic inadequacy. There's no mystery in any of this. But I repeat: that doesn't mean we have to abandon *our* core principles. When there are emergencies, some people are going to suffer. It can't be helped. But everyone has a choice between playing the victim card or standing on their own two feet and turning a bad hand into a winning one. The aftermath of the hurricane is the perfect opportunity for Floridians to rise to the occasion and grow stronger.

Jonathan Brown of *South Florida Today*: "Mr. President, the National Hurricane Center was privatized and eventually the for-profit business that replaced it went bankrupt. People are saying that, if Floridians had had early warning about the extent and force of the hurricane, lives and property could have been saved. In light of the current disaster and failure of the system, do you think the privatization of the Hurricane Center was a mistake and are you considering rebuilding it?"

President Cooper: "The answer to both of your questions is: Absolutely not! I find it truly amazing that, when things get a little tough, there are still people who think that all we should do is return to the days when government coddled its citizens. There was a time when the National Hurricane Center didn't exist and people got along just fine. Then, we went through years of pouring tax money down a rat hole to keep the place going—without any return on the dollar. Once we sold the Center off, everyone could see it was simply a losing proposition. The company that bought it was able to make money selling the land, the building, and its equipment. The CSA was saved from continuing to throw good money after bad. The CSA is not in the business of funding losing propositions."

Governor Cott: "I'd like to add my wholehearted support for President Cooper's position. The CSA federal government lost hundreds of millions of dollars propping up the money-losing National Hurricane Center that never had a chance of breaking even, let alone returning a profit. And since the Center's building was located in Miami, the state of Florida lost millions of dollars because it didn't have to pay taxes. After the for-profit company that took it over went bankrupt, an investment group bought it, and it's finally generating a healthy bottom line. All the tracking equipment was sold off and the original building was leveled. The new multi-purpose, business and residential facility is ten stories. There are shops on the ground floor, parking on two floors, offices and condos on six floors, and a state-of-the-art fitness center on the top floor, complete with an indoor-outdoor swimming pool. That's the CSA spirit of entrepreneurship that drives us in Florida. The whole country needs to keep the cash registers ringing.

Geraldine Fredericks of *Washington Today*: "Gentlemen, what do you say to victims of the disaster who have lost their homes, are literally living exposed to the elements, haven't eaten in going on four days, and who may have been injured or have health issues?"

Governor Cott: "My answer is simple: Get to work. Roll up your sleeves and start digging out and rebuilding your lives. Pay others to help you if you can afford it. Don't wait for anyone to come to your rescue because no one's coming. You live and die in your own skin. If you didn't know that before, you know it now. Floridians need to learn from this experience to better prepare themselves in the future. No one is going to be there to bail them out."

President Cooper: "I'll ditto that, Governor Cott. There is an especially good business opportunity, mostly in the central core of the state, for Floridians who have escaped the most serious loss and damage. But it's also good advice for people anywhere in the CSA. Ask real entrepreneurs and they'll tell you that one person's misery is another person's profit. That's just a simple fact. So, people who can hear this message should hop into their trucks. It won't be long before they wind up in a disaster zone—and start making money."

Agnes Richards of TV 7 Miami: "What *is* the role of government if not to come to the aid of its citizens during crises? Can you *really* believe that we're all on our own, totally alone, that there should be no social structure to help people when they are truly victims of forces beyond their control?"

President Cooper: "Ms. Richards, I can't believe what you're saying. Honestly, I guess living in the White House I have to be reminded from time to time that, as unthinkable as it sounds, there are still people who think as you do. Your questions are filled with all the socialistic buzz words that sent John Galt and his companions on strike in the first place. 'Aid'? Government should come 'to the *aid* of its citizens'? Have you any idea how feeble that thought is? You suggest that responsible adults should simply sit back and wait for someone to make everything better for them, that they have no responsibility to get themselves out of a jam. It's really unbelievable. You suggest that there should be a 'social structure to help people when they are victims of forces beyond their control'? Help and victim are words that should be banned from the English language—at least as it's spoken in the CSA. If I help you because you're a 'victim' for any reason, I make you into a victim for a second time—my victim. What a useless existence that would be! How anyone would want that is beyond me."

George Knight of *The South Florida Times*: "Governor Cott, this disaster has been called 'the rich man's hurricane,' because it has destroyed some of the most expensive homes in Florida. In many cases, property owners paid premiums for years and thought they were insured against hurricanes. But now they're discovering that those companies have gone out of business or don't have reserves to cover claims. What's their recourse? We're getting reports that some people are planning to sue the state."

Governor Cott: "Rich man's hurricane? You media people make up words like that. Mother Nature doesn't know the difference between rich and poor. And it doesn't make any difference to me and the state either. Recourse? Recourse? That word is right up there with "victim" and "help" and "aid" and all the other cop-out vocabulary that people use to get others to sympathize with them and shift the blame onto innocent businessmen, whose *only* job is to maximize profits. I am proud of the fact that, after years and years of sorting through a maze of laws and regulations, the state of Florida freed the insurance industry to compete in the marketplace without profit-killing restrictions. What used to be called consumer protections were nothing more than wealth-redistributing, socialistic schemes to defraud corporations. Sue the state? Let them try! I don't care how much money they have or who they are, whatever gripe they have is strictly between them and their insurer. The state has absolutely no responsibility or liability. They should have protected themselves before they signed a contract."

George Knight: "Governor, a follow-up question, please. Are you saying that the state of Florida has no responsibility to see to it that insurance companies operating within its borders are not committing fraud and are able to cover the policies they issue and live up to the terms of their agreements?"

Governor Cott: "Why of course! I'm saying *exactly* that. How could it be anything but that? Fraud? What's fraud? Isn't it in the eye of the beholder? One person's fraud is another person's not paying attention to the terms of an agreement. Buyer beware is standard operating procedure for anyone with half a brain. Read the fine print. And what about consumers defrauding businesses? Would you have the state protecting corporate interests against the illegal acts of individuals? Shouldn't what's good for one be good for all? The beauty of Free-for-All economics is that the sacred marketplace takes care of everything. You don't need a judge and jury with it. Consumers will spread the word about fraudulent insurance companies, others won't buy policies from them, and they'll go out of business. It's a perfect model!"

George Knight: "Governor, a follow-up question, please."

Governor Cott: "OK, but this is your last one. You're hogging the stage."

"In your scenario, the damage is done and people have to be shafted, before the word gets out that companies are being unethical and ruthless. And there's no guarantee that it will get out quickly and to enough people or that people will believe what they hear—assuming that the accusations are accurate."

"Mr. Knight, there are no guarantees in life. Grow up. Accept ultimate freedom. You lead your life alone, on your own. Don't expect anyone or anything, especially the government, to be there for you."

Phillip Cohen of *Washington Insider*: "Governor, five years ago, you signed into Florida law a sweeping bill that replaced state building codes and preempted county and local standards designed to ensure construction that was able to withstand hurricanes. Do you regret doing that— and do you plan to reinstate former building codes that deal specifically with hurricane conditions?"

Governor Cott: "In a word, no. The codes we eliminated cost developers too much, increased the price of new construction, and reduced jobs. The government has absolutely no role to play in micromanaging construction. If developers want to build to a hurricane-proof standard, the choice should be theirs and theirs alone. If customers want stronger construction, they can pay extra for it. And insurance companies can charge more or less for policies based upon criteria they establish. That's the beauty of the Free-for-All market."

Phillip Cohen: "A follow-up, please. President Cooper, with two-thirds of Florida destroyed, what steps do you plan to take from Washington to help businesses recover?"

President Cooper: "Mr. Cohen, you're obviously asking a leading question because you assume that the CSA should do something in the first place. Well, let me go on record, as I've said before: Those businesses will survive and thrive that take care of themselves, without expecting anything from anyone else. If everyone in a given business pitches in and digs out from the debris, they'll have a bright future. If they don't, they don't deserve to continue. Do you think our pioneer forefathers relied upon the government to rescue them as they tramped across the Continental Divide? Of course not! They set out to overcome unknown obstacles with the kind of resolve that made this country great. That's what we've got to keep reinforcing. To keep the CSA strong, we've got to keep individuals resolved to look no farther than the end of their nose for the power to succeed."

Governor Cott: "President Cooper, ladies and gentlemen, this concludes our press conference."

From back of the room in Tallahassee, a tall, unidentified, red-headed, young man shouts out, "President Cooper, Carey Hinton is saying that you have abandoned Floridians in their time of dire need and is making that an issue in the presidential election." But Cooper is already out of earshot.

MONDAY, AUGUST 8, 10 A.M.: THE WHITE HOUSE CABINET ROOM. President Cooper and Florida Governor Cott are meeting with the executive committee of the Corporate Council. Cooper is beaming. For the first time, he appears jubilant after the monumental embarrassment of the July 4th gala. He slowly looks around the room, shoots both arms over his head like an Olympian winning a gold medal, fists clenched, and proclaims, "Gentlemen, we're here to carve up a pie called Florida. It's huge and each one of you can get in on the ground floor. There's no limit to how much money you can make. This is pure Free-for-All economics. The recent sweeping disaster is nothing less than the windfall we've all been waiting for, but could never have imagined or engineered. It's a godsend, my fellow patriots. The storm hit mostly the richest areas of the state. Those people have got insurance. Plus, they'll personally pay extra and do anything to get their property rebuilt. You're all going to have a whole state to privatize. It could become a model for the rest of the country. I don't mean to get carried away, but I'm sure all of you can see where this is going. If you play your cards right, you'll make profits you could never have dreamed of. Governor Cott, please share your thoughts with us."

"First, I'd like to ditto President Cooper's reading of the situation and the enormous, unprecedented riches that await you," says Cott. "We're here to transform the state of Florida into Florida, Inc. As the president said, if we play our cards right, and I see no reason why we wouldn't, we can wipe away the last vestiges of state government that have stood in our way of creating a pure corporate state."

"Governor Cott and I would now like to hear your thoughts on how we might proceed to create Florida, Inc. Feel free to speak up and share your ideas. Be bold. This is a unique time in our history and we should let our imaginations run wild. With the right strategy, what happens in Florida won't stay in Florida, but it will set the pace for the rest of the CSA. That's forty-nine other ways for you to reap trillions of dollars. Yes, you heard me. That's trillions with a T!"

"Gentlemen, I'm Jonathan Smythe of Consolidated Industries. First, let me say that I totally agree with you that we have an historic opportunity to achieve John Galt's vision. I've been imagining a corporate-takeover scenario for years. I suggest that we turn Florida into seven profit centers individually owned and operated." He moves to the front of the room holding a map of the state. "I've drawn a line up the middle of the peninsula, then one east to west from just south of Fort Pierce to Sarasota, and another from just below Daytona Beach past Ocala to the west coast. I've also drawn a north-south line east of Tallahassee, creating a zone from the capital to the Alabama border. In my proposal, those seven profit centers would be for sale to the highest bidder—members of the Corporate Council, of course. Corporations could own one or more—or all seven. What used to be called government would become Florida, Inc., a board of directors made up of the owners of the zones."

"I love the overall concept, Jonathan," Cott says, "but how do we take over existing government assets and the property and other assets of existing individuals and businesses?"

"Governor, I told you I've been running various scripts in my mind for years, including how we could sell the idea to the public. You could issue an executive order, declaring the entire state a disaster. You could call it something like 'The Florida Humanitarian Relief and Restoration Initiative.' In due time, you can get the legislature to approve establishing Florida, Inc., a holding company, retroactively, to tie it up neatly in a bow. Under the Initiative, you would first declare the existing state bankrupt because it is self-insured and without the money to rebuild the physical structures it owns and to provide the services it has in the past. That would open up the door to sweeping privatization.

"In addition, private individuals and businesses would be given sixty days to establish their claims to real property. That's all we really care about because, with control of the land, we control everything.

Under powers of eminent domain granted to you in the Initiative, in the public interest, you would confiscate all undocumented property in the name of the state. Documented rights to property would be compensated at ten cents on the dollar out of state funds, less whatever insurance companies pay out. Then, you could open up the zones, like Smythe suggests, to the highest bidder."

Harold Klein of International Networks gets up to speak: "Mr. President, Governor, my fellow investors, what I've heard so far is encouraging, but let me remind you that we've got to keep our eye on the ball. We need to be practical and strategic or we'll get creamed. Before we talk about which way to carve the lines of the profit zones, we've got to be absolutely clear that we can create a clean, swift, permanent basis upon which to confiscate everything in the name of Florida, Inc. There can't be any backtracking. If we show any sign of weakness, the whole project will come tumbling down. After that, we can do whatever we wish. Our success will depend upon public relations, which have not gone all that well for us, may I remind you: The Adam case! We need an ironclad message that 'the people' will swallow."

"I agree with everything that's been said already," says Aristotle Khouris, "and I'd like to remind you that, as I emphasized when we last met, my investors have already put trillions of dollars on the table. Let me repeat, trillions, not billions, banking on the three-country European strategy that I've been putting together for the last three years. I am confident that we can add upwards of $500 billion to the Florida project. We've already run the preliminary numbers on what it would mean to our bottom line, especially because we can use some of the same tactics we've used in Europe in signing on to Florida, Inc. As you may recall, after the November election, the Worldwide Investment Trust is ready to force countries A, B, and C—you all know who they are—into default by calling loans they have no chance of repaying.

"In addition to everything that's been suggested, we can get the banks to do the same thing to property owners in Florida. Then, we can seize them and open the bidding to privatize all public services and resources. Just like we're doing overseas, we can auction off power companies, seaports, airports, national lotteries, state-owned media, national banks, railway systems, and airports. Everything will be sold at fire-sale prices. If there are any protests from state and private company workers who'll lose their jobs or who have to take a pay cut, they won't have a leg to stand on."

Mortimer Gayle, of Gayle's Department Stores, rises: "Gentlemen, gentlemen, you know that, in general, I support everything you're saying—and why you're saying it. You're talking about a grand scheme, but I've got an immediate problem. Twenty of my department stores in Florida were completely destroyed, leveled, scattered like pick-up sticks. From the way you're talking, you're gonna put me out of business. I'm already losing millions."

"Mortimer," Governor Cott says, smiling. "Mortimer, you know we *always* take care of our friends. Gayle's Department Stores will be eligible for millions in corporate incentive grants, which you'll *never* have to repay. Just tell us how much you want and we'll open the spigot. In addition, choose the ideal locations where you'd like to relocate your stores and we'll see to it that they are turned over to you. As you know, we have our ways. You don't have to be limited to the places where you used to operate. Remember: the state will be a clean slate. It belongs to us—to you, to everyone in this room. You're in on the ground floor."

President Cooper then says, "Mortimer, of course I echo the governor. In addition to getting rid of all the regulations that have hindered development in recent years, Washington is declaring a moratorium on any and all existing rules that in any way would stand in the way of your free rein to build and rebuild. I am signing an executive order to that effect this afternoon. Consider Florida yours for the taking."

"Within ten days," says Governor Cott, "you'll be receiving a VIP copy of the auction catalog listing all resources and assets within Florida so you can bid on them. In addition, based upon the suggestions you've made today, as well as those we've already received, we will be issuing a draft plan of Florida, Inc."

"Governor Cott," Franklin Reynolds of Continental Health System calls out, as he rises to speak, "there are literally millions of Floridians who remain stranded throughout the state. Daily, we're hearing reports of illnesses that could become epidemics, if they haven't already. What is being done or what do you plan to do to help those in such dire need?"

Governor Cott, shaking his head and pursing his lips in disbelief: "You have just uttered the most despicable word in the English language—'help'. I'd like to outlaw it. We don't *help* people. People help themselves. If you haven't understood that concept, if it doesn't already run through your veins, I don't understand what you're doing here."

"But, governor," Reynolds says, interrupting him. "This is a public relations problem. If you don't do something to make it look as though you have a strategy to help people—sorry if you don't like the word—it could come back to haunt you as you implement Florida, Inc. There are things you can do—window-dressing—to stop any backlash that might hamper your efforts."

"I couldn't give a shit about threats of backlash," says Cott, "and window-dressing is for department stores. No offense, Mortimer. I came into office to continue and expand Free-for-All economic policies—and not to give an inch. This is no time to back down. I'm not going to waste time listing all the accomplishments I've had since I became state CEO. But I'd like to remind you, in case any of you have forgotten, that I have made Florida the most corporate-friendly state in the nation. Now, I'm ready to take it to the next step by making it a pure corporate state. I'm delivering it to you on a silver platter, now that it's dropped into our laps. Miss this opportunity and there's no telling when another one may come our way.

"This is no time to back down. We've got total control of the Florida peninsula—and I don't have to kowtow to anyone. Mr. Reynolds, the *real* story you should know is that the marketplace is already working precisely as it should throughout devastated Florida, without 'the government' needing to intervene. Private helicopter services are flying in supplies and selling water, tents, generators, and other essential equipment. At competitive rates, they are also evacuating people who prefer, and have the means to pay, to leave. Amphibious craft are landing along the Florida coasts, bringing earth-moving and other heavy equipment to clear areas for people who are willing to begin the reconstruction process. Many are willing to pay, even before their insurance companies do an assessment.

"So, I hope you realize that the simple answer—the only answer to your question—is that Florida is helping those who can help themselves, which means we *help* no one. Those who can't afford to pay the price have only themselves to blame. None of us was put on this earth to pick up every deadbeat and fall for every hard luck story. End of story. I'm amazed that we have to keep repeating the first principle of John Galt's Restoration, but I guess that's just the cross those of us in leadership positions have to bear. Now, if you'll excuse the president and me, we've got some serious planning to do to maximize your bottom lines."

As they leave, Aristotle Khouris runs up to Governor Cott and says, "I've got a blank check for you from my international consortium as soon as you're ready to deal."

NINE

Slugged, Bugged, Mugged

THURSDAY, AUGUST 11, 10 A.M.: THE OFFICE OF THE MANHATTAN DISTRICT ATTORNEY. New York District Attorney Herman Coffey is about to begin a press conference to announce grand jury indictments of the principals of Atlas Fitness Centers and New Atlantis for manslaughter, fraud, prostitution, theft of intellectual property, suppression of evidence, and embezzlement.

DA Coffey: "Thank you all for coming here on such short notice. As a result of a six-month grand jury investigation, today I am announcing a seventeen-count indictment against Enrique Reyes, Zora Tremmon, and Albert Swift, the principals of Atlas Fitness Centers, and Professor Hilton Manfreed and the trustees of New Atlantis. This sweeping indictment, copies of which all of you will receive, alleges that the defendants engaged in a multi-faceted conspiracy, not merely for financial gain, but, as their marketing program states, to create acolytes of Free-for-All economics. They were obsessed with drugging the world on every form of Atlas to maintain and enhance the momentum of the John Galt Restoration. In the process, they consistently conspired to violate the trust of those with whom they did business. They jeopardized the public health. And they operated with a flagrant disregard for the proven, adverse effects of their products and services on individuals and the public interest. As a personal aside, I am sorry to say that, in my twenty years as district attorney, I have never seen such callous indifference to the welfare of others as these defendants exhibited. Simply put, they would stop at nothing to achieve their ends."

Rising, without waiting to be called on, Bradley Sims, of TheReporter.com says, "Mr. Coffey, how can you refer to what you call 'the public interest' when ..."

"If you don't mind, Mr. Sims," Coffey interrupts, "I'd like to finish my statement before answering questions. I'll be happy to speak to your point in a few minutes, because it raises an issue that is not only central to this case but that goes to the heart of what we have become as a corporate nation under the CSA. But first, I'd like to tell you how we got where we are today. It's important for you—and for the general public—to understand the painstaking process we went through before making today's announcement. So much was at stake in terms of individuals' reputations and finances that we always err on the side of caution.

"About eight months ago, we were made aware of the website www.notatlas.com, which had been established by a disgruntled and frustrated member of an Atlas Fitness Center in Chicago. He reported having a number of bad reactions—nausea, dizziness, vomiting—to the Atlas Energy Drink. When he spoke to his trainer, the answer he received was that it was flat-out impossible, that the drink was constantly being tested to ensure its safety and effectiveness for human consumption, that there obviously was something wrong with *him*.

"Still, every time he consumed the Energy Drink, he had the same reactions. So, he decided to find out if others had similar problems. Two hours after his website was online, it crashed because so many complaints poured in from around the country—and not only complaints, but reports of far more serious reactions. Several people were said to have collapsed and to have convulsions—and a total of twelve were said to have died in Atlas Fitness Centers across the country. In each case, center personnel, along with executives in the New York headquarters, vehemently denied any relationship between Atlas products and regimens.

"The indictment alleges that Atlas Energy Drink is harmful and that the principals of Atlas Fitness had every reason to suspect it *was* deleterious, but instead conspired to act in wanton disregard of indisputable evidence. Furthermore, it is alleged that the claim that objective scientific studies proved that Atlas Energy Drink is safe and effective is a lie. Researchers who allegedly validated the drink were actually paid to endorse it, and in all cases never even tested the product. In addition, after receiving reports of serious illness and death, management specifically did not test Energy Drink batches prepared in laboratories in China, Guatemala, and the Philippines, where there was every reason to suspect contaminated product originated.

"The indictment also alleges that the New York headquarters of Atlas Fitness was the center of a national prostitution ring with major plans for expansion. Under the guise of serving VIP clients through "Elite Services," personal fitness trainers, male and female, became paid escorts providing sexual favors. A highly lucrative commission system was added to trainers' base salary. Private suites were set aside in the building. VIP clients had access to the facility 24/7. At a recent meeting of franchisees, proprietors were counseled individually about how they could enhance their bottom line through such illicit activity.

"Furthermore, the indictment alleges that the principals suppressed evidence proving conclusively that use of the so-called Titan Whole-Body Harmony Machine can lead to irreparable damage to the lower back. In a separate action, the owner of the international patent to the machine in Norway is suing for the theft of his intellectual property, alleging that he, not Albert Swift, is the inventor of the original *Titan Hele Kroppen Harmoni Maskin* and holds all rights to its manufacture and distribution. I'll be happy to take questions. Now, Mr. Sims, what were you saying?"

"Mr. Coffey," Sims says, "how can you refer to what you call 'the public interest' when it doesn't exist in the CSA?"

"Though it is true that the phrase 'the public interest' has been virtually eliminated from the law and public policy considerations in the CSA, not all of us are immoral."

Judy White of *Business Today*: "Mr. Coffey, What is the status of Atlas Fitness Centers and New Atlantis at this moment?"

"Last week, based upon the grand jury report, Judge Cynthia Minder granted a preliminary injunction against the sales of Atlas Energy Drink, the use of the Titan Machine, and all activities of Atlas Fitness."

Judy White: "What does that mean in practical terms?"

"It has been effectively shut down. And, as of 5 p.m. yesterday, Atlas Fitness Centers sought Chapter 11 bankruptcy protection. In addition, New Atlantis has ceased all operations."

Malcolm Donnelly of *RighttoKnow.com*: "As a follow-up to Sims's question, how can you indict the defendants on the grounds that they violated what you seem to be calling 'the public interest,' when that concept has been systematically abandoned, even openly ridiculed, in the CSA? Federal regulations safeguarding consumers no longer exist. The FDA was dismantled decades ago. What is the basis for any cause of action?"

"You are absolutely correct, as a governing, societal concept 'the public interest' has long been replaced by the principle of 'the market,' Free-for-All economics, to be exact—and the entire super-structure that protected average Americans was systematically dismantled, with the complicity of 'the people,' I might add. 'The people,' as you refer to them, let it happen. They sat back and did absolutely nothing. They were seduced by the freedom they were told Free-for-All economics would bestow upon them—and everyone.

"Nonetheless, the grand jury found grounds for indictments on the basis of conspiracy. It's a cause of action that is actually boomeranging on the Free-for-All establishment. The concept remains in the laws of the CSA only because it was deemed a necessary protection for corporations against attacks from competitors, as well as from employees undercutting businesses for which they worked. We believe that it can easily be applied to Atlas Fitness because the named principals and their accomplices conspired against the interests of their franchisees, employees, and Fitness Center members. I guess you could say that it's a good-old case of karma or, if you prefer, what goes around comes around!"

Curly Franken of *The People's Reporter*: "Have individuals or groups of individuals alleging they've been harmed filed lawsuits? Are there any class action, malpractice, and product liability complaints likely?"

"No. As you know, corporations have been legally protected from those and similar causes of action for decades. Two cardinal principles of Free-for-All economics are 'buyer beware' and 'the market is the best, and only, watchdog.' In other words, pure markets are alleged to be self-correcting and moral: In time, people will discover that a product or service doesn't live up to its claims, the word will get out, consumers will stop buying, and companies will stop producing what the public doesn't want to buy. Of course, until then, a lot of damage may be done, but that doesn't seem to concern advocates of Free-for-All. No, on the grounds you mention, there is no way to protect consumers."

Reynolds Goldsmith of *Legal Times*: "Is this case likely to set a precedent?"

"I think it's too soon to draw any major conclusions from this one incident, especially without any backlash from the public. I wouldn't want to speculate. But, based upon past indifference, I doubt anything will change anytime soon."

Portia Klein of *BehindtheScenes.com*: "How was the prostitution ring exposed?"

"As you can imagine, this is a most damning aspect of the case against Atlas Fitness—and perhaps the most ironclad. As you can see in the indictment, in addition to testifying, our source, whom we call 'the red head' for his protection, provided logs of encounters, names and addresses of clients, and fees paid, as well as video of private sessions. Numerous prostitutes and clients were deposed, including Count Henry de Horsch. The count not only hired males and females for sexual favors, he invested in Atlas Fitness and entered into a profit-sharing arrangement from the 'Elite Services' at the Midtown Manhattan Atlas Center. In the end, he had no choice but to turn state's evidence in exchange for our dropping trafficking charges against him. In short, he sang like a bird!"

Jonathan Riddle of *The Times*: "Do you anticipate lawsuits by franchisees for breach of contract and fraud, other federal indictments, and legal action by international entities?"

"I'll repeat what I said, or implied, before: At this point, almost anything and everything is possible. The ramifications of this case are endless. But there's a maze of evidence still to follow and no telling exactly where it might lead. At one level, the indictments go to the heart of the CSA itself. It is no secret that Atlas Fitness Centers became the financial engine of New Atlantis, which has been the driving ideological force behind Free-for-All economics and our entire political and economic system. With those two entities now totally discredited, it is hard to imagine what the future holds. We'll just have to wait and see. Again, I want to thank all of you for coming, and I promise to let you know as soon as we have other information to report."

MONDAY, AUGUST 15, 10 A.M.: UNDISCLOSED LOCATION. In the master control room of the Prometheus Project, Zeus calls an emergency session to order.

"Olympus, Pandora, Mercury, and Adonis, thank you all for responding on such short notice. Things are happening faster than we could ever have hoped or imagined. These are the moments we have been waiting for. I hope all of you are prepared. Believe me when I tell you 'this is it.' It's 'make it or break it.' Our time has come. It's right up there with the war with the Titans. We won our first major battle at New Atlantis on June 4th , when Olympus blindsided the annual celebration of the John Galt Restoration and declared John Galt dead. As all of us saw, the smug bastards never knew what hit them—or where it came from. I laugh every time I see the furious face of that smarmy Professor Manfreed after we rattled his cage. He and his accomplices have been scratching their heads ever since. They still haven't figured out who we are. It was the first major test of StarWords and it worked to perfection.

"Before we plot our next step, we'll start with an update. As all of you know by now, Atlas Fitness Centers and New Atlantis are out of business—and not only out of business, but disgraced, under indictment for a vast conspiracy that should wind up sending all of the perpetrators to prison. And we have our very own Adonis to thank for it. He managed to infiltrate the Manhattan headquarters and, eventually, discover the secrets of the operation. Adonis, you were tight-lipped in June when you gave us your update—and we understand why, especially now. But please fill in all the blanks for us."

A picture of Adonis broadly smiling appears on screen five, his red, curly hair pulled back in a ponytail, shoulders back accentuating his bare chest. "Thank you, Zeus. But I share any credit for taking down Atlas Fitness with Olympus, of course. Once again, StarWords proved that no one can escape us. I'm sorry if it looked to you and my fellow Histheans as though I were holding anything back or just being coy. No offense intended. I had every reason to believe that I was on the verge of getting all the information I needed to expose the conspiracy at Atlas Fitness, but I still didn't have solid proof. As much as I suspected things were rotten, I wasn't prepared for just how corrupt they really were.

"When the Manhattan District Attorney announced the grand jury indictments at his press conference last Thursday, he had to be cautious and couldn't editorialize about its merits. Plus, his legalese blunted the depth and scope of the conspiracy. But I can tell you the unvarnished truth. Perhaps the most shocking thing is that Atlas Fitness Centers were *never* intended to be a legitimate business. It was a fraud and a con from the start. The company principals—Reyes, Tremmon, and Swift—were Professor Manfreed's model students at New Atlantis. They mastered—I should say learned how to exploit—the free rein presented by the Free-for-All marketplace. They never expected to get caught. They figured the system was on their side, rigged for them to make obscene profits—forever.

"One night, after he'd had several glasses of wine too many, Enrique told me the whole story of Atlas Fitness. While they were brainstorming business plans, Zora came up with the idea of 'drugging' people on Atlas. But she had said nothing more than 'We've got to find a way to get people hooked on Atlas. It will make money for New Atlantis and money for us. We've got to drug them.' Enrique ran with it: 'Suppose we come up with a drink that promises to make their dreams come true, to make them Super Atlases—that gives them energy, stimulates their brains, prepares them to succeed in the marketplace,' he suggested.

"Not to be outdone, by the next day, Swift, who had been a fitness freak for years, presented the idea of creating a holistic body balancing machine. With those two concepts, they had created a draft business plan for what they called the ultimate fitness center that would make money for them and for New Atlantis and, at the same time, make zealous converts to Free-for-All economics. With positioning like that, they knew they could get all the start-up money they needed from the Taggart Venture Fund. And they were right. Instantly, Manfreed was sold on the idea, and, from then on, there was no stopping the trio.

"Of course, there were two things missing: the miracle drink and the machine they were supposed to have. But that didn't faze them for a minute. In the Free-for-All marketplace a minor technicality like that doesn't matter. They knew that they could eventually concoct something. After all, it wasn't as though their products had to work. The CSA had done away with all consumer protection agencies and laws. So, they had free rein to sell, and make claims for, the effectiveness of anything they could dig up. Proudly, Enrique told me that he mixed the first batch of Atlas Power Drink in his kitchen. I overheard the three of them laughing that his 'secret' formula turned out to be ninety percent water and ten percent spinach juice—and saying they would never drink the stuff themselves. When Enrique reminded them that he had made the drink green so people would think of money, they laughed even harder.

"Reyes and Tremmon were shocked and delighted when Swift brought in a sketch of 'his' unique exercise machine, which he said he had developed years ago and for which he made spectacular claims. At the time, he boasted that no one had created anything like it anywhere in the world. Zora is *truly* a marketing genius. So, on the spot she began creating promotional materials. Swift was thrilled when she blurted out that independent scientific studies revealed that regular use of the machine lowers body rhythms, harmonizes the brain, and produces unique levels of physical strength.

"Then, without so much as a shred of proof, she found an ingenious way to link Reyes's drink formula with Swift's machine. She came up with the corporate name 'Atlas Fitness Center' and then developed the idea of offering a proprietary, thirty-day program that combined a regimen of the Atlas Energy Drink and the Titan Machine that would guarantee weight loss, energy gain, and total-body toning. She even made up the claim that there was scientific research to prove that the program actually cures conditions like diabetes and shows promising early signs of helping reverse the effects of spinal cord injury and Parkinson's.

"Reyes, Tremmon, and Swift set out to drug the world on Atlas, but, in the end, they drugged themselves on pure greed. In June, I said I was on to a 'dirty little secret.' But it turned out to be a big, sleazy, and profitable one. To their credit, running a high-priced whorehouse was never part of their initial business plan. They just fell into it. With all of those hot, pumped-up bodies parading around the Manhattan headquarters, it wasn't long before clients and trainers were hitting on each other.

"The idea for 'Elite Services' actually came from Count Henry de Horsch, who, with a wink and a nod, framed it as a way to establish discrete, profitable, and 'meaningful' relationships between clients and trainers. The trio read between the lines. And once they heard it, their Free-for-All market instincts went into high gear. Atlas Fitness was cash-strapped at the time, because membership revenue had slumped. All they saw were dollar signs. The count offered to fund what he called a 'state-of-the-art' expansion of headquarters, providing patrons with 24/7 access to staff.

"It seems that the count had propositioned one of the male trainers in headquarters. But, after a few awkward trysts outside the facility, he was desperate to find a totally discrete location because of his high profile and connections in Washington and specifically the White House. With the count's financial help and business savvy, the trio developed a lucrative commission schedule for trainers and facilities that catered to fetishes you can't even imagine—at least I couldn't. At their recent national sales meeting, they were already showing franchisees how to implement their own 'Elite Services.' The count even offered to write an expanded headquarters into his proposal for the private development of Central Park. Smack in the middle of the family-friendly mall and amusement park he pitched to the city, patrons would be able to fulfill any fantasy 24/7—for a hefty price.

"Eventually, they made me the head of what they called the VIP Division. I scheduled all appointments, maintained all client contact information, processed payments, and even paid commissions. Thanks to Olympus, the secrets in the VIP Division were completely recorded and exposed. No one at headquarters suspected a thing. And, when the time came, the grand jury got more than they ever imagined. The conspiracy surrounding Atlas Energy Drink and the Titan Machine outraged the grand jury. But when they saw undeniable proof that headquarters had turned into a whorehouse, including the juicy tapes, you could see the fire in their eyes. The proceedings had to be adjourned for an hour."

"Adonis," Zeus says emphatically, "we all thank you for your update and for the role you've played in bringing down Atlas Fitness and New Atlantis. You managed to disarm the enemy, ingratiate yourself, and never lose sight of the goal. But, as I know you all realize, we have to move on. We're jumping from the frying pan directly into the fire.

"Now, everyone, take a look at screen six. The hundreds of thousands of people you now see surrounding the White House are *your* people. They have been pouring into the capital since August 8th, after all of you went to work urging them to protest. We have effectively shut down Washington, D.C. and paralyzed President Cooper's administration for almost a solid week. Cooper and his Corporate Council thought that, behind closed doors, they could carve up the state of Florida and profit from the massive devastation after the worst hurricane in this country's history. The Florida governor was in on the whole plot. He and his family had even set up companies to get a piece of the action. They didn't give a damn about all the people suffering on the ground. They were blinded by dollar signs. All they cared about was the bottom line. Olympus, tell us what you did."

"Thanks, Zeus. The *real* hero of our strategy is StarWords. When we met in June, I told all of you that, when we put Manfreed into a slow burn at New Atlantis, interrupting him and declaring John Galt dead, it was just the beginning. That day, we proved the power of our audio transmission, our 'invisible voice,' as an offensive weapon. On August 8th, StarWords moved to a whole new level. It was the first test of our video interception system. We managed to foil all defensive systems at the White House and penetrate right into the Cabinet Room. Secretly, we recorded the audio and video of Cooper's top secret meeting with his Corporate Council. Frankly, as we were doing it, I almost became physically ill. Those bastards knew people were desperate—injured, even dying, in Florida. But they couldn't have cared less.

"We got it all on tape. They were plotting the ultimate free-for-all from Free-for All economics—as long as you were one of them. They named their plan Florida, Inc. They already controlled public property and assets. But, by declaring the state a disaster after the recent hurricane, they were going to confiscate all private property. I know it sounds bizarre, but that's what they were planning. For example, they were going to confiscate all land whose clear title could not be established and, where ownership could be determined, pay ten cents on the dollar, at best. Then, all assets were going to be put into Florida, Inc., an umbrella private corporation, which would sell off land, long term contracts for providing services, and literally everything in the peninsula to private businesses—for little or nothing. Mortimer Gayle was promised prime sites for his department stores. Foreign investors were proposing to take over water and power companies. They were debating whether to establish economic zones, but couldn't decide whether they should run east-west or north-south and where the lines should be drawn.

"While people in Florida were desperate, they were planning to convert the state into the equivalent of a huge department store—with themselves and their cronies as the owners. People would have to pay for everything they needed or do without. All-Florida Transport was proposing to buy the rights to all roads, create travel zones, and charge tolls to drive within them. You could buy an annual pass for one or more zones or for the whole state. If you didn't want to, or couldn't afford it, you'd simply have to walk or ride with someone else. It's unimaginable to me, even as I'm recounting it. In short, they were planning to seize what they called 'a once-in-a-generation-opportunity' to implement pure Free-for-All economics and create a sweeping corporate model that could be replicated nationwide.

"Because of StarWords, as soon as the meeting was adjourned, I was able to send a link to the transmission to Pandora. And she sent it to all Coopervilles over our secure, wireless network, and they spread the word to their local networks. In June, she reported that we could reach upwards of ten million people. Just two months later, she estimates that we now connect almost seventy-five million, and that doesn't count the millions to which those seventy-five million connect. The callous, conniving conversations between Cooper and the Corporate Council enraged everyone who heard and saw them. The video went viral worldwide. Of course, the media immediately picked up the story. Almost immediately, Mercury organized flash mobs around the country protesting Florida, Inc.

"Mercury called for a massive march on Washington. Tens of thousands—by now hundreds of thousands—of protestors have overwhelmed the capital. Within a day, the White House was surrounded and Cooper had to call in the National Guard to protect the perimeter. But they could only access the grounds by helicopter because all streets leading to the mansion were blocked. It turned into a veritable tent city, people camped out as far as the eye could see. Tuesday morning, August 9th, in the middle of the night, the president and his staff fled by helicopter to Camp David, while enflamed mobs were screaming 'Murderers,' 'Coward Cooper Kills,' 'Damn Ham,' 'Fire Cooper.'

"Of course, we were able to record his skulking away and the crowd's withering reaction. By daybreak, the picture of a cowering Cooper surrounded by security being led to the helicopter was on the front page of every newspaper. All TV programming was preempted and the video was played and replayed non-stop. The plot to profit from the Florida disaster was burning up social media platforms worldwide. One tweet summed up the situation so well it was quoted again and again: "@averageAmerican Is the CSA a country or a cash register?"

"Thank you, Olympus, and Pandora and Mercury, of course," Zeus says. "If you look closely at screen six in the upper left-hand corner, you'll see what I think is the most poignant picture of all. I've been watching it day after day. There's a large, yellow flag with a picture of a young boy on it and the words 'Cooper Killed Adam.' It refers, of course, to the brutal attack on the National Mall Cooperville when the innocent, helpless, young boy, Adam, was trampled to death and the encampment was bulldozed and turned into bonfires. The incident became a spark that ignited mass outrage—and the most compelling anti-Cooper event the world had ever seen. Most of the people who were sent on the forced march from the encampment into RFK Stadium have joined the protest camp around the White House.

"With the end of Atlas Fitness and New Atlantis, there's hope for our future. But as long as Cooper remains in office and the CSA follows the principles of Free-for-All economics, we still have much work to do. Cary Hinton must win the presidency."

MONDAY, AUGUST 15, 1 P.M.: CAMP DAVID, MARYLAND. It has been almost a week since President Cooper and his entourage arrived within the safe confines of the presidential retreat in the Catoctin Mountain Park. When Navy One, his helicopter, hovered over the grounds of the White House to whisk him away to safety, the president looked out in disbelief over what had become an occupied capital. He could hear shouts of "Cooper kills" from the crowds closest to the mansion, who suddenly had been awakened by the noise of the copter's rotors. In the middle of the night, the city was pitch black. But, here and there, the ghostly silhouettes of protestors wrapped in a shroud of night-mist could be seen in patches of light from small fires burning everywhere.

Exhausted and shocked, Cooper sat by himself—his fists drawn together, knees up, almost in a fetal position—and spoke to no one. No one spoke to him. As he looked out over the city—*his city*, he thought—all he could keep asking himself over and over was *How did this happen? How could this happen? What has gone so terribly wrong?* But once the copter reached altitude and was en route to Camp David, suddenly his attitude turned defiant. Clenching his fists as though preparing for a fight, he thought, *This must have been how the Romans felt when the barbarians overran them. Who do they think they are? I'm the president of the CSA. I'm not going to take this lying down from a bunch of nobodies. By the time I'm through with those bastards, they'll wish they had never started up with me.*

In the days since Navy One touched down at Camp David, Cooper had used its peaceful setting to plot an all-out attack on his own people—an unprecedented action in the annals of presidential history. Jimmy Carter brokered the Camp David Accords there between Egyptian President Anwar al-Sadat and Israeli Prime Minister Menachem Begin. Past American presidents had used the relaxed, country retreat as a quiet getaway. John F. Kennedy and his family enjoyed horseback riding there. Lyndon Johnson, Gerald Ford, Ronald Reagan, Bill Clinton, George W. Bush had mixed business with pleasure, hosting dignitaries and celebrities there. George W. and Barack Obama made the camp's Evergreen Chapel their primary place of worship.

But now, for Cooper, Camp David has become a war room, ground zero for "Operation Liberation," code name for routing protestors from the capital. Cooper has called a meeting of his FBI and Homeland Security Directors and Defense Secretary to finalize the attack.

"Gentlemen," he begins, "the infiltration of the inner recesses of the White House and the recording and broadcasting of our secret session on Florida, Inc. is the biggest breach in security the CSA has ever known. It is all-out treason. Two months ago, when that mystery voice invaded New Atlantis and declared John Galt dead, I warned all of you that it was just the beginning.

"Now, we must declare open war on our enemies and wipe them out once and for all. If we don't, the Galtian Restoration will have failed. *We* will have failed it. And I will go down in history as the president who lost the glory of the Corporate States of America and Free-for-All economics. I cannot, I will not, let that happen. Florida, Inc. is a golden opportunity. It comes along once in a generation, if ever. We are in a struggle for our souls.

"Thank Galt we didn't depend upon the piss-ass strategy some egghead consultant expert of Professor Manfreed's dreamed up. But where are we? The FBI has never even cracked the code behind 'beauty is truth, truth beauty.' Our men botched the attack on the National Mall. I told you to plant drugs and weapons and go to the press with the story that the squatters were a threat to national security. Instead, that kid got killed and we wound up with international headlines calling me a murderer. So, have you learned *anything* from what's happened? It's been almost a week since we've been here. Where are we with 'Operation Liberation'?"

"Mr. President," Homeland Security Director Smathers, interjects. "Mr. President, there is *absolutely* no way we can clear the capital without massive numbers of injuries and major loss of life. The pictures we've seen this morning show a sea of people camped out everywhere. The White House, the Capitol, the Mall, K Street, the Lincoln and Jefferson Memorials—everywhere the people have taken over. Think of it as the Mall Coopervi … I mean illegal encampment, multiplied by ten. It's a siege. I think we sit back and do nothing. Time and the weather are our best defense. We need simply to wait the invaders out. They'll get tired and frustrated living in tents out in the open air. They'll get hungry, and sick, and fed up with living in filth. This is the hottest time of the year in the capital. If the heat doesn't get them, the summer rains will. Yes, I've thought this through and our best strategy is to do nothing and trust in Mother Nature."

"Smathers, pack up and get the fuck out of here," Cooper says. "If doing nothing is your best professional advice, you're fired. Defense Secretary Gibbons, what's your version of 'Operation Liberation'?"

"Mr. President, as you can see from the material I've prepared, there's *only* one way to take control of the situation, the classic tactic of 'Contain and Contaminate.' It's from Offense 101, the first course for officers at the War College. First, we contain the enemy. We box 'em in. We surround his terrain with our troops and fortifications and control all means of escape. Second, we drop leaflets on 'em, telling 'em they must immediately evacuate at appointed exists or face serious consequences. Those who exit are arrested, of course. Third, we attack those who remain from the air. We alternate spraying with tear gas and water. I guarantee you, before long the whole area will be cleared—and the enemy will be behind bars.'"

"Simmons, what do you think, from the FBI's perspective?" Cooper asks.

"Mr. President, it is insanity. But I wholeheartedly support it and will be sure that the FBI gives you all the resources you need. In unprecedented times, what sounds craziest makes the most sense."

"I'm glad to hear you say that, Simmons. And Gibbons, I totally agree with your strategy and tactics. I'll be meeting with my Corporate Council just minutes from now and informing them that I intend to implement the broad outlines of your plan. In fact, I'd like you to join me at the briefing. Please make fifty copies of your proposal we can pass out. After the meeting, I'll sign a formal order, giving you the go-ahead."

Twenty minutes later, smiling broadly, almost jubilant, as though he didn't have a care in the world, Ham Cooper walks briskly into the Camp David conference room. All fifty of the members of his Corporate Council are waiting for him. The room is eerily quiet. Everyone is sitting stone-faced, staring ahead, steely eyed, arms crossed in front, lips pursed. Taking his place in the front of the room, the president asks Gibbons to pass out copies of "Operation Liberation." Half of them decline to take it. Those who do don't bother looking at it. They just look straight ahead.

"Friends, what you have in front of you is my administration's plan for restoring peace and harmony to the nation's capital. I know that all of us are troubled by the direction recent events have taken. But it is now time for us to act. And act we will—firmly and decisively. Defense Secretary Gibbons has developed what I believe is a brilliant strategy and, adding to it whatever useful perspectives and suggestions you share, I am prepared to implement 'Operation Liberation' immediately. As you can see from your copies of the proposal, it is a classic tactic of 'Contain and Contaminate,' as Secretary Gibbons has explained..."

"Mr. President," Jonathan Smythe of Consolidated Industries shouts angrily, standing up, shaking his right fist and interrupting Cooper. "Mr. President, I told you back in June that your administration appeared to have lost control when the annual celebration at New Atlantis was rattled by 'the voice from nowhere.' Since then, things have gone from bad to worse. First, there was the Adam incident. Now, we have the Florida, Inc. debacle. You haven't got a clue about your enemy—our enemy. All we know is that we're being made to look like fucking idiots, and we're losing the best chance we could have imagined to make billions. I'll be the first to say it: Mr. President, you must resign. The CSA needs new leadership. To save the future of Free-for-All economics, you've got to get out of the way."

"Mr. Smy...the," Cooper replies, seething and barely able to pronounce his name. "Mr. Smythe, I will *never* resign. For you even to suggest that I do so is..."

"Mr. Smythe, please sit down," Harold Klein of International Networks says. "Obviously, you're agitated. And you have every reason to be. We all are. But let's give Ham a chance to tell us his strategy before we take any drastic measures. We owe him that at least."

"Thank you, Harold!" Cooper continues. "As I was saying, first we will contain the protestors in the capital by surrounding them with troops and fortifications. They will only be able to escape through exists we've created. Then, we'll drop leaflets telling them to leave or face serious consequences and then..."

"Ham," Mortimer Gayle of Gayle's Department Stores says. "I'm sorry to interrupt you. But Ham, we've been friends a long time. I can't let you go on like this. It's simply too painful. I've been your loyal supporter, even when others weren't. I've defended you again and again. I've lost millions of dollars because of you. Yes, you. Don't look surprised when I say you ... "

"Mortimer, please let me add something," Aristotle Khouris says. "Ham, the members of my investment groups have told me that, as long as you remain president, they will not put any money into the CSA. Under Florida, Inc., for starters, they expected to be able to own all the airports and sea ports. But they don't believe that will ever happen now. I did my best to defend you, just like Mortimer. But they wouldn't listen. They're even afraid that, because you've lost a grip on the CSA, their effort to take over countries A, B, and C is in jeopardy."

Practically unable to speak, Cooper says, "But, gentlemen and lady... I've ... "

"Ham, Mr. President," Mortimer says somberly, rising and sympathetically shaking his head and pursing his lips. "Ham, I volunteered to be the one to tell you. You have no choice but to step down."

"But I ... You can't," Cooper says feebly.

"Yes, we can, Ham. Before coming here, the Corporate Council met in the capital so we could speak with one voice. All of us have signed a formal expression of 'No Confidence,' which, under the CSA Constitution, is tantamount to your removal from office.

"Friends, do I have to remind you about all the things I've done for you?" Cooper says pensively, pleading, slowly looking them in the eye, one by one. "Yes, I guess I do. Or, no, I should say, it appears it won't do any good. I feel like I've been poisoned, as though someone I've loved and trusted for years has slipped a fatal dose of a slow-acting drug into my favorite cocktail and is watching me die, while I figure out what's happening to me just before I lose consciousness."

"Ham," Mortimer Gayle says sadly, "please don't make this any harder on yourself—or us. You know, the old saying: 'You don't produce, you're outta here. Business is business.' They're your words. How many times have you told us you delivered them when you had to clean house? All of us consider ourselves your friends. We all hope you'll still think of us that way, too. We've prepared a written statement for you to sign before releasing it to the press. As you will see, it simply says that, effective immediately, you have chosen to resign to spend more time with your family—and that you have withdrawn as a candidate for president. You throw your unqualified support to Vice President Moreland and to his replacing you on the November ballot. You thank all the citizens of the CSA, and its leading investors, and your Corporate Council for always standing with you. For security reasons, you will not be able to return to the White House. You may remain at Camp David until you apprise us of where you will be living, but you have no longer than seven days in any event. We will provide you with your farewell address to the nation, which you will deliver one week from today. Again, we all wish to remain your friends and wish you well."

TEN

Enlisting, Evading, Enflaming

MONDAY, AUGUST 29, 11 A.M.: SOUTH OCEAN DRIVE, PALM BEACH, FLORIDA. For the past three weeks, if astronauts had been poised in outer space looking down on the CSA, they would have reported a mystifying phenomenon. For hundreds of miles, from every direction, clogging major roads and interstate highways, caravans of thousands of cars, trucks, and people on foot, bicycles, and motorcycles have created an almost unbroken chain headed to the Florida border. Since August 8th, when the full extent of the devastation caused by Hurricane Dick, the category 5+ storm that hit the Sunshine State, became clear, the Prometheus Project, in collaboration with Coopervilles nationwide, fired up "the people" to mobilize—and mobilize they did. And they keep coming.

Along the way, reporters stopped Mr. B, the "mayor" of the Central Park Cooperville, on I-95, outside of Savannah, Georgia, among the first to head to Florida. "Do you *really* have to ask what we're doing and why we're doing it?" he replied in disbelief to a question he thought particularly naïve. "Have you seen pictures of what's happened? Surely, you can see for yourselves. It's the same old pattern: the CSA has abandoned its people. Florida has become the biggest

Cooperville in the nation. There's no government to rescue the millions of people stranded and desperate. They are *literally* crying for help. But, as we learned, right after the disaster, Cooper and his mob cynically connived in the comfort of the White House to make money from the misery of millions of helpless people. So, who better than all of us who have suffered to take charge when other victims are homeless and devastated?"

"But this has been called 'the rich man's hurricane,'" said one reporter. "Most of the people affected are well off. Why should you help?"

"Young lady, I'm sorry to say that if you can ask such a question, you'll *never* understand my answer. Let's just leave it at that. I've got to get going. There's work to do. Honestly, I don't have time for silly chatter."

Along the route, once the media began reporting on the path of "the people's march," as they dubbed it, people who live nearby have been bringing food and water, tents, generators, and other vital supplies to the side of the road. They even set up portable toilets and showers. Local doctors and nurses have staffed medical tents. As one doctor put it, "Who can sit by when homeless people rush to help homeless people?" Volunteer patrols protect the marchers at night. Unfortunately, almost all roadside hotels and motels, convenience stores, restaurants, and gas stations refused to cooperate. As one franchisee of a national motel chain put it, "I've got to follow company policy. I've been told, all of us have been told, that anyone who can afford the price of a room is welcome. I ain't in the charity business. My investors want profits or this place goes belly up and I'm outta a job. I ain't gonna let no commie-lovin' socialists clog up my toilets."

In Palm Beach, in the headquarters of "the people's" hurricane relief effort, a tent pitched where rubble has been cleared from the flattened condominium at 100 Worth Avenue, Mr. B, Wilson Brackett, III, head of internal affairs from the Central Park Cooperville, and

Alma Parks, head of services, hold their daily assessment meeting of the statewide relief effort. Mr. B, along with other Cooperville leaders from around the country, surveyed the damage and needs throughout the peninsula and set up a coordinated plan to dispatch volunteers, based upon their skills, where they were needed most. They established three major points of entry (I-10 from the west, I-75 and I-95 from the north). As volunteers enter Florida, they are assigned to one of eight service zones, then given jobs and directions to get them there. Daily, Parks updates the "needs" database, based upon reports from coordinators in the field. She has also established a census program that identifies the name and vital information for every volunteer, including where they are working. Everyone is issued a personal wristband when they cross an entry point. So far, 45,000 volunteers have flooded into the state—and hundreds more arrive every day.

"We still don't have an accurate body count, and we probably never will," Mr. B says, shaking his head from side to side and pursing his lips in disbelief. "It's hard to imagine. One minute millionaires around here are living in mansions, the envy of everyone, thinking nothing can happen to them. Then, all of a sudden, they're just like the rest of us, homeless and dazed, not knowing what to do next. There's a group of about twenty men who still can't face up to what's happened. They keep asking me, 'Where's Tallahassee when we need them? Where's the federal government?' All I can reply is, 'Where have you been? Didn't you hear what the president and *your* governor were plotting with the Corporate Council? That wasn't made up stuff. It was real. Those were their very words. You elected these guys! Didn't you understand their agenda? Didn't you understand that they've been out to screw you all long?'"

"I know how you feel, Mr. B," Brackett adds. "Most people don't 'get it' until it's too late and, as soon as things get better for them, they go back to business-as-usual. But I can't think of all that at the moment. We've got *real* work to do, right in front of us. We've almost got wireless service back in place statewide. But we've still got a major problem with explosions and fires from gas leaks. Most are under control. But we never know when or where the next one's gonna erupt. In many places, you can smell the gas in the air. Otherwise, we've been making real progress. We've established eight service hubs across the state: four on the west side (Tallahassee, Gainesville, Tampa, and Naples), another three on the east side (Miami, Daytona Beach, and Jacksonville), and one in mid-central (Orlando). Since most major roads are now at least passable from Orlando, our central distribution point, we've finally been able to distribute portable showers, blankets, sleeping bags, toilets, generators, drinking water, and the like across the state."

"That's great, Wilson! Where's all the stuff coming from?" Alma Parks asks.

"Haven't any idea," says Brackett. "All I know is it's coming in—and going out as fast as we can get it to people. And that's all I care about. The Prometheus Project sends daily updates nationwide listing what we need. Many volunteers are bringing supplies, stuff people have donated who've helped them along their route."

"I wish I was having as much luck as you are," Parks laments. "I'm seriously short of medical personnel—and supplies. Many, many victims have run out of their medications. We're trying to get prescriptions refilled, but, unless their conditions are life-threatening, they are low priority. We've got seriously wounded victims, some who haven't had any medical attention at all, living in the open—without even a tent or a sleeping bag. This morning I saw a woman with her broken arm in a makeshift sling, walking around dazed. By now, the whole world's gotta know that Florida is a war zone. We've got dead and dying everywhere. But we haven't even begun to get a handle on the situation."

"Ever since volunteers from Cooperville have arrived," Mr. B adds obviously troubled, "the biggest problem we're having is with the guys who *know* what's happened here and who only want to make a buck off of other people's misery. They've been planting saboteurs in our feeding tents, or showing up themselves, saying that our stuff is contaminated and offering to sell food and water. In one case, they held up a dead rat they said had been found in a vat of soup, but which they brought in to scare people. They're parking their helicopters on roads that we've cleared, making it impossible for our trucks to get through. People have been shouting them down. Some have attacked their helicopters with bats. Some of the money-grubbers have even been trying to hack into our wireless system to keep us from reaching people who might donate supplies. They won't do anything unless people can pay. They stood by and let a house burn down because the owners didn't have the cash to pay their fee. I don't know what we can do, but we've got to do something.

"There's some great news, however. Last night, we had confirmation that supplies from Mexico, Cuba, Venezuela, and Panama will be arriving at the Port of Tampa within two days. Phase two of the European relief effort is under way, as well. Supply ships should soon arrive at the Port of Palm Beach. Don't despair, Alma, the whole world *is* watching—and helping—even if Washington and Tallahassee are doing nothing."

Farther south on South Ocean Boulevard, where the historic Mar-a-Lago mansion was located before the hurricane leveled it, a large feeding tent has been set up in a clearing. As in similar tents across the state, preparations for the midday meal are well under way. Today, trucks from the Orlando central food distribution center arrived at 3 a.m. to supply the day's rations. Volunteers began their preparations immediately. The first feeding went on schedule from 6 a.m. to 9 a.m. But several hundred men, women, and children are already in line for the next feeding. By the time the meal is over, hundreds more will have shown up. They don't start serving until noon, so a young, red-headed man is making his way along the line, passing out snacks, especially to help quiet the ever-hungry kids. Mothers nursing infants and frail, older victims are let into the tent whenever they want.

"I've got a box of granola bars," a young woman calls out to the red-head. "Thanks," he says, relieved. "I was just about to run out. How about a granola bar?" he says to the next person in line, a stately, white-haired woman, who appears to be in her eighties.

"A what?" she asks.

"A granola bar. It's *really* good for you. You'll be getting lunch in a few minutes, but this will be good for you in the meantime."

"Young man, please over here," the next woman in line says to the red-head, stepping out of the line and moving out of the older woman's earshot.

"Mrs. Winthrop doesn't understand you. She can't understand you. She has dementia. I'm her nurse. You see that pile of rubble over there, two blocks up, where the tower is sticking out? That was her mansion. Her family's lived in Palm Beach since 1925. It was designed by Addison Mizener himself. She and her husband lived in it year-round after she inherited it from her mother. Her husband died five years ago. She always said she didn't need to go anywhere in the world because she had everything she needed right here in Palm Beach. 'Look around, Millie,' she'd say to me. 'Can you imagine ever being anywhere else?' She always said that summer was her favorite time of the year. 'All those silly people leave,' she'd laugh. 'That's when I have paradise all to myself.' I'll see that she eats the granola bar. Thank you so much. I don't know what we'd do without you and all the kind people who are helping us."

MONDAY, OCTOBER 24, 8 P.M.: THE WASHINGTON D.C. CONVENTION CENTER. "Welcome, ladies and gentlemen here in our audience and those of you watching throughout the Corporate States of America and around the world. My name is Joshua Redding, and I am the moderator of tonight's presidential debate. In two weeks, on Tuesday, November 8th, voters will go to the polls to elect the next leader of the CSA and free-market nations around the globe. Make no mistake about it. You are watching history-in-the-making tonight. And you'll make history at the polls. No matter where people see themselves on the political spectrum, everyone agrees that this is an historic occasion.

"I don't have to remind you that, in recent months, the nation has been rocked by popular uprisings and boycotts—what some have called terrorist attacks—that have shut down businesses and whole cities. A president has stepped down and withdrawn from the upcoming election. As a result of a scandal, New Atlantis, the intellectual breeding ground of the Galtian Restoration has closed its doors. It is an understatement to say that the nation is in turmoil. Mortimer Gayle of the president's Corporate Council has been quoted saying, 'This election is a watershed for the nation. We will move forward with the Free-for-All economic policies and reaffirm the rock-bed principles that have made our beloved market great, or we will backslide into a shameful and dispiriting socialism that will doom us to self-defeat and shame.'

"Predictably, Mr. B, the 'mayor' of the Central Park Cooperville, couldn't disagree more. One of the leaders continuing to coordinate relief efforts after the recent, devastating hurricane in Florida, Mr. B says in a written statement, 'Unless you're blind, if you want to understand what's desperately wrong with the CSA, remember the misery going on in the Sunshine State. Every day, I look into the faces of the victims who have been abandoned. That's right, abandoned. They could be any one of us. They *are* each and every one us. And yet, citizens of the CSA have been made to believe that there's no longer a collective *us*. There's only I and me. The message is: I grab whatever I can for me—to hell with everyone else. I don't recognize the country I grew up in—and that I believed in.'"

"With those words as a bit of background," Redding continues, "the two candidates seated before you couldn't be more different.

Former vice president, now president, H. R. 'Bill' Moreland became CSA president and CEO at one of the most volatile times in our history. Cary Hinton calls herself 'an ordinary citizen on an extraordinary mission' to take back the country. Tonight, you will get to listen to them fully explain their positions and decide which of their visions is best for your future—and America's. President Moreland goes first."

Bill Moreland stands up, arches his back, buttons his jacket, looks back in the direction of Cary Hinton, then walks slowly to the podium. Four years ago, he was Ham Cooper's first choice to replace his then-VP, Harold Harmington, who decided not to run again, which quashed the ethics investigation against him. Moreland accepted with alacrity. Though his colleagues at Benson, Benson, Trickman, Schlosser & Schlag, the securities firm in which he was senior vice president, were eager to capitalize on his place within the administration, most hardly knew him or noticed he was gone. A diamond-in-the-rough that nothing could polish, he was successful throughout his life because he was smart enough to play dumb. Agreeable, lazy, seemingly devoid of ambition, the human equivalent of an odorless, colorless, harmless gas—his chief virtue was that he never appeared to pose a threat to anyone, except his family. Heirs to a mining fortune in Colorado, they trembled at the possibility that he, the eldest of three sons, would ever be responsible for managing their collective interests. So, he was sent East on a trumped up 'business development' mission, from which he was never allowed to return.

The consummate yes-man and proud of it, even telling anyone who would listen that he wasn't "here" to make waves, mild Bill rose up the corporate ladder in various financial institutions—never remaining long enough in one place to be held accountable; landing comfortably near the top but never so high as to provoke jealousy; keeping his mouth shut, his ears open, and his hands clean. He stood for anything, everything, and nothing—often at the same time. If he came across a body on the sidewalk, chances are he'd walk over or around it. Nothing touched him—and he touched nothing. So, nothing stood in his way.

To Ham Cooper, Moreland was the running mate he had always wanted. He was perfectly content rarely to attend meetings, never to be called upon for his opinion, and thrilled to stand in for Cooper at ceremonial trivialities, like ribbon-cuttings and state funerals, especially state funerals. So, two months ago, when Cooper resigned, it shocked everyone that "mild Bill" became "wild Bill" as soon as he walked into the Oval Office. A Dr. Jekyll turned Mr. Hyde, Moreland appeared to take special delight in firing half of Cooper's staff, minutes after swearing to the oath of office—and letting the rest know they were on borrowed time. "Things is gonna be different 'round here," he proclaimed, smashing his fist on his desk. He then held a press conference denouncing the former president, demanding a thorough investigation into the case against Atlas Fitness Centers and New Atlantis—"no matter where it leads," he said—and pledging that his administration would "gush" (his exact word) in a new beginning for the CSA.

At the podium, Moreland stands for a full minute without saying a word, sucking in a mouthful of air, or so it seems. Then, he looks to the left and says, "*a-rh* I am John Galt," then to the right and repeats, "I am John Galt." Finally, he stares straight ahead and, extending and raising both arms above his head, fists clenched, says, "Believe in me. I *am* John Galt. Just look here. Look at my tie. The gold dollar sign I so proudly wear is the symbol of everything that's great about the CSA. *a-rh* There's almost nothing more to say—except, it's a sin to be poor."

Cary Hinton scowls and shifts uncomfortably in her seat.

After waiting about thirty seconds, Moreland sucks in another breath, then continues. "*a-rh*, My fellow investors, I know that word bothers some of the socialist caste," he says, knitting his brow, turning and pointing to Hinton.

"Watch it, Bill! Remember, I get the last word," Hinton flings back at him, pointing with her right index finger.

"Investors! Every man, woman, and child in the CSA has the privilege of being an investor in our Free-for-All e-con-o-mee. If they're smart enough to take advantage of that glorious opportunity, they can be richer than they ever imagined. If they don't, well, they're not even worth talking about, *a-rh*. In the CSA, you freely invest whatever you choose to invest and wherever you chose to invest. And, *a-rh*, you profit or you lose. That's the game we play. And if you're in the right place at the right time, you may make the rules you play by, which is even better. It's as simple as that, *a-rh*.

"At the end of the day, the *only* thing that matters is that you win and that you win big—*real* big! Alotta people *still* don't 'get it.' They pussy-foot around, talkin' about mush: our debt to society, the common good, the poor and the hungry. Well, I couldn't care less about any of that stuff. And I have no patience for losers. You are your own God. You're not responsible for anyone else, and no one else is responsible for you—and me. Glory be to me! I just *love* saying that. In fact, I love saying it *so* much, I'm gonna say it again. Glory be to me! That's true freedom! It's what makes us and our markets the envy of the world, *a-rh*. And it's not to be taken for granted. It took years for us to win—and decades to defend."

"We can never rest. Our whole glorious way of life is under attack," he says, again turning towards Cary Hinton, scowling and shaking his head in disapproval. "Evil people are out to take everything away from us, *a-rh*. Some of our weak sisters find my mas-sage hard to take. But I say that's *their* problem. We are a diff'rent breed of people—and proud of it. We are an excep-tional breed of people. We choose ourselves for greatness. It's a heavy burden to bear. We gotta be strong. We gotta meet our destiny. As Free-for-All economics spreads around the globe *a-rh*, the rest of the world is either with us or against us. All of you are smart enough to guess which is the rendition for them to choose."

Smirking, quickly turning and looking at Cary Hinton again, then back at the audience, he continues, "At times like this, I feel like I'm teaching kindergarten, *a-rh*. Ms. Hinton's words are inflammable. For months, she's been talking up her half-baked propaganda and talking down the principles that have made the CSA great. Well, I'm here to throw cold water on her fire, *a-rh*. And I want all of you to be firemen in my fire house. She'll give us a three-alarmer if she wins, you betta believe it. I'm not gonna let her destroy the greatest marketplace in the world. Election Day is your chance to honor Atlas and to rededicate yourself to John Galt.

"Number One: Remember, there ain't no such thing as 'the common good' that the goody-goody lady over there harps on. Deadbeats love the sound of those words, *a-rh*. They tell couch potatoes, illegal aliens, welfare mothers, drug addicts, perverts, moochers, freeloaders, lazy good-for-nothing takers that there's always gonna be dumb fools who will take care of them. That's what you get with Miss Hinton: a bunch of blood-suckers feeding off you.

"Well, you can trust good 'ol Bill Moreland to tell you there ain't no 'common good.' It's just the fig leaf, *a-rh*. You heard me, a fig leaf. Some people are ashamed of what they got. But we all know what's under there—and they should be proud of what they got, unless it ain't much of anything. You're not your brother's keeper, *a-rh*. Don't fall for the scam. There are no good Samaritans. In the CSA, no one's comin' to get you when you're down-and-out, and you don't need to high-tail it to bail anyone out. Get what you can, as long as you can, 'cause when you can't, no one's gonna be there for ya, *a-rh*.

"Number Two: Miss Hinton and her supporters bad-mouth rich people. Oh, how they chew 'em up and spit 'em out. Rich people this, and rich people that, *a-rh*. You name it: Rich people are responsible for the bad weather, high prices, your hemorrhoids. Yes, blame everything on the rich! Well, let's get *real* clear about how the rich get rich: They are cree-ative. What's that? They make things—that sell. That's right! They're on-the-make. As the saying goes, 'It ain't cree-ative un-less it sells.' Cree-ative artists don't piddle around in some studio painting. They paint what sells, what they make people wanna buy. They don't care if it's a bowl of fruit or a sailboat. They don't care if you hang it over the refrigerator or put it under the bed—as long as they get rich. Free-for-All inventors don't just fiddle around with gadgets for the fun of it. They make something, anything. Then, they sell the hell out of it. They *make* people want to buy it, *a-rh*, whether they want to buy it or not. That's *real* cree-ativity!

"Number Three: Don't let Cary Hinton and her crew get the gov-'rnment back in the business of running the economy—and your life, *a-rh*. We've spent years giving the gov'rnment away. Don't fall for the propaganda that we *need* gov'rnment. If you can find it on the Inter-net, you don't *need* gov'rnment to do it. And since you can find almost everything on the Internet … well, all of you are smart enough to fig-ure out what comes after that.

"I'll give you an example of how gov'rnment buttin' in can stomp on good people like ants. 'Bout thirty years ago, gov'rnment high-and-mighty, know-it-all bureaucrats in Washington, in cahoots with tree-hugging environmentalists, dreamed up some reg-u-lay-tions 'bout logging on federal lands. Just like that, someone did some half-ass study and decided they had to pro-tect the forests, *a-rh*. You know, for 'the common good.' Well, before that, some hard-working men had been making a good living. But it got so bad, if a kid broke a branch off a tree, he could have gone to jail.

"Well, I'm from the school of 'if you've seen one tree, you've seen 'em all.' The great thing about Mother Nature is she's out there makin' things grow. If you just leave her alone, you'll get all the trees you could ever want—or need. Mother just loves making trees. You can have non-stop trees—as long as you leave Mother alone. She gets testy when you meddle in her business. You can chop down a whole forest and, *a-rh*, after you plant a few seeds, which cost you nothing, in time all those trees will grow back so you can chop 'em down again, make a pile a money, and chop 'em down again. It's perfect—if you just get the gov'rnment out of the damn way.

"Mother Nature *wants* you, me, all of us to chop down trees or she wouldn't have made it so they can grow back. Mother Nature loves Free-for-All economics, *a-rh*. Mother Nature is all *for* free markets. You better believe that one of the proudest moments of my life was when we lifted all restrictions on logging and let the market take off. Ask the loggers who are making money hand-over-fist if it was a good idea. And the same goes for bankers, oil and gas companies, developers, and everyone else you can think of. Man, now that we've got gov'rnment out-of-the-way, everything's a-boomin'. So, I rest my case. The choice is yours, CSA investors," he says, looking intently into the camera. "By now, you should know to vote for me on November 8th. It's a sin to be poor! I rest my case, *a-rh*," he says, quickly returning to his seat.

"Thank you, President Moreland, Ms. Hinton, the floor is yours," Joshua Redding says.

"Thank you, Mr. Redding. Bring him in," she shouts when she reaches the podium. A young, red-headed man hurries up to her with a manikin dressed and made up to look like Ham Cooper. The audience first gasps, then erupts in laughter.

Moreland jumps out of his chair, shouting, "I object. What the hell kinda cheap stunt ..."

"Cheap, is it, Moreland?" Hinton asks. "I'll tell *you* what's cheap— the way *you* and Ham here connived and cheated average men, women, and children all across this country. Did you forget that we've got every word of the fraud you were part of on tape? Or are you going to pretend you didn't know about the deal to make billions from the misery in Florida? Everyone has heard the plotting between the prez and his Corporate Council. You may be standing here, but I *really* want all the good people of this country to remember you're just as guilty as former President Ham Cooper," she says, putting her arm around the manikin.

"How dare you? I object, I object," Moreland shouts.

"Down boy, if you don't mind, Moreland, I have the floor now. I sat and listened to your poison. I didn't interrupt you, and I expect the same basic courtesy from you, unless…" she breaks off, as he sits down. "That's better!" she adds, first looking at him, then turning to the audience. "You're gonna hear a *lot* more from President Cooper before I'm through—and Moreland, you ain't gonna like it.

"No more Moreland! No more Moreland! Less is more with Moreland!" Hinton starts to chant. "Two months of Moreland is more than we can stand! Moreland says that he feels like he's teaching kindergarten, that my words have been 'inflammable' and that some people don't get his 'massage.' Well, we get it. We just reject it. Mr. Moreland is flat-out wrong about *everything*—except one thing. I *have* come to light one huge fire, 'the people's' fire—and to put another one out, his! It's time Free-for-All economics went up in smoke. By the time I finish with him tonight, he's gonna wish he was in kindergarten, because, with a little help from my friend Ham here, I'm gonna put him through Hell and in Hell," she says smiling and putting her left arm around the shoulders of the manikin and stroking the top of its head. "Aren't we, Ham? But first, I've got my own *choice* words for Mr. Moreland.

"Listen up there, wild Bill: I'm gonna tell it to the people straight. Atlas Energy Drink! Atlas Fitness Centers! Florida! Cooperville! Free-for-All economics—all of it is the social equivalent of date rape. For sixty-seven years, almost seven long deceitful decades, you and people like you have drugged the good, honest, decent people of this country into thinking you were doing something good for them. But you give yourself away when you pronounce 'e-con-o-mee.' Because your Free-for-All agenda is a con, and all of you only think me, me, me. You speak in tongues—forked tongues.

Moreland shouts, "That's an outrage! She needs to be stopped!"

But Hinton ignores him and continues. "Outrage? I'll tell you what's an outrage! If you ever took a slug of Atlas Energy Drink, you know it wasn't only a fraud, it could have killed you. How much lower can you go? Atlas Fitness Centers pimped people out to raise millions to prop up New Atlantis. If you've seen the disaster in Florida, you know what it's like where there's no government, people rot and die, and vulture capitalists swoop in and feed off them. And as for Coopervilles, well, now, they're gone but we've got Billvilles. That's the glory of Free-for-All economics for ya! And you'll get more and more of that if you elect Moreland! I honestly don't know how people can look themselves in the mirror, knowing how they've lied and deceived people. How much is enough? How many cars, mansions, planes, and yachts are enough when they are bought with money from ripping other people off and from selling public assets at fire-sale prices? 'Beware of false prophets, which come to you in sheep's clothing, but inwardly they are ravening wolves.'

"Put me in the Oval Office and I won't plot with corporate bottom-feeders to line their pockets. I'm here to declare a return of the States of America to 'the people.' I am one of 'the people.' I am proud to represent 'the people.' I'm the 'Beauty is truth, truth beauty' candidate. The head of the FBI told Cooper he suspected those words were code for a radical gay-socialist-communist-artist cabal, possibly even part of an international plot. He said he put his 'crack' cryptographers on it, but he still hasn't figured it out. I know some of you want me to tell you what those silly-sounding words mean. But I'm gonna let them roll around in your heads while you listen to what I have to say. You're all smart enough to figure them out for yourselves by the time I'm through.

"I'm the *only* one who's ever dared to challenge Ham Cooper and, now, his lackey 'wild Bill.'

"I strenuously object," Moreland says, jumping up again. "No one calls me a lackey."

"I strenuously object to your strenuous objection—and to your *being* the lackey you are! You've called me worse and I've never tried to shut you up. Now sit down and take it like a man. Moreland and his henchmen have told bald-faced lies about me and what I stand for. They call me a socialist, communist, freeloader, moocher. But nothing could be further from the truth. So, I'm going to set the record straight.

"My story is the story of every American. It's so common a story, that too many people take it for granted, have forgotten its theirs— or don't want to be reminded of it. Perhaps, they are ashamed to admit that their grandparents and parents ever had to struggle or weren't to the manor born. Well, I'm proud of my story: My grandparents and their families fled persecution in Eastern Europe—the *real* kind of persecution, the kind of persecution that *kills* people— and came to this 'promised land.' That's *literally* how they saw America—as a promised land, their salvation. They worked hard, didn't expect anyone to give them anything, and saved their money so their children could get educated. Those children educated their children, and so on. They never asked anyone for anything. But if someone else needed their help, they were *always* there for them.

"Communist? Socialist? Freeloader? Moocher? With that kind of background and upbringing? You've gotta be kidding! I believe in a meritocracy. I believe everyone should have the same chance to prove they're the best one to do any job. I don't care about the color of someone's skin, their sex, ethnic background, religion, lifestyle preference, anything. If I need surgery, I don't care if my doctor is green or blue—only that she's the best in her field. That's what the *real* America is, that's what it has *always* been about, and that's what it will be again—if you elect me. That's not what Free-for-All economics is about. It's about inherited wealth and an old boys' network that takes from everyone so the rich can have it all and the powerful and their sons and daughters can rule. They want everybody's toys. But 'what is a man profited, if he shall gain the whole world and lose his own soul?' Join me in sending them packing. No more Moreland," she says, smirking and turning toward him.

"What a silly man! Wild Bill says Mother Nature believes in Free-for-All economics. He says that if you've seen one tree you've seen them all. Well, I say, if you've heard one defender of Free-for-All, you've heard them all. They're all for logging all right—logrolling. You know, politicians' saying you vote my bill and I'll back yours. They're just a bunch of back scratchers. Their idea of free is free for all of their corporate cronies, everyone else be damned. I've got a different kind of story about a tree. It sums up the difference between Wild Bill and me. It's the difference between the worlds we each want for you.

"This is a true story. Many years ago, a man and his wife bought a plot of land, on which they planned to build their dream house. The man told their architect that he wanted the house built literally around the largest tree in the middle of the property. It physically sickened him, but he had resigned himself to the fact that almost all of the heavily wooded area would have to be cleared. But he couldn't face killing the stately oak. Both the architect and the builder argued that the plan was not just impractical but ill-advised, even dangerous, for any number of reasons. He insisted. They insisted. They simply could not agree. And then, the man's wife suggested building the house higher on the lot in back of the tree, pointing out that, with the raised elevation, the view from the picture window in the living room would take in the whole city. They all agreed.

"The house on the hill behind the tree was also on the crest of a hill. So, it stood out from all the other houses around it. The driveway was steep and especially difficult to access when it snowed. Typically, a plow needed to clear it. Every fall, the oak leaves inundated the walk. Quickly, the family grew used to walking up the drive and the stairs. Visitors were usually breathless. Some even cursed, and couldn't figure out why the house had to be higher than everything around it. But especially in the fall, even the winded marveled at the symphony of color—leaves turning purple, red, yellow, orange—that could be seen for miles around only from the picture window and another front room of the house.

"After nearly a quarter of a century, the man and his wife agreed to sell the house. Their realtor warned that the hill would be a liability and suggested lowering the price to entice buyers. But the man disagreed. The first two prospective buyers got into a bidding war and drove the price up—because they fell in love with the tree and the view from the picture window. The house sold for fifty percent more than the original asking price, higher than any other house in the neighborhood.

"I know this story is true, because my father and mother built the house. It's where I called home for the first twenty-one years of my life. I walked up the steep driveway. I groused, but helped rake the forests of leaves that fell on the walk. I cursed when a plow was late getting to us, and I had to help clear the snow. But I spent countless hours looking out of that picture window—summer, fall, winter, and spring—and marveling at the commanding view. In fact, I think more about the incredible view than any of the minor discomforts of living there. After more than thirty years, recently, I drove by it. I didn't have the heart to ask the currently owners if I could go inside—just too many memories. But I reveled in the place from the outside. The tree is still there, bigger than ever and covered with the leaves of late spring.

"No, Mr. Moreland, I can tell you without a doubt that, if you've seen one tree you haven't seen them all. 'Beauty is truth, truth beauty.' You *can* have it all in the *real* America. You can achieve harmony and balance. You *can* have the best of both worlds. You can follow your human, caring, soulful instincts and you may even be rewarded in dollars and cents beyond what you might have imagined. Free-for-All economics takes all that away from you. It is a Godless greed, a cancer upon nations, a parasite living off the people—and killing their humanity. It is un-American, un-Christian, un-Jewish, un-Buddhist, un-Hindu, un-Moslem—an un-believable hypocrisy. It tramples every decent instinct in the hearts and minds of man. It goes against the grain of every civilized nation. It takes, and takes, and takes until there is nothing left to give—and yet it still looks for more.

"'Beauty is truth, truth beauty.' The quality of mercy isn't some abstract notion; it is real. In the *real* America, we don't leave people in Florida to rot and die unless they can afford to pay their way out of misery. We don't turn our back on them so they wind up in Billvilles. 'The quality of mercy is not strain'd. It droppeth as the gentle rain from heaven upon the place beneath. It is twice blessed. It blesseth him that gives and him that takes.' For generations mercy was the lifeblood that ran through the veins of our people, until the Free-for-All vampires sucked the life out of them. 'For I was hungered, and ye gave me meat: I was thirsty, and ye gave me drink: I was a stranger, and ye took me in: Naked, and ye clothed me: I was sick, and ye visited me: I was in prison, and ye came unto me.' Ask yourself, 'Or what man is there of you, whom if his son ask bread, will he give him a stone?' And ask yourself how you would—and should—answer, and what we've come to in this country today.

"Beauty is truth, truth beauty. I pledge to restore the balance we've lost between people and profit. We don't live in an either-or world. We can have both. We've had too much of Atlas for too long. We need the fire of Prometheus to bring us back to life. I pledge allegiance to 'the people' of America and to create a nation in which *all* people are *truly* equal.

"And ladies and gentlemen, and especially Mr. Moreland, I am not the only one who has seen the light," she says, smirking and putting her arm around the Ham Cooper manikin. "I'm sorry to have kept you waiting so long, my friend. But I always keep the best for last. I will now read the statement from former CSA president Ham Cooper that he never got to deliver. As you will recall, the transmission of his farewell address to the nation failed and you never heard from him again. That's because he went off the script that his Corporate Council had prepared for him. Here's what he intended to say..."

Moreland runs forward to try to seize Hinton's copy of Cooper's speech out of her hands, but before he reaches her, Redding stands in his way. "President Moreland, we agreed on an open and uncensored debate. Please return to your seat." Moreland skulks back in disgust.

"As I was saying, Ham Cooper was supposed to say the words his Corporate Council wrote for him. Instead, here are the words he tried to deliver: 'I owe every man, woman, and child in the CSA an apology for the most recent actions taken by myself and members of my administration. Many years ago, when I first became president, I *really* believed in the honesty and integrity of the principles of Free-for-All economics. I *really* thought that they would lead to an economy in which *everyone* would prosper. But I no longer believe that. I have seen this once great and generous nation turned over to greedy, selfish operatives, and I am ashamed that I have allowed myself to conspire with them. I hope you will forgive me and accept my apology.'

"Of course, Ham Cooper was muzzled. The transmission of his speech was stopped. Because of a twenty-second delay, no one watching heard so much as a word of his confession. He was led off the set by uniformed police and escorted to his home, where he is being kept under virtual house-arrest.

"I rest my case, ladies and gentlemen. On Tuesday, November 8th, I ask you to vote for me. 'Beauty is truth, truth beauty.'

After the debate, Hinton chooses to drive to her hotel alone because her staff have some loose ends to tie up and she doesn't want to wait. Besides, her adrenaline was flowing and she was eager to unwind. As she drives out of the parking garage, it is snowing. How odd! How very odd! October and snowing, she says to herself. And how innocent the capital looks, as though it were nestled in swaddling clothes. The cold, white snow hides our differences, masks our warts, and, if only for a few fleeting moments, deludes us into thinking that maybe, just maybe, we—honest, ordinary, decent people—can fulfill our higher destiny, in spite of the odds. I take the falling snow as a sign of good things to come. I owe it to "the people" never to give up hope.

ELEVEN

Missed, Dissed, Kissed

TUESDAY, OCTOBER 25, 10 A.M.: ALEXANDRIA, VIRGINIA. At Hinton Campaign Headquarters, preparations are under way for a press conference. Originally called for 9 a.m., it has been rescheduled for 11 a.m. because of the bad weather. On a TV monitor, staffers are watching the news. On one side of a split screen, from his helicopter, unfazed by the severely limited visibility, "Bart the Channel 4 Weatherman" is sweeping across metropolitan Washington showing the shocking pictures of the snow storm that has been blanketing the area since about 9 p.m. last night. "Cars are stranded everywhere," he says laughing. "It's slow going on major roads. Many back streets haven't even been plowed. Trees and power lines are down. What a blast, folks! I feel as though I'm driving a snowmobile. It's nowhere near winter, but we're getting pummeled. And it looks like it's gonna continue for several hours. I guess Mother Nature didn't check her calendar. Don't be crazy like me. Drive carefully. Don't go out unless you have to. And watch out for patches of black ice. It doesn't take much for you to lose control of your car and end up in a ditch or wrapped around a tree."

On the other side of the monitor, there's a picture of Cary Hinton and Bill Moreland together at last night's debate. Under it, in the lower-third of the screen, are the question "Who won?" and numbers to which viewers may call in or text their votes. Nationwide, post-presidential-debate patter has been firing up the media since the talking heads went at it last night. Morning newspaper headlines categorically declare the winner and loser: "Hinton Scores," "Moreland Bores," "Cary Galls Galt," and "Cooper Cops Out." Predictably, morning drive-time chatter is non-stop and breaks down along partisan lines. Talk radio and TV pundits are dissecting candidates' words more intently than a high-school English teacher diagramming a sentence. "Ham Cooper is a lily-livered traitor" were the first words out of Ross Bullman's mouth, the self-proclaimed "voice of reason" and host of the nationally syndicated radio show of the same name. "Five of George Carlin's 'seven dirty words' apply to Hinton," he declares. "One of them rhymes with stunt. She took a cheap shot at Moreland with the Cooper-look-alike manikin."

On "The Voice of Reason," Harrison Paul of The Paul Poll, the "dean" of conservative opinion-sniffers, told Bullman that "the race is far from over. I've seen bigger margins than Hinton supposedly has after last night evaporate overnight, especially in the last two weeks before an election. One mistake, like proof that a candidate farts in public, and it could be all over, even for a front-runner. We're in the make-it-or-break-it phase. There's almost no time to recover from any negatives that come out. And believe me, both campaigns will go negative, right up to the end. Get out your barf bags. It's gonna get nastier than we've ever seen it."

Since 6 a.m., Channel 4 anchors Evander Jack and Melissa Harden, hosts of the capital's most watched morning show, have been saying how they thought that Moreland came across as nothing more than warmed-over Cooper and that, after the former prez threw him under the bus, unless he finds his groove in the next two weeks, he's toast. They've reported that all the overnight polls agree that Cary Hinton was the hands-down winner—by between seven and fifteen percent—but also reveal that a surprisingly high number of likely voters is still undecided.

At 11 a.m., Evander Jack says, "Hold on Melissa, ladies and gentlemen. We're interrupting our scheduled programming for breaking news from the Cary Hinton Campaign Headquarters." The receptionist in the Hinton office mutes the TV. An ashen-faced Randall Griffin, Cary Hinton's campaign manager, steps up to a sea of microphones and cameras. With him is a uniformed police officer.

"Ladies and gentlemen, Cary Hinton is missing," he says, barely able to contain himself. There's an audible gasp from the room. He pauses and takes a deep breath. "Last night after the debate, my last words to her were, 'I'll come to your room at 6:30 a.m., just to be sure you're up and ready to leave for the airport.' She and I, along with key field staff, were about to begin our long-planned, two-week, final campaign swing through the country. But this morning when I went to her room, I was immediately surprised when I didn't see the rental car she was driving when she left the D.C. Convention Center last night. It crossed my mind that she might be out buying newspapers to read reviews of the debate. But she wouldn't drive out in this weather, I reminded myself. I knocked on the door, but she didn't answer.

"The night shift at the motel was still on. So, I then went to the front desk and asked if anyone had seen her arrive last night or leave this morning. When no one said they had, I identified myself and told them the woman registered as Lois Kent was really presidential candidate Cary Hinton. Because of security considerations, they wouldn't give me a key to her room or even come with me and open the door. So, I had no choice but to call the Alexandria, Virginia Police Department. Police Chief Alan Porter, who's with me now, was immediately notified and arrived on the scene, shortly after three squad cars. Once we entered Cary's room, it was clear that she hadn't been there last night. The bed was made and mints were on the pillow. The light on the night-stand was on. The briefcase she was carrying was nowhere to be found.

"Once Chief Porter assessed the situation, and after I notified Cary's immediate family, he alerted the F.B.I. and the Secret Service. Because of the obvious political sensitivities of this situation, he also contacted the White House. At this time, I'd like to introduce Chief Alan Porter, who has an update for you."

"At 11 a.m., a nationwide, all-points missing person's bulletin was issued for Cary Hinton," Chief Porter says. "A full-scale investigation is now under way. We consider this a matter of national security. At this time, I have no details beyond what Mr. Griffin has just told you. We will be issuing updates, but not until we have further information to report. As you can imagine, our investigation is severely hampered because of the snow storm. So please bear with us."

"Chief, do you suspect foul play?" a reporter asks.

"At this time, we cannot rule anything out. But let me stress that I'm not saying yes or no. I don't want anyone to jump to any conclusions. That would be dangerous and irresponsible. This is an ongoing investigation and we are taking absolutely nothing for granted. But it's also highly politically charged—and suspicious—as you can well imagine. So, we are not going to speculate about anything—and I mean anything. We're just after the facts. And of course, we hope there's a simple explanation for all this and we find Cary Hinton safe and sound right away."

"A follow-up, Chief, please. Why did you wait so long to go nationwide with the news of the disappearance?"

"By standard operating procedures, we did not wait long at all. Usually, we don't issue an all-points bulletin about a missing adult within twenty-four hours. For obvious reasons, this case is different, however. We first had to notify all the parties Mr. Griffin mentioned. Then, we had to map out our search-and-response plan with the District of Columbia police. They've got their jurisdiction. We've got ours. Since 7 a.m., officers on the ground have been retracing the like-liest routes Ms. Hinton might have driven back to the hotel to see if she had been involved in an accident, especially in light of the snow storm. So far, there's no indication of that. Also, a special detachment has been interviewing people along all likely routes to see if anybody saw anything suspicious or unusual."

"For the record, Mr. Griffin," says a second reporter, "where were you staying at?

"The Alexandria Inn," says Griffin. "It's just down the street from our offices, which is why we always stay there."

"Chief, you mentioned that you've notified the White House. What's been the response?"

"So far, we haven't heard anything from President Moreland or anyone in his administration."

"Mr. Griffin," a woman in the back row shouts, "were any special security measures in place? Did she have Secret Service protection? And if not, why not?"

"No, I'm sorry to say. There were no special security measures in place to protect Cary Hinton. For decades, the federal government has reduced or eliminated all security services. It has specifically re-fused to supply any kind of protection for candidates, even those for president—and even those who may have received death threats. And yes, to save you asking, yes, we've received death threats. Cary was also adamant about not having any bodyguards with her. She thought it sent the wrong message—that she was scared or that there was any reason for others to be concerned. I don't mean to cut this short. But we're inundated. As you can imagine, this is a troubling time for all of us. Thank you all for coming. Of course, we will update you as soon as we know anything."

After the press conference, pandemonium engulfs the media. Vir-tually all TV and radio programming has been pre-empted. Mad-dashing reporters swarm to stake out the scene at Hinton Campaign

Headquarters, the Alexandria Inn, and the Washington D.C. Convention Center. The White House press room is practically empty, however. The press corps has been alerted to a possible briefing, but no time has been given. A written statement from the press secretary has been handed out. It expresses the administration's concern and urges everyone to remain calm and not jump to any conclusions— and to pray.

No matter, the general consensus and working hypothesis among members of the press is a doomsday scenario. On air, some commentators are speculating that Cary Hinton has been abducted and is probably already dead. It's already being called "The Cary Kidnapping" and "The Hinton Hijacking." This is just *too* coincidental, most pundits have already concluded. And the beat from the pundits goes on: Her stellar performance in the debate with Moreland made her a marked woman. She suddenly turned into a real threat to her political adversaries and she had to be disposed of. These guys play for keeps. They've invested too much for too long to see it all disappear because of some upstart woman who thinks she can change the world.

In the words of veteran, foreign Washington-watcher and D.C. bureau chief for *Die Anschaung*, Gregory von Belden, "An incident like this could rock the nation to its foundation with sweeping international implications. If foul play is responsible for the disappearance of Cary Hinton, this government will not be able to survive—and I fear for the country. It will have lost the confidence of the people and the world. There is no telling what the consequences will be, but they will be catastrophic in the long term and the short term. I don't know what the schemers behind this plot could have been thinking. But they have overplayed their hand and it will boomerang on them. I doubt that Cary Hinton will ever be found—dead or alive. Of course, at this time, this is just my personal, gut feeling. But I have to go with it—and say what I have to say."

1 P.M.: THE WHITE HOUSE PRESS ROOM. The room is packed, not a seat to be had. Members of the media stand lined up along the walls. The aisles are impassible; the murmur is deafening. Conversations boil over. Fingers point. Hands wave. But the room immediately falls silent as Press Secretary Fred Blastic steps up to the podium. "On behalf of the Moreland Administration," he begins matter-of-factly, "I want to make this official statement about the circumstances and wild allegations surrounding the whereabouts of Cary Hinton.

"First of all, the Moreland Administration categorically denies any involvement in the alleged disappearance of Cary Hinton. No one, I repeat absolutely no one, in this administration has had anything to do with it or knows anything more about it than has been generally reported thus far. Like everyone else, all we know is that Cary Hinton did not return to her hotel room last night and has apparently disappeared.

"Second, we consider it unscrupulous and unethical for the media and others to suggest that we have hatched a plot to destroy a political rival. The ceaseless chatter, branding us as a bunch of lowlife thugs who would resort to such an obvious and unsophisticated tactic, must immediately be stopped. And we ask that, in the national interest, there be a voluntary halt to such idle, destructive, and politically motivated speculation. We do not wish to have to invoke the black-out provisions of the Free Speech Act.

"Third, in light of new intelligence information that we have just received, we regret to report that, at this time, we have every reason to believe that Cary Hinton has not disappeared *against* her will, but that her so-called disappearance has actually been engineered by her campaign. It is a cheap trick and part of a carefully orchestrated plot to discredit the Moreland Administration, right before the election. Preliminary information we've received would indicate that Cary Hinton has gone into hiding of her own free will—and she will reappear when she and her campaign operatives think the timing is to her advantage. This is raw politics at its worst. We strenuously condemn it. Within the hour, we expect to receive further information confirming the details of the plot, so we will update you shortly. That's all for now."

All at once, practically everyone in the room shouts, "What? What? What did he say?" At least half the reporters jump up, waving their hands to be recognized. But Blastic quickly withdraws from the podium, shakes his head, says, "No, no, no questions at this time," and escapes through the side door.

The agitation in the room is palpable—heads bobbing in every direction. "What the fuck? Do these guys actually believe they're gonna be able to get away with walking away from such an irresponsible accusation?" Gregory von Belden says out loud, shaking his head in disbelief, while trying to make his way through the exiting crowd.

3 P.M.: HINTON CAMPAIGN HEADQUARTERS, ALEXANDRIA, VIRGINIA. Hinton campaign manager Randall Griffin makes his way through the overflow crowd to the podium in the front of the room. "Ladies and gentlemen, thank you all for coming. I'm genuinely sorry to bring you out in this terrible weather. To those of you camped outside in your vans, I wish we could accommodate all of you in here, but we simply don't have room, as you can see. As far as the ongoing investigation into the disappearance of Cary Hinton, I have nothing new to report. Mother Nature just doesn't seem to want to cooperate with us. This bizarre snowstorm that doesn't seem to want to go away is making it extremely difficult to trace the route Cary drove and to track down the flood of leads we've been getting. But of course, the search is under way and has been expanded nationwide from the D.C. metropolitan area. As soon as we have any news to report, we will immediately notify you.

"In the meantime, in no uncertain terms, the Hinton campaign must denounce the outrageous accusations made a couple of hours ago by White House Press Secretary Fred Blastic on behalf of the Moreland Administration. Frankly, we are shocked and dismayed by the slanderous statements, suggesting that we orchestrated Cary Hinton's disappearance as part of some crazy strategy to win the presidency—and that we're hiding her somewhere until it's strategically to our advantage to bring her back. We all know how low the Cooper Administration went to carry out its schemes—and where it got them in the end.

"We had hoped Moreland would raise the bar higher. But it appears to be déjà vu all over again. This is not a time for politics, but I guess some people are so desperate to hang on to power, that they have lost all sense of honesty and decency—especially since their candidate was trounced in yesterday's debate. Moreland pledged that things would be different after Cooper was forced out of office—and they are. They are now worse than they were and than we ever imagined they could be. To suggest in public, in the White House, before national and international journalists, a scenario so outrageous, and frankly so stupid, tells you everything you need to know about how Moreland and his people think. Cary Hinton debated Moreland brilliantly. In a single appearance, she tapped into the heart and soul of this nation. She said things people have been longing to hear, but never thought they'd hear again. Moreland mumbled, bumbled, and stumbled—and repeated the same-old same-old we've been hearing for decades.

"All of you know that, across the country and around the world, newspaper headlines are declaring Cary the hands-down winner of the debate. Political pundits are singing her praises. People in the street are holding spontaneous rallies and vigils for her. Social media sites are jammed with positive messages of support. That's not the kind of response anyone in her right mind hides from. She had absolutely no reason intentionally to disappear. That would be a ludicrous strategy. As she proved last night, the more she gets 'out there' before the public, the better it is for her. We would have been nuts to pull a stunt like the White House is suggesting. Cary Hinton will win at the ballot box— and win big. She will be found. We will get to the bottom of her disappearance. And she will be your next president. Apparently, after two months in office our accidental president is now giddy with power and will say anything to win in November. We hope he and Mrs. Moreland didn't unpack too many things in the White House and choose new carpet and drapes, because they won't be there too much longer. I'll be happy to answer a few questions."

Reporter 1: "The Moreland campaign has just launched a new, grizzly, negative ad against Cary Hinton. It shows a menacing, bald-headed, black buzzard, with a wing span of at least six feet, soaring overhead in a lazy circle, swooping down on a dead cow's carcass. And as soon as it lands, its head morphs into Hinton's face and the carcass turns into a map of the CSA. At the beginning, there's menacing, bird-like screeching, then a voice says, 'She'll eat you dead or alive. Cary Hinton, a menace to the CSA—and you.' Would you care to comment?"

Griffin: "Comment? The adjective that comes to my mind for that sickening display of bad taste is disgust. When I first saw it, I couldn't believe my eyes. In all my years in politics, I've never seen anything like it. It's beyond me to think that any credible candidate, let alone the sitting president of any nation, could possibly approve such a low-life message in his name. We considered it tasteless when it began running last week, but we wrote it off to Moreland's desperation, even before last night's debate. But since it continues to run, in light of Cary's disappearance, early this morning, our campaign immediately lodged a formal complaint with the Moreland campaign. As of now, we've heard nothing, however. We are asking everyone to call the White House and Moreland Campaign Headquarters to express their outrage and demand that all advertising be suspended until Cary

Hinton is found. We fully understand that, after Cary ate Moreland during the debate, he and his people don't know what's hit them. All they can think about is that when Cary wins, they see the Galtian Restoration going down the drain, after sixty-seven years—and they don't want to be the ones to have to take the blame for it."

Reporter 2: "This morning Chief Porter said that nothing is being ruled out in Ms. Hinton's disappearance, even that it may be the work of international terrorists. Do you have anything more to add to that at this time?"

Griffin: "No. Believe me when I tell you that the *last* thing I want to find out is that anyone at home or abroad has conspired to do something unspeakable to Cary. People running for office always have to fear for their safety—and their lives. It's just common sense. But I shudder to think what the effect on the country would be if terrorists are to blame. I'm absolutely sure there's a simple explanation for her disappearance and she's safe and unharmed. And I'm not about to cast suspicion on anyone. I remind you that Chief Porter has emphasized that nothing is being ruled out, but that no one should jump to any conclusions. I just wish the Moreland Administration and campaign acted with sensitivity and restraint. I have time for one more question."

Reporter 3: "Would you please comment on the rumor that is circulating that Cary Hinton has a history of clinical depression and, on two prior occasions within the past five years, she actually dropped out of sight for several days."

Griffin: "It is total and utter nonsense. There isn't a shred of truth to it. It's just another example of the desperation of the Moreland Administration to smear Cary Hinton. On that note, again thanks for being here. I'll share any news and updates as soon as we get them."

WEDNESDAY, OCTOBER 26, 10 A.M.: WASHINGTON, D.C. At about 7 p.m. last night, the snow finally stopped. Overnight, plows went to work clearing streets, the job complicated because of the abandoned cars that had to be towed, downed power lines, and splintered trees. The sky is crystal clear. The sun is bright. The temperature is already a balmy sixty degrees. Shovelers are delighted they can finally clear driveways and sidewalks, but grouse at the backbreaking challenge of heaving the heavy slush of melting snow. Putting his professional imprimatur on the obvious, "Bart the Weatherman" has declared this "the damnedest weather" he's ever seen. "One day it's winter; the next it's almost summer. What is this world coming to?" he asks, crossing the line from meteorology into cosmology.

The quirky Washington weather aside, there is still no news other than Cary Hinton's disappearance, and still no new news about that. But precisely because there are no fresh facts, speculation is rampant—and partisan. From TV and radio pundits to watercooler gossips, there seems to be general agreement that "they," whoever they may be, are withholding information—and that's a bad sign. If you are anywhere in public in the Corporate States of America, or around the world for the matter, you are in danger of using up at least some of your fifteen minutes of fame by giving your reaction to Hinton's disappearance to one of scores of roving reporters. Increasingly, the general consensus is that people are bracing for the worst. No surprise, on the website www.wherescary.com, imaginations and accusations runs wild. Comments range from "Who cares about Cary?" to "I cud uv told ya this was gonna happen" and "It's all because of them damn imargrunts."

In the meantime, President Moreland is getting hammered in the polls. According to the just-released Paul Poll, sixty-five percent of respondents believe Moreland *definitely* had something to do with Hinton's disappearance, twenty-five percent say he *may have* had something to do with it, and ten percent aren't sure. The results are even more devastating for the president in the daily Mackyasack FasTrack of likely voters: seventy-five percent say her disappearance was *definitely* politically motivated, twenty percent say Moreland *may have* had something to do with it, and a mere five percent aren't sure. Privately, Moreland's advisors say he's cooked.

THURSDAY, OCTOBER 27, 1 P.M.: WASHINGTON, D.C. Because of ice and frozen snow on the ground, like tightrope walkers, three men steady themselves as they approach a blue, four-door Ford sedan in a ditch on a forty-five degree angle behind a clump of trees on Patriot Lane, an unpaved, side road in a new residential development of Arlington, Virginia. At 11 a.m., a dedicated signal from the StarWords global communications system of the Prometheus Project was finally restored after suddenly going dead Monday night at about 11 p.m. Once the location of the vehicle was established, they rushed to the scene.

Peering in from the driver's side window, they see the body of Cary Hinton. Her eyes are closed; she is lying back in the bucket seat like an astronaut heading into space, but isn't moving. The air bag is inflated in front of her, as well as on the passenger's side. They can't tell if she's breathing. The doors are locked. Armed with a tool kit, they try to pry the driver's side door open with a long, flat, notched metal strip. The noise they make awakens Hinton. She opens her eyes with a start and lurches forward. "Oh, my God!" she says. "Oh, my God, you're alive!" they shout. "She's alive!" They ask her to unlock the door, but she appears either not to understand them or to be unable to move her left arm.

In about a minute, they pop the lock and open the door. "Are you okay?" the young, red-headed man leading the group asks.

"I think my left hand is broken," she answers. "I don't have any strength in it. And the airbag burned my face when it popped. Otherwise, I think I'm okay."

"Stay still, and don't try to move," the red-head instructs her.

"I haven't been able to. I've just been lying here waiting for someone to find me, I don't know for how long. What took you so long? Has it been long? How long has it been?"

"Save your energy, Ms. Hinton," the red-head says. "We'll get you out of here in just a few minutes. Officer Wales, who came with us, is coordinating everything with Chief Porter. But, for your own safety, we can't move you until the police rescue helicopter gets here. It's on its way."

FRIDAY, OCTOBER 28, 10 A.M.: BAXTER MEMORIAL HOSPITAL, WASHINGTON, D.C. Smiling for the first time in almost four days, a jubilant Randall Griffin emerges from the left side of the hospital auditorium and makes his way to the podium. "Thank you all for being here," he says to the overflow crowd of media in the hospital auditorium. "And thank you for sticking with us since Tuesday. I know that many of you spent cold nights in vans parked outside our campaign headquarters, waiting for breaking news. As you all learned yesterday, as soon as we could confirm it, Cary Hinton is alive and—I am thrilled to report—well.

"Except for some facial burns from the airbag, a broken arm and sprained wrist, her doctors say she's in great shape. She was a little dehydrated and very hungry, as you can imagine. She always carries a water bottle with her. So that really came in handy! She's had a thing or two to say to those of us who kid her about needing to have her bottle. In fact, in a couple of minutes, she'll be joining us. The doctors want her to stay in the hospital and rest for another day. But they've done every test imaginable, and there's absolutely nothing wrong with her. Her arm is in a cast and the sprain is bandaged. Otherwise, she's back to her old self. And speaking of the devil who gave us the scare of our lives, here's Cary, now."

As a smiling Hinton walks confidently to the podium from behind the stage, the entire audience stands and applauds.

"How sweet it is to be here—and see all of you!" she proclaims, shaking the sling on her left hand and raising her right hand over her head in a triumphal fist. "Thank you, thank you, thank you from the bottom of my heart. Please sit. I don't know where to begin, except to say that I'm sorry I caused everybody so much trouble. I didn't mean to. I was just trying to drive home after the debate, not cause an international incident. And I still want to go home! I'm really a good driver.

"Of course, all of you want to know what *actually* happened to me. So, let me tell you the little that I can remember. Monday evening, at about 10:30, I left the Convention Center after the debate in one of the two cars the campaign rented. I was alone. The rest of our team stayed behind to tie up some loose ends—like talking to the press, some of you, in fact. You all know how that goes," she adds, rolling her eyes and laughing. "I had no idea that it had already started snowing heavily, but I didn't think anything of it when I drove out of the garage. I've driven in blizzards, and I didn't have very far to go.

"I started out on 14th Street, crossed into Virginia, got onto the George Washington Parkway, exited onto North Washington Street, turned left onto Cameron, and then I thought I saw the right turn Randall always takes, a short-cut through a new residential development. It winds up just a couple of blocks from our motel. But, by then, it was snowing very hard and the road was slippery. I suddenly lost control of the car. The next thing I knew, I guessed that it was morning because there was light coming through the snow covering the windows. But it could have been afternoon. I had no idea what time it was, though. I never wear a watch and I couldn't start the car to check the clock. The air bag was in my face.

"I had absolutely no idea where I was. I couldn't see out because the windows were covered with snow. The car was on an angle. I was still in my seat belt, which I undid, of course. The only pain I felt was when I tried to move my left arm or hand. I had no feeling in my left wrist. I counted the time by the light and dark coming through the snow on the windows. After what I guessed were two days, it began to melt, so I could see out. But that didn't do me much good, because all I saw were trees. I always have a bottle of water with me—everybody laughs at me for it—but that was all the nourishment I had for (what I've been told was) almost two-and-a-half days. Those sips never tasted so good. Lucky for me, I had two bottles with me and I know how to pace myself. That's where I was until I was rescued yesterday. And it's all I know about what happened. I'll be happy to answer a few questions."

"Welcome back, Cary," a smiling young woman reporter says. "It's great to see you doing so well! Please comment on the charge by the Moreland Administration that you and your campaign staged your disappearance to get publicity and voter sympathy."

"Take a look at me. Do I look like something staged? All I can say is, poor Bill. That tells you everything you need to know about Moreland and how unfit he is to be president. It's just another outrageous, illogical, bizarre statement to come out of the White House. It's what I expected from Ham Cooper, but hoped Moreland wouldn't stoop to. His campaign is doomed—and he knows it. So, he'll say anything and everything to smear me. I won the debate Monday night. Why would I intentionally go into hiding?"

"Do you feel that foul play might have been involved in your accident?" a second reporter asks. "Were you being followed? Did you feel any force being applied to push your car off the road, say from another vehicle?"

"I'm sorry, but I really can't say. It all happened so fast. I think they call it hydroplaning. I felt as though my car suddenly picked itself up, slid off the ground and barreled ahead. I felt as though something was pushing me from behind, but I can't say for sure. It all happened so fast, I didn't have time to look in the rear view mirror."

Griffin steps forward: "Sorry to interrupt, Cary, but I've just had a text message from Alexandria Police Chief Porter. Since the police towed the car Cary was driving to their forensics lab, they've been going over it looking for clues. At the moment, they can't rule anything out— or in—as a cause of the accident. But they are assessing what appears to be damage to the back bumper to determine if any force that could have caused hydroplaning might have been applied there. We've got time for one more question. As you can see, Cary's doing great. But the doctors want her to rest today."

"What's next, Cary?" an older, gray haired man calls out.

"Starting bright and early tomorrow, we hit the campaign trail. There's nothing holding us back! We're gonna win this election. We're gonna take this country back. But expect the Moreland camp to get downright dirty until Election Day. As the expression goes, 'You ain't seen nothin' yet.' But let me assure you, we're ready for them."

TUESDAY, NOVEMBER 8, 10:30 P.M.: ELECTION DAY. By all accounts, war broke out in the days after the rescue of Cary Hinton, as almost every political pundit predicted. Two hours after she was found, Moreland addressed the nation from the Oval Office. Desperate because of his declining poll numbers after their debate, he denied that he or anyone in his campaign had anything to do with Hinton's disappearance and accused her "pee-ple" (as he called them) of "malicious, unfounded, mealy-mouthed" slander and keeping that rumor alive. "Why didn't she want security," he said, "unless it was so she could get away with staging her own disappearance?" When asked if he *seriously* thought her plan would have included driving into a ditch and having her car buried in snow, breaking her arm, spraining her wrist, and lying helplessly in a cold car for days, he answered that Hinton was a "snake," and he wouldn't put anything past her.

Meanwhile, day after day, reports of dirty tricks from the Moreland campaign—all of them denied—grabbed the headlines. Routinely, likely Hinton voters who requested absentee ballots were sent return envelopes that went to bogus addresses—and were promptly thrown in the trash. Voters were warned not to vote online because there were reports that systems had been hacked so all Hinton votes were switched to Moreland or automatically canceled, without voters' being sent an error message. There were death threats against Hinton organizers and Hinton herself.

Moreland volunteers passing themselves off as members of non-partisan get-out-the-vote organizations canvassed neighborhoods. They identified likely Hinton voters and signed them up for rides to the polls, but no one ever showed up on Election Day. Phones to polling places and election offices were jammed, so people having ballot problems or difficulty proving they were eligible to vote were never able to get their issues resolved.

In a relentless barrage of negative TV ads, Moreland threw the book at Hinton. Each one opened with blaring trumpets, a picture of John Galt with a dollar sign superimposed on it, and a stentorian voice declaring, "Keep John Galt Alive. Don't let the Hinton hoax destroy Free-for-All economics!" After that, each one heaped a different set of smears on her. One alleged that she was born a man, Conrad Heppenstahl, in East Germany, but underwent a sex change operation ten years ago, and so, being foreign-born, is disqualified from being president. As Heppenstahl, a committed communist and socialist for most of his/her life, Hinton was said to have made routine visits to Cuba to plan deals with powerful comrades before infiltrating the CSA as the woman he/she is today. The ad also alleges that Heppenstahl/Hinton's parents were Nazis, an obvious explanation for Moreland's claim that Hinton is anti-Semitic and anti-Israel.

Other ads picture Hinton in black face, lip-syncing Al Jolson singing "Mammy," and accusing her of making assorted, subliminal, "coded," racist remarks. Yet another says she will propose legislation to limit families to no more than two children and require forced abortions, vasectomies, tubal ligations, and sterilizations to achieve population goals determined by the state. Yet another accuses Hinton of wanting Spanish and Chinese declared the official language of the country, so, in the words of the voice-over, "all them furn-ers can take over the CSofA."

Hinton runs a single ad. As the music of "This Land Is Your Land" plays in the background, she stands in front of a panorama that dissolves into pictures of Americans of both sexes, differing ages, races, and ethnic backgrounds, which alternate with scenes from across the country—from the Statue of Liberty to the skyline of Chicago, the Mississippi River, mid-West wheat fields, the bayous of Louisiana, the Grand Canyon, the Rockies, and the Golden Gate Bridge. She simply says, "I am Cary Hinton. I am running for president of this great country. I pledge to be president of all of you and for all of you. Please vote for me on Tuesday, November 8th. Beauty is truth, truth beauty."

On the ground, for weeks, the Prometheus Project launched a nationwide mobilization of the residents of Coopervilles. Volunteers fanned out to register voters. Today, at 4 a.m. local time across the country, tens of thousands of men and women poured out of the camps and scoured neighborhoods urging people to vote and helping them get to the polls. A special contingency trained in the martial arts surrounded polling places to keep voters from being intimidated by thugs hired by the Moreland campaign. Others saw to it that voters whose registrations were frivolously challenged were able to vote.

Minutes ago, at 10:30 p.m. Eastern Time, with the polls already closed for thirty minutes or more on the West Coast, all TV networks called the election for Cary Hinton by a margin of twenty-five percent, one of the biggest landslides in history. At the Washington Convention Center, where Hinton supporters are gathered, Randall Griffin walks to the podium and says, "Ladies and gentlemen, President-elect Cary Hinton."

To thunderous applause, she emerges from stage left and walks to the podium.

"Thank you, all of you," she says, putting both hands to her lips and blowing kisses to the audience. "As of this moment, President Moreland refuses to concede ..." She is interrupted by boos. "No, no, even if he never man-ups, his fire has gone out. Together, we have accomplished what looked to many like the impossible. We have sent a message around this great nation and throughout the world that a government 'of the people, by the people, and for the people' will never die, as long as there is a spark of life in even one person that can light the fire of freedom in others. It is now up to all of us to preserve, protect, and defend our hard-won victory. It will not be easy. We shall face resistance from those who may continue to see us as their opponents. But I want everyone to know that I pledge to work for a strong, just, and prosperous nation—for all. Beauty is truth, truth beauty. Thank you, and good night!"

TWELVE

Reclaim, Rename, Proclaim

SATURDAY, JUNE 2.: NEW PROMETHEUS (FORMERLY NEW ATLANTIS), WESTCHESTER, NEW YORK. In the post-election euphoria, just for the fun of it, some people call themselves Hintians or Caryites. Others prefer Prometheans. But they really treat it like an inside joke. Publicly, they proudly proclaim themselves only Americans, pure and simple. At her inauguration in January, Cary Hinton said, "Test my sincerity. We need to light the fire of unity and carry the torch of bipartisanship throughout the land. I will work with anyone who will work with me. We must restore balance in the country. In our light, others will see the light. We hold the flame, pass the fire, so others will thrive and be inspired. Beauty is truth, truth beauty."

On this, the first Saturday of June, seven months after Moreland and his crew and sixty-seven years of Free-for-All economics went down to defeat, Hinton supporters in droves are making a pilgrimage to the dedication of New Prometheus, the former New Atlantis. The sky is a blue-blue, dotted with cotton-ball clouds; the air crisp and refreshing, odd for late spring; there is a gentle breeze. A line of motley vehicles is backed up for at least three miles on the highway south of the main entrance. Spilling from the sidewalk onto the road, three abreast, throngs are arriving on foot. The first car waiting to turn in is a late model van with a Kansas license plate. Behind it is a motor home with "Cooperville Express" painted on its side. Next is a bright-yellow school bus. Above the entrance, over the massive iron gates, are the words "Of the people, by the people, for the people."

Hinton immediately went for the jugular when she set out to create New Prometheus. "The people need a visual symbol that times have *really* changed," she told her advisers. So, she made it a top priority to reclaim and rename the disgraced, bankrupt New Atlantis in the image of the United People of America and turn it into a legitimate think-tank for the honest, wholesome exchange of ideas. "If anyone wants to debate the plusses and minuses of Free-for-All economics, socialism, capitalism, the barter system, whatever, they may do so freely, openly, and without prejudice or recrimination at New Prometheus," she insisted.

Hinton had all the money and support she needed for the development of New Prometheus from the Countess Isabella de Horsch, her biggest campaign contributor, who's back to being Idabelle Sue Raft—and loving it. The now-disgraced Count Henry thought he rid himself of her for good when he threw her out of his limousine, penniless (he thought), on Fifth Avenue, like a used Kleenex. But she's rolling in dough (his!) and has the last laugh. The "air-head," who he thought didn't know how to add, had siphoned millions from his accounts without his suspecting a thing and made copies of incriminating business records that "mysteriously" found their way to the media and the IRS. "Every woman better know how to sock her own secret stash away, any way she can, or she's a damn fool," she told her friend LuAnn Buford. "Men are not to be trusted—at least not the men I've known." She contacted Cary Hinton through her campaign and became one of her closest and most valued advisors.

As visitors make their way into New Prometheus up "Main Street" (formerly Taggart Drive), strategically placed monuments remind everyone of why and how the Galtian Restoration died. At the first turn on the left, stretched proudly across two giant oaks, is the first "John Galt Is Dead" banner that flew over New Atlantis a year ago. At the next right is the "Taj Mahal" from the Manhattan Cooperville, which Billy Buford built for the love of his life, LuAnn. The one-room shack was transported and reassembled, piece by piece—corrugated tin roof, the door that Billy insisted on painting red for good luck, the Chinese wind chime—as though it were a Michelangelo sculpture. Even the cow-bell was refastened next to the front door. Next to the Taj is a black marble gravestone engraved in gold with the words "R.I.P. Billy Buford." Idabelle posted a $50,000 reward for information leading to the arrest and conviction of Billy's murderer, but to date no one has come forward or been found.

At the next left, sits a ten foot tall, wire-mesh basket filled with empty bottles of Atlas Energy Drink and a smashed Titan Whole-Body Harmony Machine. Strewn around them are fifty naked manikins in various exercise postures and nameless grave-markers. At the next turn is the bronze statue of the frail, innocent, young victim Adam, helplessly lying on the ground, a horse poised above him, on the verge of trampling him to death. Behind "Do Not Cross—US" tape is an unbroken picket line made up of fifty life-size sculptures—men, women, and children holding hands—that stretches about 120 feet along the road. At the end of the line, at the crest of the road, is a mob of fifty people huddled together around a flagpole, at the top of which is a flag with the words The United People of America.

Below, a vast, open expanse of manicured lawn stretches in a gentle decline to the walls of the People's Pavilion (formerly d'Anconia Pavilion). The octagon-shaped, flying-saucer-like building continues to dominate the landscape. In the island in front of it, a flame burns from a massive torch, in front of which, on a marble slab are the words "Fire: The Gift of Prometheus." The massive, gold dollar sign that used to dominate the gleaming, copper roof has been replaced by a sculpted metal flame emerging from a torch, an exact replica of the live flame below.

Overnight, hundreds camped out in RV's and on the lawn in tents and sleeping bags. According to the security officers who signed them in, they came from all fifty states (even Hawaii!). Hard times made many of them tough and resilient, but not callous. For years, many had lived in Coopervilles out of desperation, but made the best of it. But now, because the economy had improved under Hinton's policies, all the encampments have disappeared, so they were enjoying a night out-of-doors—by choice, under compassionate stars. Last night, a spontaneous folk concert started at 9 p.m. No less than twelve guitars, four banjos, three recorders, and two harmonicas appeared out of nowhere—and, like wandering troubadours, kept the music playing into the early morning hours. Starting at 6 a.m., people were cooking breakfast; the smell of coffee and bacon was everywhere.

Since the doors opened at 11 a.m., the crowd has been streaming into the 7,000-seat People's Pavilion. By the standards of haute couture, it is a rag-tag, motley crew, indeed; but by the guiding principles of representative government, it is a pure, robust picture of democracy-in-the-flesh, a parade of boundless diversity: men, women, and children of all sizes, shapes, and colors, sharing one priceless thing in common—a look of pure joy, almost innocence, on their faces, as though they've been freed from some indescribable oppression, they're drugged on the pure joys of life, and are loving every minute of it.

The lobby of the Pavilion is bare except for a towering twenty-four foot, muscular, bronze statue of Prometheus in the middle. The monumental figure is crouching and in chains attached to a boulder. He's struggling to free himself, plaintively looking straight ahead, his eyes saying "help me." Every muscle in his body is taut; his veins are almost popping. In his outstretched right hand, he holds a palm-full of clay, like that from which he created humanity; in his left, he holds a lighted torch, with which he gave fire, life and knowledge, empowering his creation. The midday light from a skylight intensifies the agony of the right side of his face and the ecstasy of the left. This is the quintessential hero—Prometheus, at once suffering but beyond suffering, struggling to regain his freedom, but nourished by the notion that he is paying the ultimate price for sacrificing himself for the betterment of the world. On the front of the pedestal are the words "In your light, let there be light."

There is no price of admission. There are no trinkets or souvenirs to buy. It's open seating, no reserved places, strictly first-come, first served. On the middle of the three walls at the back of the stage, a 10' x 20' national flag is mounted—one large white star in the middle, fifty alternating red and blue stripes behind it. "Of the people" is painted in black on the wall to the left of the flag; under the flag, "By the people"; and on the wall to its right, "For the people." On the remaining five walls surrounding the audience, stained glass windows carry different messages: "Equality for All," "Justice for All," "Empowerment for All," "Freedom for All," and "Opportunity for All."

At 2 p.m., all 7,000 seats are filled and people are standing along the walls. Outside, thousands have gathered before giant TV screens to watch the program. Over the loudspeaker, the voice of Randall Griffin says, "Ladies and gentlemen, the President of the United People of America, Cary Hinton." And from stage left, Hinton strides forward in slow, sure steps, waving to the crowd, which is on its feet and chanting "Car-y, Car-y, Car-y!" When she reaches the podium, she smiles as she drinks in the audience, pointing to people she recognizes and mouthing a silent "Hey, there" when she sees them. After five uninterrupted minutes, like a happy seal, she waves both hands up and down, signaling the crowd to be seated. Instead, they shout "Car-y, Car-y, Car-y" even louder. She laughs and shakes her head. "You're too much," she shouts. Finally, after about another five minutes, they take their seats.

"Wow," Cary says, clearly overcome. "You are too much, too too much." She pauses to breathe in and compose herself. "You all know why we are here," she continues. "But I never tire of saying it: We are here to dedicate New Prometheus, your home and the home of the Flames of Democracy and the United People of America. It is nothing less than a reawakening, a new birth of true freedom and self-fulfillment on this continent."

"Yes, yes, yes," the audience shouts, again jumping to their feet and applauding, taking their seats after about five minutes.

"It has been a long, hard struggle to reach this day. And we are here *only* because of all of you and others like you. We pause as well to remember those who are no longer with us, but who are part of the spirit of this day and the new spirit that has swept across this land: The young Adam whose life was cut short in the vicious attack on the National Mall Cooperville; Billy Buford, an economic refugee from the evils of Free-for-All economics, who was murdered in the Manhattan Cooperville; and all the others, whose names we may never know, but who will forever be part of us.

"Since my inauguration in January, the Constitutional Convention has met to establish the principles and the shape of the government of the United People of America. Through social media like Facebook and Twitter, through town halls and videoconferences, its members have listened to the citizens of this great country. Today, we have come together to affirm and breathe life into the spirit of their words—your words—and to dedicate ourselves to achieving their goals—your goals.

"It is with great pride and commitment, my fellow Americans, that I read the preamble to our new Constitution: 'From this day forward, let the word go out to all people and places of the world. We, the men and women of the United People of America, declare our free, complete, and independent sovereignty and our dedication to the Five Flames of Democracy as expressed in the inviolable principles of Equality, Justice, Empowerment, Freedom, and Opportunity for all.'"

Next to the podium stands a five foot high candelabrum with five large candles in it. "To dedicate ourselves to the first Flame of Democracy, I'd like to call upon Mr. B, the 'mayor' of the Central Park Cooperville, to light the candle representing 'Equality for All.'" As Mr. B makes his way from the right side of the pavilion, where he has been standing against the wall, Hinton continues, "Known only as Mr. B while he organized and protected the thousands of homeless men, women, and children who were victims of Free-for-All economics, he still prefers to go by that name. Mr. B was the last person to leave the Central Park Cooperville—and he was glad the chapter in our history that created the need for it is over. But he has told me that he cherishes his time in Cooperville as Mr. B because he came to know the greatest people in this country—average, decent, caring, hard-working men, women, and children who may be down on their luck but who are full of spirit. No one embodies our belief in equality for all more than Mr. B."

After Mr. B lights the candle and leaves the stage, Hinton declares: "We light the flame of 'Equality for All,' never taking it for granted. From the radical idea of total equality, the heart and soul of this nation flows. It is our lifeblood. Each and every citizen of the United People of America, regardless of our differences, enjoys the same inalienable rights. A right extended to one is extended to all, without exception. A right denied one is denied to all, without exception. For the first time in the history of this country, that means women have equal rights; they are no longer second-class citizens. Fundamental rights may not be abrogated or abridged. The majority rules, but any vote that tramples on or takes away the inalienable right or rights of individuals and minorities is null and void."

Next, Hinton calls on LuAnn Buford to light the flame symbolizing "Justice for All." As Buford joins her on stage, Hinton says, "No one knows the crippling effects of injustice more than LuAnn Buford.

To this day, the murderer of her husband Billy has never been found and brought to justice. And she suffers the hurt and anguish of that every day, because in the Corporate States of America she and her husband were abandoned. Agents of the law did not keep them safe or come to their defense when their rights were violated." As Buford returns to her seat, Hinton continues, "Throughout the United People of America, every man, woman, and child must rest assured that the law protects them; that Justice is blind; that they don't just *have* equal rights, they are *treated* equally before the law; and that there is a single, impartial system of justice. Judges, whether elected or appointed, must rule free of political and personal bias.

"Idabelle Sue Raft, will you please join me?" As the former Countess de Horsch makes her way to the stage, Hinton says, "Idabelle is without a doubt the 'Mother of New Prometheus.' Everyone in the United People of America owes her a debt of thanks. At the lowest point in my campaign for president, when I had almost no money and little moral support, Idabelle appeared out of nowhere. A total stranger, she contacted my campaign office and asked, 'How can I help?' I had no idea how to answer. So, I said, 'I need whatever you've got to give.' Well, that turned out to be time, money, and commitment. From that day forward, Idabelle was there for me—no matter what I needed, how much I needed, or when I needed it." As Idabelle lights the candle, Hinton continues, "She is the perfect person to light the flame of 'Empowerment for All.'

"Idabelle's contribution has funded the establishment of New Prometheus out of the ashes of New Atlantis. We are here today because of her—and only her. Count Henry de Horsch, a symbol of Free-for-All economics gone wild if there ever was one, used her and abused her and then got rid of her when it suited him. He had no idea that she had taken charge of her life, had empowered and protected herself—at his expense. Idabelle has given us the last laugh: Look around! The count has been the arch-enemy of everything we stand for. But now, thanks to Idabelle, his money has made New Prometheus possible—not to mention my presidency."

As Idabelle returns to her seat, Hinton asks a child to join her on the stage, chosen at random from the audience. "What's your name, sweetheart?"

"Susanne."

"How old are you?"

"Six."

"And where are you from?"

"Oklahoma."

"That's a long way away. Who are you here with?"

"My momma and my poppa."

"Well, they should be very proud of you. I'm going to hold you up and help you light the next candle." After she does so, Susanne returns to her parents.

"Susanne lit the fourth flame, signifying 'Freedom for All.' Who better to do it than a six-year-old who has her whole life ahead of her and for whom freedom means her ability to realize her full potential, whatever she chooses for herself?

"Finally, Roger, please join me." As he gets up from the front of the pavilion, where he has been sitting on the floor and walks toward the stage, Hinton says, "Like so many others who once lived in Coopervilles around the country, Roger still chooses to use only his first name, even though he is now working and able to provide for his wife Anne. I have asked him to light the flame signifying 'Opportunity for All' because he is Adam's father, the young Adam who was brutally assassinated when police swarmed the National Mall Cooperville."

Shaking Roger's hand as he takes his place next to her, she says, "I know how hard this is for you and Anne. I know that there is never a day or a moment when you don't think of Adam, the frail young boy for whom every day, even the best day, was a struggle to stay alive. He never had the opportunity to reach his full and glorious potential."

Stephen L. Goldstein

As Roger lights the candle, she continues, "Today, and every day, in Adam's name, we dedicate ourselves to providing opportunity for every man, woman, and child in the United People of America. The UPA is a meritocracy. There are no inherited rights or privileges. You are rewarded in this country because you are the best at what you do. Our constitution outlaws political parties that too often stifle opportunity and the private financing of campaigns that favors special interests over the public interest. It establishes term limits for all elected officials, including members of Congress, of course. The spirit of Adam lives. John Galt is dead!

"And now, ladies and gentlemen, please stand and join with me in reciting the Pledge of Allegiance: "I pledge allegiance to the flag of the United People of America and to the republic for which it stands, one nation, indivisible, with equality, justice, empowerment, freedom, and opportunity for all."

"I've heard just about all I can stomach," Mortimer Gayle shouts as he stands and identifies himself as head of the Corporate Council of Presidents Cooper and Moreland. Shaking his right fist at Hinton, he yells angrily, "You're filling their heads with socialist propaganda, lies, and deceit. I represent the *only* people, the *real* people, who made and who make this country great . . . "

The audience stands up and interrupts with boos. One man hollers, "It's not *just* you! It's *everyone!*" A woman in the back screams, "Put that lying corporate thief in jail!"

"No, no, that's all right! Calm down, everyone," Hinton says, holding both hands up, Buddha-like, palms facing the crowd. "Let him continue. He's angry and upset, so let's try to put ourselves in his shoes. Go on Mr. Gayle. This is your chance to get everything out. We're listening."

"There wouldn't be a thriving economy without us. There wouldn't be a country without us. We create jobs. We pay salaries. We take *all* the risks. *We* are the people who have made this country great. You

225

can't survive or thrive or stay alive without *us*. Remember what happened when John Galt and the others went on strike. You're dooming this country to extinction with your pie-in-the-sky talk. You're fooling everyone if you think they can do anything without us. The people you say are everything really are nothing without us. And you'll find that out soon enough. Big deal: You've been in office for six months. At the end of the next six months, if you keep filling people's heads with such rubbish, the country will be bankrupt."

"Thank you for sharing, Mr. Gayle," Hinton responds. "Let me remind you that I was elected by the people of this country, the same people whom you would appear to consider trash, beneath you, insignificant in the scheme of things—your scheme of things. Moreland and his gang—you, too, I'm sure—did everything they could to keep me from winning. But all of you failed! How many millions did you and your corporate cronies contribute to Moreland? It must really kill you that, for the first time, your money didn't do you any good. You couldn't buy what you wanted. Isn't that what you think, that everything has a price and, as long as you can pay it, no matter what you had to do to get the money or who you might have hurt, you're entitled to get what you want?

"Well, now, it's time for you to listen and to face reality, if you have the guts to. 'The people' have been awakened. They've felt their power. And they're standing up for themselves. The game you've played is over. You lost. You've thrown your flames at us. But we don't return fire. We're not aiming for you, Mr. Gayle, or anyone else. It may sound hokey to you. But look at what's burning beside me—the flames of equality, justice, empowerment, freedom, and opportunity for everyone, including you. They're real! There's absolutely nothing phony about it. We mean what we say. Don't look so surprised. You're one of us. It's not beneath you to be one of 'the people.' I know it may shock you, but equality, justice, and all the other values are not just campaign slogans we use to fool people into voting for us. We believe them. We live by them. They are the blood that runs through our veins. They are all that matters to us.

"Have you been asleep for the past hour? Has nothing that has been said here registered on you? Do the words 'for all' mean nothing to you? Are you really so callous or dense or deaf or are you just pretending not to understand who we are and what we stand for? I'd like to give you the benefit of the doubt, but you make it very hard, Mr. Gayle. What did you think when you saw Susanne come up and light the Flame of Freedom? Nothing? Dollar signs? How could you not look at her and see the promise of tomorrow in her just being alive? How could you not feel a responsibility, a desire, a commitment to make the world a better place so she can thrive? She could become a researcher who finds a cure for cancer. Or she could thrive as a writer or artist or musician. Or she could become a mother whose greatest joy in life is to care for her husband and children. Surely, something in you wants the best for her, though you'll never see her again. You know she exists, like millions of others. She's you and me.

"And what about Roger, mourning the death of Adam? Aren't you outraged and ashamed to think that an innocent, frail, young boy was trampled to death by a cop on a horse sent by the man you elected president, because he didn't want to be reminded of the economic disaster he and people like you created? Can you feel the helplessness of a father holding the crushed bones and lifeless flesh of his son in his arms? Can you hear the screams of disbelief of a mother who first learns that the spark of life she brought into the world has been snuffed out? Or are certain people like you so blinded by greed that you are incapable of feeling. Do you only see numbers on your corporate balance sheet and care about profits in your pocket? Are you dead to other people?

"Obviously, you still don't understand or you have a short memory or both. Do you only choose to remember John Galt's strike? Don't you remember what happened when your stores were swarmed, when 'the people,' the ones you think don't matter, went on strike, and you couldn't do any business? Haven't you learned that it takes two to tango? You and others like you are just *some* of 'the people who have made this country great,' to use your words. It appears that you still don't accept that you are not the *only* people who count. That kind of thinking, and the behavior that follows from it, was what was wrong with the CSA: It produced wild, unchecked, anti-democratic greed. And it led to your downfall.

"Don't shake your head dismissing me," she warns him, pointing with her right index finger. "And don't you dare call what I stand for socialism. Yes, I can read your mind. I stand for democratic capitalism, for ensuring a level playfield on which each and every person in this country can achieve his or her potential—a pure meritocracy. That's a far cry from what you and Free-for-All marketers want and wanted—and got for decades: a system rigged so you could reap millions, make that billions, from average, hard-working men and women: All for some but none for all!

"You seem to forget you were caught red-handed and the whole world has heard your heartless scheming. Everyone knows that you were at the secret meeting with Cooper and your partners in crime to profit after the hurricane hit Florida. It was a crime, you know. Everyone heard how you plotted to make millions off of other people's misery. People were literally dying, but you were thinking only of how you could steal their land out from under them and put your department stores in better locations than they were in before the hurricane hit. I honestly don't know how people like you sleep at night.

"For decades, we've heard your mantra, and the mantra of Free-for-All economics, that government is the cause of all of our problems, not their solution. It's wasteful, unproductive, and obstructionist, you and others have insisted. On the flip side of your broken record, you've repeated that business does everything right and good. But we know the truth, we know that Free-for-All economics is a smoke-screen for you to lie, cheat and steal.

"We've done it your way for decades. Boy, I've got to hand it to you and the others. You sold 'the people' a bill of goods and they fell for your promises of the good life! You rolled them, and they just rolled over for you. The Corporate States destroyed the lives of millions of Americans. But times have changed—forever. People finally woke up and saw that business and government don't mix. A successful business and good government operate under a different set of values and goals. Boards of directors and Wall Street don't reward CEOs because they create a lot of jobs. Investors and owners are interested in bloated profits, not big payrolls. Our republic was not conceived as a series of profit centers created to line the pockets of corporations. You can no longer invoke our founding fathers while you pervert their ideals and twist their words. In the United People of America, there's a firewall between business and government. And anyone who tries to cross it gets burned big-time.

"Of course, under some circumstances, government and business may be complementary. When it is in the public interest, government should support the for-profit sector—certainly not create unreasonable barriers to success. But breach the firewall, tilt the balance to profit over people, and you get the corporate welfare state, except no more!

"Have you forgotten what happened when your money put CEOs in the Oval Office? Ham Cooper was incompetent, but at least he self-destructed. Ironically, he and his Administration, in cahoots with New Atlantis, did away with all regulations on the development, testing, and distribution of prescription drugs and medications—which led to the Atlas Energy Drink fraud and criminal prosecution and his getting forced out of office. But most of his predecessors were downright thieves. The first president of the CSA was Boss Roper. He was in the front pocket, the back pocket, the hip pocket, under the thumb, and on the short leash of big business. He made the case for naming the country the Corporate States of America—and, once that was done, he replaced his cabinet with a Corporate Council that drafted a new constitution that transferred executive power to them. It was a coup, but the people hardly knew what hit them.

"Everyone said Roper had a 'ten-gallon smile,' because when he took a bribe, he always tipped his hat, smirked, and put the checks under it. More than once, he'd forget he had a fresh stash under there, play the gentlemen to a passing lady, and scramble to pick up the 'letters from his pen pals,' as he called them. He signed over government leases for oil and gas rights for just enough money to make them seem like legal transactions and deregulated energy prices so they went up fifty percent in two years. He peppered his rhetoric with populist twaddle and a homegrown twang, promising to rescue America from bad government. But he made his *real* money from the company he founded, but which he turned over to his son, that raked in billions from a no-bid contract to sell computers made in Mongolia that had no hard drives to what was left of federal agencies.

"And then there was President 'Bucks' Cott. His real name was Burton, but no one ever called him that. He had a sign on his desk that read 'Your bucks stop here.' It took him three terms in the Oval Office, but, when he was through, he had turned every government agency and health program over to private businesses—half of which he'd invested in and the other half his wife owned. And these are the good guys you made president, Mr. Gayle—because eventually we knew what they were up to, even if we couldn't stop it.

"But the crowning glory of the CSA was the Political Stock Exchange and Commodities Market, an idea Hilton Manfreed hatched at New Atlantis. H.R. 'Horse' Trott was president then. They called him 'Horse,' because he was famous for trotting out of any jam he got himself into and letting everyone else take the blame. Well, the two of them held a news conference to announce the PSECM. As Manfreed explained it, it was just another example of 'the beauty' of the market: like pork bellies, the futures of elected officials and candidates would be publicly traded. That way, politicians could make millions, and average Americans could buy and sell them and make a profit. Under the Exchange, Trott could have become a stock corporation while he was running for president. Investors who were smart enough to buy shares in his IPO could have made a killing when he was elected and his price-per-share skyrocketed. When I was elected, I announced that my first act as president would be to disband the PSECM by executive order. Immediately, prices plummeted. That was the quickest way I knew to clear out the Congress. I'm guessing you took a big hit, Mr. Gayle. But you know how it is in the marketplace: You take risks. You win some. You lose some. This time you lost big. But you can win again by working for 'the people.'

"Mr. Gayle, the CSA turned this country into the equivalent of a dead land crab—an empty shell, picked apart and left to rot on the beach. You've gotta feel the desperation that average people feel. You've gotta get your humanity back. I'm convinced it's still there, although you haven't really tapped into it for a while. I forgive you. We all forgive you. Now, you've gotta forgive yourself enough to do the right thing. I'm not asking you blindly to believe me. I'm not a saint. But I'm sure as hell not a sinner, either. I'm asking you to work with me to make things happen as we all want them to. You give a little. I give a little. I give a lot. You give a lot. Before you know it, we may actually be able to work together. It isn't gonna take a miracle for this to happen; it's gonna take rational people coming together. If you're ready to come to the table and work together with others as an equal partner to create a fair and just society, I welcome you, we welcome you. But I stress the word *together*, Mr. Gayle. Profit, yes, of course you're entitled to it, but not at *any* cost—especially not at the cost of your soul! The days of profit over people are over.

"Thanks for hearing me out, Mr. Gayle. I rest my case. You don't have to tell me now whether you're on board. Only time will tell. I'm ready whenever you are. Together, we can change the world. If not,

I'm gonna do my best to do it with everybody and anybody I can find. 'Beauty is truth, truth beauty.'

"Before we leave here today, there is another group of people whom I want to acknowledge, though they insist upon remaining anonymous. Without them, we would not be here, I would not be here, and there would be no United People of America. The world knows them as members of the Prometheus Project. Individually, they are known as Zeus, Olympus, Pandora, Mercury, and Adonis. Individually, each is enormously powerful. Together, once aroused, they are unstoppable. They remain the sworn enemies of the followers of Atlas, who so drug themselves, that they lose reason and judgment and turn their victims into objects of crass exploitation. The Prometheus people are living breathing human beings, but they are also symbols of the undying spirit of 'the people,' a force beyond any one person's or any group of people's ability to trample and suppress forever. They rose up before and they and others like them will rise up again if we, or others, betray their trust."

As Pete Seeger's version of "This Land Is Your Land" is piped in over the loudspeaker, Hinton walks down from the stage and makes her way over to Mortimer Gayle, who's taken aback.

"Come with me," she says, smiling, beckoning him to join her, then taking him by the hand so together they walk up the middle aisle of the pavilion, shaking hands with and greeting people. Leaning against the back wall of the pavilion is a young, red-headed man. When Hinton reaches him, she shakes his right hand with hers, then places her left hand warmly over both of theirs. He's the last person she sees before she exits by the back door.

The young red-head thinks to himself, *How much has changed! How much remains to be done!* Exactly one year ago today, Hilton Manfreed tried to humiliate him when he dared to ask a question about the morality of Free-for-All economics. He laughs now thinking of how, a little later that day, he smirked as he watched Manfreed's minions leaving the d'Anconia Pavilion, outraged at the "John Galt Is Dead" banner flying over head. Just a year ago, he had no idea that those four words would spark a revolution.

Startled by a loud ringing, he quickly reaches into his pocket to silence what he assumes is his cell phone, only to discover that it isn't the source of the noise. He wonders what tomorrow will bring, and the day after, and the day after, and a year from now—and if he should wonder at anything or just take one day at a time, instead of killing the moment as usual with premonitions of what might be. Something is definitely troubling him. He can't put it into words. But he can see it— a fuzzy, amorphous grayness that gives him a funny feeling in his stomach, like nothing he's ever felt before, a feeling that could foreshadow impending delight or doom, but without a clear cause or even the certainty that it's simply one or the other. *It might be both,* he thinks. *Here I go again, driving myself crazy. I can never just let things be.*

The ringing gets louder. *What the hell is that? Who the hell can that be?* he wonders. *Am I the only one who hears that infernal noise?* But as aware as he is of "something out there," he refuses to let it or any of life's petty annoyances distract him. Nothing is going to keep him from relishing every minute of being at New Prometheus this minute, today. History is being made, and he can say he has been here from the beginning. It's been like a dream-come-true.

EPILOGUE
Ego vidi somnium

6 A.M.: WEST 79TH STREET, MANHATTAN. Awakened from a sound sleep by a loud ringing, Dan Ryan grabs for his pants from the floor and reaches into its left pocket to silence what he assumes is his cell phone, only to discover that it isn't the source of the noise. *Who's calling me so early?* he wonders. He checks his alarm clock, but it isn't coming from there, either. "Go away. Stop ringing," he shouts out loud. But it only seems to be getting louder. Finally, he forces himself to get out of bed and traipses over to the other side of the room, looking for his land line, which is buried under a pile of newspapers.

"Hello," he says abruptly, only half awake.

"Hey, champ, this is your wake-up call," the voice on the other end says, laughing.

"Who the hell is this? What wake-up call?"

"It's Oscar! Your boss," the unbearably cheerful voice announces. "All you red-heads are alike—hot under the collar. Did you forget you have a job, which gives you a paycheck, which should make you happy to hear from me, day or night? Are you feeling all right? Have you forgotten about today, Saturday, at New Atlantis? I told you I'd call you this morning to be sure you meet up with the crew by 7:30 so you can set up the remote from there."

"What are you talking about—New Atlantis?" Ryan snaps back. "There is no New Atlantis. It went bankrupt! It's New Prometheus now!"

"Are you tryin' to punk me, Dan? Have you been smoking something or popping pills?"

"There's nothing wrong with me, Oscar. What day is today?"

"It's Saturday, June 4th. Yesterday was Friday, June 3rd. Tomorrow will be Sunday, June 5th. That's how it usually goes: Friday, Saturday, Sunday…"

"You don't have to give me grief, Oscar. But what about the election? Cary Hinton won. She's the president now, isn't she? Ham Cooper had to resign. Are you absolutely sure New Atlantis didn't go bankrupt?"

"Dan, I don't know what's gotten into you. The election isn't until November. And, I'm sorry to break the news to you, but Cary Hinton's never gonna be elected president of the CSA. Are you crazy? Cooper's still president. And nothing's happened to New Atlantis. The last I heard, it's going as strong as ever, and they're still raking in the bucks. You must have a fever and be delirious."

"No. I'm okay, at least I think I'm okay," Ryan says hesitating.

"Are you sure? I can try to get a replacement for you if you're not feeling well."

"No, I'm okay. But it was all so real. Everything was *so* real. And everything turned out *so* well," Ryan says dreamily. "I dreamt that life was beauty, but I woke to find it was duty."

"Dan, seriously, what's goin' on?"

"Oscar, let me go. I have to shower. I'll meet the crew and go to New Atlantis. Honestly, I'm feeling fine."

"And when am I gonna get your column?"

"I'll have it for you first thing on Monday."

Once he's showered and dressed, Ryan looks out on 79th Street. But it's not the cars or the pavement or the trees or the macadam he's seeing; it's the blank spaces between what's there. He thought of how, as a kid, he used to envy Christopher Robin, who could fool everyone into believing that he had "sneezles and wheezles that bundled him into his bed" and kept him rolled up in a ball, safe from the world-not-of-his-making—or of his imagining or preference. Then, he laughed at himself for remembering. All at once, he realized that the fuzzy, amorphous grayness that he pictured and that had given him a funny feeling in his stomach was gone. And suddenly, he felt that there were more knowns than unknowns in his life. He turned on his computer and opened the file for his latest column, in which he had yet to type a word, and entered the following notes:

"I had a dream of what America could be—again ..."

"If I am not for myself who will be for me? If I am only for myself what am I? And if not now, when?"

"Beauty is truth, truth beauty."

"I have miles to go before I sleep."

That's all I need to know to write my column, he said to himself. The fire is still there, and it now feels more like a blaze.

He then writes an email to Oscar that he plans to send Monday morning, right after he files his column:

Oscar,

Effective immediately, I resign. Thanks for helping me discover that I have a *real* job to do. *Liberté, égalité, fraternité!* I'm not worried about payday. But please direct deposit my next check. I may be manning the barricades or leading a charge. Where you see any smoke, there's likely to be my fire.

-Dan

The End of the Beginning

CPSIA information can be obtained at www.ICGtesting.com
Printed in the USA
LVOW061959250512

283408LV00001B/1/P